International bestselling author **Tess Gerritsen** gave up a career as a practising physician to write full time. She draws upon her experiences to bring all the tension and terrors of her thrillers to life. She lives in Camden, Maine, with her physician husband and two sons.

TESS
GERRITSEN

STOLEN

This work was first published as *Thief of Hearts*
by Harlequin Enterprises Limited in 1995.

MIRA

*MIRA is a registered trademark of Harlequin Enterprises Limited,
used under licence.*

*Published in Great Britain 2008.
MIRA Books, Eton House, 18-24 Paradise Road,
Richmond, Surrey, TW9 1SR*

First published in 1995 by Harlequin Enterprises Limited under
the title *Thief of Hearts*. This edition published January 2008.

© Terry Gerritsen 1995

ISBN: 978 0 7783 0195 0

59-0108

*Harlequin Mills & Boon policy is to use papers that are
natural, renewable and recyclable products and made from
wood grown in sustainable forests. The logging and
manufacturing processes conform to the legal environmental
regulations of the country of origin.*

*Printed and bound in Spain
by Litografia Rosés S.A., Barcelona*

In memory of Jum Heacock

"In thy face I see the map
of honour, truth and loyalty."

—*Henry VI, Part III*
William Shakespeare

PROLOGUE

SIMON TROTT stood on the rolling deck of the *Cosima,* and through the velvety blackness of night he saw the flames. They burned just offshore, not a steady fire, but a series of violent bursts of light that cast the distant swells in a hellish glow.

"That's her," the *Cosima*'s captain said to Trott as both men peered across the bow. "The *Max Havelaar.* Judging by those fireworks, she'll be going down fast." He turned and yelled to the helmsman, "Full ahead!"

"Not much chance of survivors," said Trott.

"They're sending off a distress call. So someone's alive."

"Or was alive."

As they neared the sinking vessel, the flames suddenly shot up like a fountain, sending out sparks that seemed to ignite the ocean in puddles of liquid fire.

The captain shouted over the roar of the *Cosima*'s engines, "Slow up! There's fuel in the water!"

"Throttling down," said the helmsman.

"Ahead slowly. Watch for survivors."

Trott moved to the forward rail and stared across the watery inferno. Already the *Max Havelaar* was sliding backward, her stern nearly submerged, her bow tipping toward the moonless sky. A few minutes more and she'd sink forever into the swells. The water was deep, and salvage impractical. Here, two miles off the Spanish coast, was where the *Havelaar* would sink to her eternal rest.

Another explosion spewed out a shower of embers, leafing the ripples with gold. In those few seconds before the sunlike brilliance faded, Trott spotted a hint of movement off in the darkness. A good two hundred yards away from the *Havelaar,* safely beyond the ring of fire, Trott saw a long, low silhouette bobbing in the water. Then he heard the sound of men's voices, calling.

"Here! We are here!"

"It's the lifeboat," said the captain, aiming the searchlight toward the voices. "There, at two o'clock!"

"I see it," said the helmsman, at once adjusting course. He throttled up, guiding the bow through drifts of burning fuel. As they drew closer, Trott could hear the joyous shouts of the survivors, a confusing babble of Italian. How many in the boat? he wondered, straining to see through the murk. Five. Perhaps six. He could almost count them now, their arms waving in the searchlight's beam, their heads bobbing in every direction. They were thrilled to be alive. To be in sight of rescue.

"Looks like most of the *Havelaar*'s crew," said the captain.

"We'll need all hands up here."

The captain turned and barked out the order. Seconds later the *Cosima*'s crew had assembled on deck. As the bow knifed across the remaining expanse of water, the men stood in silence near the bow rail, all eyes focused on the lifeboat just ahead.

By the searchlight's glare Trott could now make out the number of survivors: six. He knew the *Max Havelaar* had sailed from Naples with a crew of eight. Were there two still in the water?

He turned and glanced toward the distant silhouette of shore. With luck and endurance, a man could swim that distance.

The lifeboat was adrift off their starboard side.

Trott shouted, "This is the *Cosima!* Identify yourselves!"

"Max Havelaar!" shouted one of the men in the lifeboat.

"Is this your entire crew?"

"Two are dead!"

"You're certain?"

"The engine, she explodes! One man, he is trapped below."

"And your eighth man?"

"He falls in. Cannot swim!"

Which made the eighth man as good as dead, thought Trott. He glanced at *Cosima*'s crew. They stood watching, waiting for the order.

The lifeboat was gliding almost alongside now.

"A little closer," Trott called down, "and we'll throw you a line."

One of the men in the lifeboat reached up to catch the rope.

Trott turned and gave his men the signal.

The first hail of bullets caught its victim in midreach, arms extended toward his would-be saviors. He had no chance to scream. As the bullets rained down from the *Cosima,* the men fell, helpless before the onslaught. Their cries, the splash of a falling body, were drowned out by the relentless spatter of automatic gunfire.

When it was finished, when the bullets finally ceased, the bodies lay in a coiled embrace in the lifeboat. A silence fell, broken only by the slap of water against the *Cosima*'s hull.

One last explosion spewed a finale of sparks into the air. The bow of the *Max Havelaar*—what remained of her—tilted crazily toward the sky. Then, gently, she slid backward into the deep.

The lifeboat, its hull riddled with bullet holes, was

already half submerged. A *Cosima* crewman heaved a loose anchor over the side. It landed with a thud among the bodies. The lifeboat tipped, emptying its cargo of corpses into the sea.

"Our work is done here, Captain," said Trott. Matter-of-factly he turned toward the helm. "I suggest we return to—"

He suddenly halted, his gaze focused on a patch of water a dozen yards away. What was that splash? He could still see the ripples of reflected firelight worrying the water's surface. There it was again. Something silvery gliding out of the swells, then slipping back under the water.

"Over there!" shouted Trott. "Fire!"

His men looked at him, puzzled.

"What did you see?" asked the captain.

"Four o'clock. Something broke the surface."

"I don't see anything."

"Fire at it, anyway."

One of the gunmen obligingly squeezed off a clip. The bullets sprayed into the water, their deadly rain splashing a line across the surface.

They watched for a moment. Nothing appeared. The water smoothed once again into undulating glass.

"I know I saw something," said Trott.

The captain shrugged. "Well, it's not there now." He called to the helmsman, "Return to port!"

Cosima came about, leaving in her wake a spreading circle of ripples.

Trott moved to the stern, his gaze still focused on the suspicious patch of water. As they roared away he thought he spotted another flash of silver bob to the surface. It was there only for an instant. Then, in a twinkling, it was gone.

A fish, he thought. And, satisfied, he turned away. Yes, that must be what it was. A fish.

CHAPTER ONE

"A SMALL BURGLARY. That's all I'm asking for." Veronica Cairncross gazed up at him, tears shimmering in her sapphire eyes. She was dressed in a fetching off-the-shoulder silk gown, the skirt arranged in lustrous ripples across the Queen Anne love seat. Her hair, a rich russet brown, had been braided with strands of seed pearls and was coiled artfully atop her aristocratic head. At thirty-three she was far more stunning, far more chic than she'd been at the age of twenty-five, when he'd first met her. Through the years she'd acquired, along with her title, an unerring sense of style, poise and a reputation for witty repartee that made her a sought-after guest at the most glittering parties in London. But one thing about her had not changed, would never change.

Veronica Cairncross was still an idiot.

How else could one explain the predicament into which she'd dug herself?

And once again, he thought wearily, it's faithful old chum Jordan Tavistock to the rescue. Not that

Veronica didn't need rescuing. Not that he didn't want to help her. It was simply that this request of hers was so bizarre, so fraught with dire possibilities, that his first instinct was to turn her down flat.

He did. "It's out of the question, Veronica," said Jordan. "I won't do it."

"For me, Jordie!" she pleaded. "Think what will happen if you don't. If he shows those letters to Oliver—"

"Poor old Ollie will have a fit. You two will row for a few days, and then he'll forgive you. That's what will happen."

"What if Ollie doesn't forgive me? What if he— what if he wants a…" She swallowed and looked down. "A divorce," she whispered.

"Really, Veronica." Jordan sighed. "You should have thought about this before you had the affair."

She stared down in misery at the folds of her silk gown. "I didn't think. That's the whole problem."

"No, it's obvious you didn't."

"I had no idea Guy would be so difficult. You'd think I broke his heart! It's not as if we were in love or anything. And now he's being such a bastard about it. Threatening to tell all! What gentleman would sink so low?"

"No gentleman would."

"If it weren't for those letters I wrote, I could

deny the whole thing. It would be my word against Guy's, then. I'm sure Ollie would give me the benefit of the doubt."

"What, exactly, did you write in those letters?"

Veronica's head drooped unhappily. "Things I shouldn't have."

"Confessions of love? Sweet nothings?"

She groaned. "Much worse."

"More explicit, you mean?"

"Far more explicit."

Jordan gazed at her bent head, at the seed pearls and russet hair glimmering in the lamplight. And he thought, *It's hard to believe I was once attracted to this woman.* But that was years ago, and he'd been only twenty-two and a bit gullible—a condition he sincerely hoped he'd outgrown.

Veronica Dooley had entered his social circle on the arm of an old chum from Cambridge. After the chum bowed out, Jordan had inherited the girl's attentions, and for a few dizzy weeks he'd thought he might be in love. Better sense prevailed. Their parting was amicable, and they'd remained friends over the years. She'd gone on to marry Oliver Cairncross, and although *Sir* Oliver was a good twenty years older than his bride, theirs had been a classic match between money on his side and beauty on hers. Jordan had thought them a contented pair.

How wrong he'd been.

"My advice to you," he said, "is to come clean. Tell Ollie about the affair. He'll most likely forgive you."

"Even if he does, there's still the letters. Guy's just upset enough to send them to all the wrong people. If Fleet Street ever got hold of them, Ollie would be publicly humiliated."

"You think Guy would really stoop so low?"

"I don't doubt it for a minute. I'd offer to pay him off if I thought it would work. But after all that money I lost in Monte Carlo, Ollie's keeping a tight rein on my spending. And I couldn't borrow any money from you. I mean, there are some things one simply *can't* ask of one's friends."

"Burglary, I'd say, lies in that category," noted Jordan dryly.

"But it's not burglary! I wrote those letters. Which makes them *mine*. I'm only retrieving what belongs to me." She leaned forward, her eyes suddenly glittering like blue diamonds. "It wouldn't be difficult, Jordie. I know exactly which drawer he keeps them in. Your sister's engagement party is Saturday night. If you could invite him here—"

"Beryl detests Guy Delancey."

"Invite him anyway! While he's here at Chetwynd, guzzling champagne—"

"I'm burgling his house?" Jordan shook his head. "What if I'm caught?"

"Guy's staff takes Saturday nights off. His house will be empty. Even if you *are* caught, just tell them it's a prank. Bring a—a blow-up doll or something, for insurance. Tell them you're planting it in his bed. They'll believe you. Who'd doubt the word of a Tavistock?"

He frowned. "Is that why you're asking *me* to do this? Because I'm a Tavistock?"

"No. I'm asking you because you're the cleverest man I know. Because you've never, ever betrayed any of my secrets." She raised her chin and met his gaze. It was a look of utter trust. "And because you're the only one in the world I can count on."

Drat. She would have to say that.

"Will you do it for me, Jordie?" she asked softly. Pitifully. "Tell me you will."

Wearily he rubbed his head. "I'll think about it," he said. Then he sank back in the armchair and gazed resignedly at the far wall, at the paintings of his Tavistock ancestors. Distinguished gentlemen, every one of them, he thought. Not a cat burglar in the lot.

Until now.

AT 11:05, THE LIGHTS WENT out in the servants' quarters. Good old Whitmore was right on schedule as usual. At 9:00 he'd made his rounds of the house, checking to see that the windows and doors were locked. At 9:30 he'd tidied up downstairs, fussed a bit in the kitchen, perhaps brewed himself a pot of tea. At 10:00 he'd retired upstairs, to the blue glow of his private telly. At 11:05 he turned off his light.

This had been Whitmore's routine for the past week, and Clea Rice, who'd been watching Guy Delancey's house since the previous Saturday, assumed that this would be his routine until the day he died. Menservants, after all, strived to maintain order in their employers' lives. It wasn't surprising they'd maintain order in their own lives, as well.

Now the question was, how long before he'd fall asleep?

Safely concealed behind the yew hedge, Clea rose to her feet and began to rock from foot to foot, trying to keep the blood moving through her limbs. The grass had been wet, and her stirrup pants were clinging to her thighs. Though the night was warm, she was feeling chilled. It wasn't just the dampness in her clothes; it was the excitement, the anticipation. And, yes, the fear. Not a great deal of fear—she had enough confidence in her own ability to feel certain she wouldn't be caught. Still, there was always that chance.

She danced from foot to foot to keep the adrenaline pumping. She'd give the manservant twenty minutes to fall asleep, no longer. With every minute that passed, her window of opportunity was shrinking. Guy Delancey could return home early from the party tonight, and she wanted to be well away from here when he walked in that front door.

Surely the butler was asleep now.

Clea slipped around the yew hedge and took off at a sprint. She didn't stop running until she'd reached the cover of shrubbery. There she paused to catch her breath, to reevaluate her situation. There was no hue and cry from the house, no signs of movement anywhere in the darkness. Lucky for her, Guy Delancey abhorred dogs; the last thing she needed tonight was some blasted hound baying at her heels.

She slipped around the house and crossed the flagstone terrace to the French doors. As expected, they were locked. Also as expected, it would be an elementary job. A quick glance under her penlight told her this was an antique warded lock, a bit rusty, probably as old as the house itself. When it came to home security, the English had light years of catching up to do. She fished the set of five skeleton keys out of her fanny pack and began trying them, one by one. The first three keys didn't fit. She inserted the fourth, turned it slowly and felt the tooth slide into the bolt notch.

A piece of cake.

She let herself in the door and stepped into the library. By the glow of moonlight through the windows she could see books gleaming in shelves. Now came the hard part—where was the Eye of Kashmir? Surely not in this room, she thought as the beam of her penlight skimmed the walls. It was too accessible to visitors, pathetically unsecured against thieves. Nevertheless, she gave the room a quick search.

No Eye of Kashmir.

She slipped out of the library and into the hallway. Her light traced across burnished wood and antique vases. She prowled through the first-floor parlor and solarium. No Eye of Kashmir. She didn't bother with the kitchen or dining areas—Delancey would never choose a hiding place so accessible to his servants.

That left the upstairs rooms.

Clea ascended the curving stairway, her footsteps silent as a cat's. At the landing she paused, listening for any sounds of discovery. Nothing. To the left she knew was the servants' wing. To the right would be Delancey's bedroom. She turned right and went straight to the room at the end of the hall.

The door was unlocked. She slipped through and closed it softly behind her.

Through the balcony windows moonlight spilled in, illuminating a room of grand proportions. The twelve-foot-high walls were covered with paintings. The bed was a massive four-poster, its mattress broad enough to sleep an entire harem. There was an equally massive chest of drawers, a double wardrobe, nightstands and a gentleman's writing desk. Near the balcony doors was a sitting area—two chairs and a tea table arranged around a Persian carpet, probably antique.

Clea let out an audible groan. It would take hours to search this room.

Fully aware of the minutes ticking by, she started with the writing desk. She searched the drawers, checked for hidden niches. No Eye of Kashmir. She moved to the dresser, where she probed through layers of underwear and hankies. No Eye of Kashmir. She turned next to the wardrobe, which loomed like a monstrous monolith against the wall. She was just about to swing open the wardrobe door when she heard a noise and she froze.

It was a faint rustling, coming from somewhere outside the house. There it was again, louder.

She swiveled around to face the balcony windows. Something bizarre was going on. Outside, on the railing, the wisteria vines quaked violently. A silhouette suddenly popped up above the tangle of leaves. Clea caught one glimpse of the man's head, of his blond hair gleaming in the moonlight, and she ducked back behind the wardrobe.

This was just wonderful. They'd have to take numbers to see whose turn it was to break in next. This was one hazard she hadn't anticipated—an encounter with a rival thief. An incompetent one, too, she thought in disgust as she heard the sharp clatter of outdoor pottery, quickly stilled. There was an intervening silence. The burglar was listening for sounds of discovery. Old Whitmore must be deaf, thought Clea, if he didn't hear *that* racket.

The balcony door squealed open.

Clea retreated farther behind the wardrobe. What if he discovered her? Would he attack? She'd brought nothing with which to defend herself.

She winced as she heard a thump, followed by an irritated mutter of "*Damn* it all!"

Oh, Lord. This guy was more dangerous to himself than to her.

Footsteps creaked closer.

Clea shrank back, pressing hard against the wall. The wardrobe door swung open, coming to a stop just inches from her face. She heard the clink of hangers as clothes were shoved aside, then the hiss of a drawer sliding out. A flashlight flicked on, its glow spilling through the crack of the wardrobe door. The man muttered to himself as he rifled through the drawer, irritated grumblings in the queen's best English.

"Must be mad. That's what I am, stark raving. Don't know how she talked me into this…."

Clea couldn't help it; curiosity got the better of her. She eased forward and peered through the crack between the hinges of the door. The man was frowning down at an open drawer. His profile was sharply cut, cleanly aristocratic. His hair was wheat blond and still a bit ruffled from all that wrestling with the wisteria vine. He wasn't dressed at all like a burglar. In his tuxedo jacket and black bow tie, he looked more like some cocktail-party refugee.

He dug deeper into the drawer and suddenly gave a murmur of satisfaction. She couldn't see what he was removing from the drawer. *Please,* she thought. *Let it not be the Eye of Kashmir.* To have come so close and then to lose it….

She leaned even closer to the crack and strained to see over his shoulder, to find out what he was now sliding into his jacket pocket. So intently was she staring, she scarcely had time to react when he unexpectedly grasped the wardrobe door and swung it shut. She jerked back into the shadows and her shoulder thudded against the wall.

There was a silence. A very long silence.

Slowly the beam of the flashlight slid around the edge of the wardrobe, followed cautiously by the silhouette of the man's head.

Clea blinked as the light focused fully on her face. Against the glare she couldn't see him, but he could see *her.* For an eternity neither of them moved, neither of them made a sound.

Then he said, "Who the hell are *you?*"

The figure coiled up against the wardrobe didn't answer. Slowly Jordan played his torchlight down the length of the intruder, noting the stocking cap pulled low to the eyebrows, the face obscured by camouflage paint, the black turtleneck shirt and pants.

"I'm going to ask you one last time," Jordan said. "Who are you?"

He was answered with a mysterious smile. The sight of it surprised him. That's when the figure in black sprang like a cat. The impact sent Jordan staggering backward against the bedpost. At once the figure scrambled toward the balcony. Jordan lunged and managed to grab a handful of pant leg. They both tumbled to the floor and collided with the writing desk, letting loose a cascade of pens and pencils. His opponent squirmed beneath him and rammed a knee into Jordan's groin. In the onrush of pain and nausea, Jordan almost let go. His opponent got one hand free and was scrabbling about on the floor. Almost too late Jordan saw the pointed tip of a letter opener stabbing toward him.

He grabbed his opponent's wrist and savagely wrestled away the letter opener. The other man struck back just as savagely, arms flailing, body twisting like an eel. As Jordan fought to control those pummeling fists, he snagged his opponent's stocking cap.

A luxurious fountain of blond hair suddenly tumbled out across the floor, to ripple in a shimmering pool under the moonlight. Jordan stared in astonishment.

A woman.

For an endless moment they stared at each other, their breaths coming hard and fast, their hearts thudding against each other's chests.

A woman.

Without warning his body responded in a way that was both automatic and unsuppressibly male. She was too warm, too close. And very, very female. Even through their clothes, those soft curves were all too apparent. Just as the state of his arousal must be firmly apparent to her.

"Get off me," she whispered.

"First tell me who you are."

"Or *what?*"

"Or I'll—I'll—"

She smiled up at him, her mouth so close, so tempting he completely lost his train of thought.

It was the creak of approaching footsteps that made his brain snap back into function. Light suddenly spilled under the doorway and a man's voice called, "What's this, now? Who's in there?"

In a flash both Jordan and the woman were on their feet and dashing to the balcony. The woman was first over the railing. She scrambled like a monkey down the wisteria vine. By the time Jordan hit the ground, she was already sprinting across the lawn.

At the yew hedge he finally caught up with her and pulled her to a halt. "What were you doing in there?" he demanded.

"What were *you* doing in there?" she countered.

Back at the house the bedroom lights came on, and a voice yelled from the balcony, "Thieves! Don't you come back! I've called the police!"

"I'm not hanging around *here*," said the woman, and made a beeline for the woods.

Jordan sighed. "She does have a point." And he took off after her.

For a mile they slogged it out together, dodging brambles, ducking beneath branches. It was rough terrain, but she seemed tireless, moving at the steady pace of someone in superb condition. Only when they'd reached the far edge of the woods did he notice that her breathing had turned ragged.

He was ready to collapse.

They stopped to rest at the edge of a field. The sky was cloudless, the moonlight thick as milk. Wind blew, warm and fragrant with the smell of fallen leaves.

"So tell me," he managed to say between gulps of air, "do you do this sort of thing for a living?"

"I'm not a thief. If that's what you're asking."

"You act like a thief. You dress like a thief."

"I'm not a thief." She sagged back wearily against a tree trunk. "Are you?"

"Of course not!" he snapped.

"What do you mean, *of course not?* Is it beneath your precious dignity or something?"

"Not at all. That is— I mean—" He stopped and shook his head in confusion. "What *do* I mean?"

"I haven't the faintest," she said innocently.

"I'm *not* a thief," he said, more sure of himself now. "I was…playing a bit of a practical joke. That's all."

"I see." She tilted her head up to look at him, and her expression was plainly skeptical in the moonlight. Now that they weren't grappling like savages, he realized she was quite petite. And, without a doubt, female. He remembered how snugly her sweet curves had fit beneath him, and suddenly desire flooded through his body, a desire so intense it left him aching. All he had to do was step close to this woman and those blasted hormones kicked in.

He stepped back and forced himself to focus on her face. He couldn't quite make it out under all that camouflage paint, but it would be easy to remember her voice. It was low and throaty, almost like a cat's growl. Definitely not English, he thought. American?

She was still eyeing him with a skeptical look. "What did you take out of the wardrobe?" she asked. "Was that part of the practical joke?"

"You…saw that?"

"I did." Her chin came up squarely in challenge. "*Now* convince me it was all a prank."

Sighing, he reached under his jacket. At once she jerked back and pivoted around to flee. "No, it's all right!" he assured her. "It's not a gun or anything. It's just this pouch I'm wearing. Sort of a hidden backpack." He unzipped the pouch. She stood a few feet away, watching him warily, ready to sprint off at the first whiff of danger. "It's a bit sophomoric, really," he said, tugging at the pouch. "But it's good for a laugh." The contents suddenly flopped out and the woman gave a little squeak of fright. "See? It's not a weapon." He held it out to her. "It's an inflatable doll. When you blow it up, it turns into a naked woman."

She moved forward, eyeing the limp rubber doll. "Anatomically correct?" she inquired dryly.

"I'm not sure, really. I mean, er…" He glanced at her, and his mind suddenly veered toward *her* anatomy. He cleared his throat. "I haven't checked."

She regarded him the way one might look at an object of pity.

"But it *does* prove I was there on a prank," he said, struggling to stuff the deflated doll back in the pouch.

"All it proves," she said, "is that you had the foresight to bring an excuse should you be caught. Which, in your case, was a distinct possibility."

"And what excuse did *you* bring? Should you be caught?"

"I wasn't planning on getting caught," she said, and started across the field. "Everything was going quite well, as a matter of fact. Until you bumbled in."

"What was going quite well? The burglary?"

"I told you, I'm not a thief."

He followed her through the grass. "So why did *you* break in?"

"To prove a point."

"And that point was?"

"That it could be done. I've just proven to Mr. Delancey that he needs a security system. And my company's the one to install it."

"You work for a *security* company?" He laughed. "Which one?"

"Why do you ask?"

"My future brother-in-law's in that line of work. He might know your firm."

She smiled back at him, her lips immensely kissable, her teeth a bright arc in the night. "I work for Nimrod Associates," she said. Then, turning, she walked away.

"Wait. Miss—"

She waved a gloved hand in farewell, but didn't look back.

"I didn't catch your name!" he said.

"And I didn't catch yours," she said over her shoulder. "Let's keep it that way."

He saw her blond hair gleam faintly in the darkness. And then, in a twinkling, she was gone. Her absence seemed to leave the night colder, the darkness deeper. The only hint that she'd even been there was his residual ache of desire.

I shouldn't have let her go, he thought. *I know bloody well she's a thief.* But what could he have done? Hauled her to the police? Explained that he'd caught her in Guy Delancey's bedroom, where neither one of them belonged?

With a weary shake of his head, he turned and began the long tramp to his car, parked a half mile away. He'd have to hurry back to Chetwynd. It was getting late and he'd be missed at the party.

At least his mission was accomplished; he'd stolen Veronica's letters back. He'd hand them over to her, let her lavish him with thanks for saving her precious hide. After all, he *had* saved her hide, and he was bloody well going to tell her so.

And then he was going to strangle her.

CHAPTER TWO

THE PARTY AT Chetwynd was still in full swing. Through the ballroom windows came the sounds of laughter and violin music and the cheery clink of champagne glasses. Jordan stood in the driveway and considered his best mode of entry. The back stairs? No, he'd have to walk through the kitchen, and the staff would certainly find *that* suspicious. Up the trellis to Uncle Hugh's bedroom? Definitely not; he'd done enough tangling with vines for the night. He'd simply waltz in the front door and hope the guests were too deep in their cups to notice his disheveled state.

He straightened his bow tie and brushed the twigs off his jacket. Then he let himself in the front door.

To his relief, no one was in the entrance hall. He tiptoed past the ballroom doorway and started up the curving staircase. He was almost to the second-floor landing when a voice called from below.

"Jordie, where on earth have you been?"

Suppressing a groan, Jordan turned and saw his sister, Beryl, standing at the bottom of the stairs. She was looking flushed and lovelier than ever, her black hair swirled elegantly atop her head, her bared shoulders lustrous above the green velvet gown. Being in love certainly agreed with her. Since her engagement to Richard Wolf a month ago, Jordan had seldom seen her without a smile on her face.

At the moment she was not smiling.

She stared at his wrinkled jacket, his soiled trouser legs and muddy shoes. She shook her head. "I'm afraid to ask."

"Then don't."

"I'll ask anyway. What happened to you?"

He turned and continued up the stairs. "I went out for a walk."

"That's all?" She bounded up the steps after him in a rustle of skirts and stockings. "First you make me invite that horrid Guy Delancey—who, by the way, is drinking like a fish and going 'round pinching ladies' bottoms. Then you simply vanish from the party. And you reappear looking like that."

He went into his bedroom.

She followed him.

"It was a long walk," he said.

"It's been a long party."

"Beryl." He sighed, turning to face her. "I really

am sorry about Guy Delancey. But I can't talk about it right now. I'd be betraying a confidence."

"I see." She went to the door, then glanced back. "I *can* keep a secret, you know."

"So can I." Jordan smiled. "That's why I'm not saying a thing."

"Well, you'd best change your clothes, then. Or someone's going to ask why you've been climbing wisteria vines." She left, shutting the door behind her.

Jordan looked down at his jacket. Only then did he notice the leaf, poking like a green flag from his buttonhole.

He changed into a fresh tuxedo, combed the twigs from his hair and went downstairs to rejoin the party.

Though it was past midnight, the champagne was still flowing and the scene in the ballroom was as jolly as when he'd left it an hour and a half earlier. He swept up a glass from a passing tray and eased back into circulation. No one mentioned his absence; perhaps no one had noticed it. He worked his way across the room to the buffet table, where a magnificent array of hors d'oeuvres had been laid out, and he helped himself to the Scottish salmon. Breaking and entering was hard work, and he was famished.

A whiff of perfume, a hand brushing his arm, made him turn. It was Veronica Cairncross. "Well?" she whispered anxiously. "How did it go?"

"Not exactly clockwork. You were wrong about the butler's night off. There was a manservant in the house. I could have been caught."

"Oh, no," she moaned softly. "Then you didn't get them…."

"I got them. They're upstairs."

"You *did?*" A smile of utter happiness burst across her face. "Oh, Jordie!" She leaned forward and threw her arms around him, smearing salmon on his tuxedo. "You saved my life."

"I know, I know." He suddenly spotted Veronica's husband, Oliver, moving toward them. At once Jordan extricated himself from her embrace. "Ollie's coming this way," he whispered.

"Is he?" Veronica turned and automatically beamed her thousand-watt smile at Sir Oliver. "Darling, there you are! I lost track of you."

"You don't seem to be missing me much," grunted Sir Oliver. He frowned at Jordan, as though trying to divine his real intentions.

Poor fellow, thought Jordan. Any man married to Veronica was deserving of pity. Sir Oliver was a decent enough fellow, a descendant of the excellent Cairncross family, manufacturers of tea biscuits. Though twenty years older than his wife, and bald as a cue ball, he'd managed to win Veronica's hand— and to keep that hand well studded with diamonds.

"It's getting late," said Oliver. "Really, Veronica, shouldn't we be going home?"

"So soon? It's just past midnight."

"I have that meeting in the morning. And I'm quite tired."

"Well, I suppose we'll have to be going, then," Veronica said with a sigh. She smiled slyly at Jordan. "I think I'll sleep well tonight."

Just see that it's with your husband, thought Jordan with a shake of his head.

After the Cairncrosses had departed, Jordan glanced down and saw the greasy sliver of salmon clinging to his lapel. Drat, another tuxedo bites the dust. He wiped away the mess as best he could, picked up his glass of champagne and waded back into the crowd.

He cornered his future brother-in-law, Richard Wolf, near the musicians. Wolf was looking happy and dazed—just the way one expected a prospective bridegroom to look.

"So how's our guest of honor holding up?" asked Jordan.

Richard grinned. "Giving the old handshake a rest."

"Good idea to pace oneself." Jordan's gaze shifted toward the source of particularly raucous laughter. It was Guy Delancey, clearly well soused and leaning close to a buxom young thing. "Unfortunately,"

Jordan observed, "not everyone here believes in pacing himself."

"No kidding," said Wolf, also looking at Delancey. "You know, that fellow tried to put the make on Beryl tonight. Right under my nose."

"And did you defend her honor?"

"Didn't have to," said Richard with a laugh. "She does a pretty good job of defending herself."

Delancey's hand was now on Miss Buxom's lower back. Slowly that hand began to slide down toward dangerous terrain.

"What do women see in a guy like that, anyway?" asked Richard.

"Sex appeal?" said Jordan. Delancey did, after all, have rather dashing Spanish looks. "Who knows what attracts women to certain men?" Lord only knew what had attracted Veronica Cairncross to Guy. But she was rid of him now. If she was sensible, she'd damn well stay on the straight and narrow.

Jordan looked at Richard. "Tell me, have you ever heard of a security firm called Nimrod Associates?"

"Is that based here or abroad?"

"I don't know. Here, I imagine."

"I haven't heard of it. But I could check for you."

"Would you? I'd appreciate it."

"Why are you interested in this firm?"

"Oh…" Jordan shrugged. "The name came up in the course of the evening."

Richard was looking at him thoughtfully. Damn, it was that intelligence background of his, an aspect of Richard Wolf that could be either a help or a nuisance. Richard's antennae were out now, the questions forming in his head. Jordan would have to be careful.

Luckily, Beryl sauntered up at that moment to bestow a kiss on her intended. Any questions Richard may have entertained were quickly forgotten as he bent to press his lips to his fiancée's upturned mouth. Another kiss, a hungry twining of arms, and poor old Richard was oblivious to the rest of the world.

Ah, young lovers, sizzling in hormones, thought Jordan and polished off his drink. His own hormones were simmering tonight as well, helped along by the pleasant buzz of champagne.

And by thoughts of that woman.

He couldn't seem to get her out of his thick head. Not her voice, nor her laugh, nor the catlike litheness of her body twisting beneath his….

Quickly he set his glass down. No more champagne tonight. The memories were intoxicating enough. He glanced around for the tray of soda water and spotted his uncle Hugh entering the ballroom.

All evening Hugh had played genial host and proud uncle to the future bride. He'd happily guzzled champagne and flirted with ladies young enough to be his granddaughters. But at this particular moment Uncle Hugh was looking vexed.

He crossed the room, straight toward Guy Delancey. The two men exchanged a few words and Delancey's chin shot up. An instant later an obviously upset Delancey strode out of the ballroom, calling loudly for his car.

"Now what's going on?" said Jordan.

Beryl, her cheeks flushed and pretty from Richard's kissing, turned to look as Uncle Hugh wandered in their direction. "He's obviously not happy."

"Dreadful way to finish off the evening," Hugh was muttering.

"What happened?" asked Beryl.

"Guy Delancey's man called to report a burglary at the house. Seems someone climbed up the balcony and walked straight into the master bedroom. Imagine the cheek! And with the butler at home, too."

"Was anything stolen?" asked Richard.

"Don't know yet." Hugh shook his head. "Almost makes one feel a bit guilty, doesn't it?"

"Guilty?" Jordan forced a laugh from his throat. "Why?"

"If we hadn't invited Delancey here tonight, the burglar wouldn't have had his chance."

"That's ridiculous," said Jordan. "The burglar—I mean, if it *was* a burglar—"

"Why wouldn't it be a burglar?" asked Beryl.

"It's just—one shouldn't draw conclusions."

"Of course it's a burglar," said Hugh. "Why else would one break into Guy's house?"

"There could be other…explanations. Couldn't there?"

No one answered.

Smiling, Jordan took a sip of soda water. But the whole time he felt his sister's gaze, watching him closely.

Suspiciously.

THE PHONE WAS RINGING when Clea returned to her hotel room. Before she could answer it, the ringing stopped, but she knew it would start up again. Tony must be anxious. She wasn't ready to talk to him yet. Eventually she would have to, of course, but first she needed a chance to recover from the night's near catastrophe, a chance to figure out what she should do next. What Tony should do next.

She rooted around in her suitcase and found the miniature bottle of brandy she'd picked up on the airplane. She went into the bathroom, poured out a splash into a water glass and stood sipping the drink, staring dejectedly at her reflection in the mirror. In

the car she'd managed to wipe away most of the camouflage paint, but there were still smudges of it on
her temples and down one side of her nose. She
turned on the faucet, wet a facecloth and scrubbed
away the rest of the paint.

The phone was ringing again.

Carrying her glass, she went into the bedroom and
picked up the receiver. "Hello?"

"Clea?" said Tony. "What happened?"

She sank onto the bed. "I didn't get it."

"Did you get in the house?"

"Of course I got in!" Then, more softly, she said,
"I was close. So close. I searched the downstairs, but
it wasn't there. I'd just gotten upstairs when I was
rudely interrupted."

"By Delancey?"

"No. By another burglar. Believe it or not." She
managed a tired laugh. "Delancey's house seems to
be quite the popular place to rob."

There was a long silence on the other end of the
line. Then Tony asked a question that instantly chilled
her. "Are you sure it was just a burglar? Are you sure
it wasn't one of Van Weldon's men?"

At the mention of that name, Clea's fingers froze
around the glass of brandy. "No," she murmured.

"It's possible, isn't it? They may have figured

out what you're up to. Now *they'll* be after the Eye of Kashmir."

"They couldn't have followed me! I was so careful."

"Clea, you don't know these people—"

"The hell I don't!" she retorted. "I know *exactly* who I'm dealing with!"

After a pause Tony said softly, "I'm sorry. Of course you know. You know better than anyone. But I've had my ear to the ground. I've been hearing things."

"What things?"

"Van Weldon's got friends in London. Friends in high places."

"He has friends everywhere."

"I've also heard…" Tony's voice dropped. "They've upped the ante. You're worth a million dollars to them, Clea. Dead."

Her hands were shaking. She took a desperate gulp of brandy. At once her eyes watered, tears of rage and despair. She blinked them away.

"I think you should try the police again," Tony said.

"I'm not repeating that mistake."

"What's the alternative? Running for the rest of your life?"

"The evidence is *there.* All I have to do is get my hands on it. Then they'll *have* to believe me."

"You can't do it on your own, Clea!"

"I can do it. I'm sure I can."

"Delancey will know someone's broken in. Within twenty-four hours he'll have his house burglarproof."

"Then I'll get in some other way."

"How?"

"By walking in his front door. He has a weakness, you know. For women."

Tony groaned. "Clea, no."

"I can handle him."

"You *think* you can—"

"I'm a big girl, Tony. I can deal with a man like Delancey."

"This makes me sick. To think of you and…" He made a sound of disgust. "I'm going to the police."

Firmly Clea set down her glass. "Tony," she said. "There's no other way. I have some breathing space now. A week, maybe more before Van Weldon figures out where I am. I have to make the most of it."

"Delancey may not be so easy."

"To him I'll just be another dimwitted bimbo. A rich one, I think. That should get his attention."

"And if he gives you too much attention?"

Clea paused. The thought of actually making love to that oily Guy Delancey was enough to nauseate her. With any luck, it would never get that far.

She'd see to it it never got that far.

"I'll handle it," she said. "You just keep your ear

to the ground. Find out if anything else has come up for sale. And stay out of sight."

After she'd hung up, Clea sat on the bed, thinking about the last time she'd seen Tony. It had been in Brussels. They'd both been happy, so very happy! Tony had had a brand-new wheelchair, a sporty edition, he called it, for upper-body athletes. He had just received a fabulous commission for the sale of four medieval tapestries to an Italian industrialist. Clea had been about to leave for Naples, to finalize the purchase. Together they had celebrated not just their good fortune but the fact they'd finally found their way out of the darkness of their youth. The darkness of their shared past. They'd laughed and drunk wine and talked about the men in her life, the women in his, and about the peculiar hazards of courting from a wheelchair. Then they'd parted.

What a difference a month made.

She reached for her glass and drained the last of the brandy. Then she went to her suitcase and dug around in her clothes until she found what she was looking for: the box of Miss Clairol. She stared at the model's hair on the box, wondering if perhaps she should have chosen something more subtle. No, Guy Delancey wasn't the type to go for subtle. Brazen was more his style.

And "cinnamon red" should do the trick.

"I'VE CHECKED THE NAME Nimrod Associates," said
Richard. "There's no such security firm. At least, not
in England."

The three of them were sitting on the terrace,
enjoying a late breakfast. As usual, Beryl and Richard
were snuggling cheek to cheek, laughing and darting
amorous glances at each other. In short, behaving
precisely as one would expect a newly engaged
couple to behave. Some of that snuggling might be
due to the unexpected chill in the air. Summer was
definitely over, Jordan thought with regret. But the
sun was shining, the gardens still clung stubbornly to
their blossoms and a bracing breakfast on the terrace
was just the thing to clear the fog of last night's champagne from his head.

Now, after two cups of coffee, Jordan's brain was
finally starting to function. It wasn't just the champagne that had left him feeling muddled this morning;
it was the lack of sleep. Several times in the night he'd
awakened, sweating, from the same dream.

About the woman. Though her face had been
obscured by darkness, her hair was a vivid halo of
silvery ripples. She had reached up to him, her fingers
caressing his face, her flesh hot and welcoming. As
their lips had met, as his hands had slid into those
silvery coils of hair, he'd felt her body move against

his in that sweet and ancient dance. He'd gazed into her eyes. The eyes of a panther.

Now, by the light of morning, the symbolism of that nightmare was all too clear. Panthers. Dangerous women.

He shook off the image and poured himself another cup of coffee.

Beryl took a nibble of toast and marmalade, the whole time watching him. "Tell me, Jordie," she said. "Where did you hear about Nimrod Associates?"

"What?" Jordan glanced guiltily at his sister. "Oh, I don't know. A while ago."

"I thought it came up last night," said Richard.

Jordan reached automatically for a slice of toast. "Yes, I suppose that's when I heard it. Veronica must have mentioned the name."

Beryl was still watching him. This was the downside of being so close to one's sister; she could tell when he was being evasive.

"I notice you're rather chummy with Veronica Cairncross these days," she observed.

"Oh, well." He laughed. "We try to keep up the friendship."

"At one time, I recall, it was more than friendship."

"That was ages ago."

"Yes. Before she was married."

Jordan looked at her with feigned astonishment.

"You're not thinking…good Lord, you can't possibly imagine…"

"You've been acting so *odd* lately. I'm just trying to figure out what's wrong with you."

"Nothing. There's nothing wrong with me." *Save for the fact I've recently taken up a life of crime,* he thought.

He took a sip of tepid coffee and almost choked on it when Richard said, "Look. It's the police."

An official car had turned onto Chetwynd's private road. It pulled into the gravel driveway and out stepped Constable Glenn, looking trim and snappy in uniform. He waved to the trio on the terrace.

As the policeman came up the steps, Jordan thought, *This is it, then. I'll be ignominiously hauled off to prison. My face in the papers, my name disgraced…*

"Good morning to you all," said Constable Glenn cheerily. "May I inquire if Lord Lovat's about?"

"You've just missed him," said Beryl. "Uncle Hugh's gone off to London for the week."

"Oh. Well, perhaps I should speak with you, then."

"Do sit down." Beryl smiled and indicated a chair. "Join us for some breakfast."

Oh, lovely, thought Jordan. What would she offer him next? *Tea? Coffee? My brother, the thief?*

Constable Glenn sat down and smiled primly at the cup of coffee set before him. He took a sip, careful not to let his mustache get wet. "I suppose," he said, setting his cup down, "that you know about the robbery at Mr. Delancey's residence."

"We heard about it last night," said Beryl. "Have you any leads?"

"Yes, as a matter of fact. We have a pretty good idea what we're dealing with here." Constable Glenn looked at Jordan and smiled.

Weakly, Jordan smiled back.

"A matter of excellent police work, I'm sure," said Beryl.

"Well, not exactly," admitted the constable. "More a case of carelessness on the burglar's part. You see, she dropped her stocking cap. We found it in Mr. Delancey's bedroom."

"*She?*" said Richard. "You mean the burglar's a woman?"

"We're going on that assumption, though we could be wrong. There was a very long strand of hair in the cap. Blond. It would've reached well below her—or his—shoulders. Does that sound like anyone you might know?" Again he looked at Jordan.

"No one I can think of," Jordan said quickly. "That is—there *are* some blondes in our circle of acquaintances. But not a burglar among them."

"It could be anyone. Anyone at all. It's not the first break-in we've had in this neighborhood. Three just this year. And the culprit might even be someone you know. You'd be surprised, Mr. Tavistock, what sort of misbehavior occurs, even in your social circle."

Jordan cleared his throat. "I can't imagine."

"This woman, whoever she is, is quite bold. She entered through a downstairs locked door. Got upstairs without alarming the butler. Only then did she get careless—caused a bit of a racket. That's when she was chased out."

"Was anything taken?" asked Beryl.

"Not so far as Mr. Delancey knows."

So Guy Delancey didn't report the stolen letters, thought Jordan. Or perhaps he never even noticed they were missing.

"This time she slipped up," said Constable Glenn. "But there's always the chance she'll strike again. That's what I came to warn you about. These things come in waves, you see. A certain neighborhood will be chosen. Delancey's house isn't that far from here, so Chetwynd could be in her target zone." He said it with the authority of one who had expert knowledge of the criminal mind. "A residence as grand as yours would be quite a temptation." Again he looked directly at Jordan.

Again Jordan had that sinking feeling that the good Constable Glenn knew more than he was letting on. *Or is it just my guilty conscience?*

Constable Glenn rose and addressed Beryl. "You'll let Lord Lovat know of my concerns?"

"Of course," said Beryl. "I'm sure we'll be perfectly all right. After all, we do have a security expert on the premises." She beamed at Richard. "And he's *quite* trustworthy."

"I'll look over the household arrangements," said Richard. "We'll beef up security as necessary."

Constable Glenn nodded in satisfaction. "Good day, then. I'll let you know how things develop."

They watched the constable march smartly back to his car. As it drove away, up the tree-lined road, Richard said, "I wonder why he felt the need to warn us personally."

"As a special favor to Uncle Hugh, I'm sure," said Beryl. "Constable Glenn was employed by MI6 years ago as a 'watcher'—domestic surveillance. I think he still feels like part of the team."

"Still, I get the feeling there's something else going on."

"A woman burglar," said Beryl thoughtfully. "My, we *have* come a long way." Suddenly she burst out laughing. "Lord, what a relief to hear it's a *she!*"

"Why?" asked Richard.

"Oh, it's just too ridiculous to mention."

"Tell me, anyway."

"You see, after last night, I thought—I mean, it occurred to me that—" She laughed harder. She sat back, flush with merriment, and pressed her hand to her mouth. Between giggles she managed to choke out the words. "I thought *Jordie* might be the cat burglar!"

Richard burst out laughing, as well. Like two giddy school kids, he and Beryl collapsed against each other in a fit of the sillies.

Jordan's response was to calmly bite off a corner of his toast. Though his throat had gone dry as chalk, he managed to swallow down a mouthful of crumbs. "I fail to see the humor in all this," he said.

They only laughed harder as he bore the abuse with a look of injured dignity.

CLEA SPOTTED GUY DELANCEY walking toward the refreshment tent. It was the three-minute time-out between the third and fourth chukkers, and a general exodus was under way from the polo viewing stands. Briefly she lost sight of him in the press of people, and she felt a momentary panic that all her detective work would be for nothing. She'd made a few discreet inquiries in the village that morning, had learned that most of the local gentry would almost certainly be headed for the polo field that afternoon. Armed with that tip, she'd called Delancey's house, introduced herself as Lady So-and-So, and asked the butler if Mr. Delancey was still meeting her at the polo game as he'd promised.

The butler assured her that Mr. Delancey would be at the field.

It had taken her the past hour to track him down in the crowd. She wasn't about to lose him now.

She pressed ahead, plunging determinedly into the Savile-Row-and-silk-scarf set. The smell of the polo field, of wet grass and horseflesh, was quickly overpowered by the scent of expensive perfumes. With an air of regal assuredness—pure acting on her part—Clea swept into the green-and-white-striped tent and glanced around at the well-heeled crowd. There were dozens of tables draped in linen, silver buckets overflowing with ice and champagne, fresh-faced girls in starched aprons whisking about with trays and glasses. And the ladies— what hats they wore! What elegant vowels tripped from their tongues! Clea paused, her confidence suddenly wavering. Lord, she'd never pull this off….

She glimpsed Delancey by the bar. He was standing alone, nursing a drink. *Now or never,* she thought.

She swayed over to the counter and edged in close to Delancey. She didn't look at him, but kept her attention strictly focused on the young fellow manning the bar.

"A glass of champagne," she said.

"Champagne, coming up," said the bartender.

As she waited for the drink, she sensed Delancey's gaze. Casually she shifted around so that she was almost, but not quite, looking at him. He was indeed facing her.

The bartender slid across her drink. She took a sip and gave a weary sigh. Then she drew her fingers slowly, sensuously, through her mane of red hair.

"Been a long day, has it?"

Clea glanced sideways at Delancey. He was fashionably tanned and impeccably dressed in autumn-weight cashmere. Though tall and broad shouldered, his once striking good looks had gone soft and a bit jowly, and the hand clutching the whiskey glass had a faint tremor. *What a waste,* she thought, and smiled at him prettily.

"It has been rather a long day." She sighed, and took another sip. "Afraid I'm not very good in airplanes. And now my friends haven't shown up as promised."

"You've just flown in? From where?"

"Paris. Went on holiday for a few weeks, but decided to cut it short. Dreadfully unfriendly there."

"I was there just last month. Didn't feel welcome at all. I recommend you try Provence. Much friendlier."

"Provence? I'll keep that in mind."

He sidled closer. "You're not English, are you?"

She smiled at him coyly. "You can tell?"

"The accent—what, American?"

"My, you're quick," she said, and noted how he puffed up with the compliment. "You're right, I'm

American. But I've been living in London for some time. Ever since my husband died."

"Oh." He shook his head sympathetically. "I'm so sorry."

"He was eighty-two." She sipped again, gazing at him over the rim of her glass. "It was his time."

She could read the thoughts going through his transparent little head. *Filthy rich old man, no doubt. Why else would a lovely young thing marry him? Which makes her a rich widow....*

He moved closer. "Did you say your friends were supposed to meet you here?"

"They never showed." Sighing, she gave him a helpless look. "I took the train up from London. We were supposed to drive back together. Now I suppose I'll just have to take the train home."

"There's no need to do that!" Smiling, he edged closer to her. "I know this may sound a bit forward. But if you're at loose ends, I'd be delighted to show you 'round. It's a lovely village we have here."

"I couldn't impose—"

"No imposition at all. I'm at loose ends myself today. Thought I'd watch a little polo, and then go off to the club. But this is a far pleasanter prospect."

She looked him up and down, as though trying to decide if he could be trusted. "I don't even know your name," she protested weakly.

He thrust out his hand in greeting. "Guy Delancey. Delighted to make your acquaintance. And you are…"

"Diana," she said. Smiling warmly, she shook his hand. "Diana Lamb."

CHAPTER THREE

IT WAS THREE minutes into the fourth chukker. Oliver Cairncross, mounted on his white-footed roan, swung his mallet on a dead run. The *thwock* sent the ball flying between the goalposts. Another score for the Bucking'shire Boys! Enthusiastic applause broke out in the viewing stands, and Sir Oliver responded by sweeping off his helmet and dipping his bald head in a dramatic bow.

"Just look at him," murmured Veronica. "They're like children out there, swinging their sticks at balls. Will they never grow up?"

Out on the field Sir Oliver strapped his helmet back in place and turned to wave to his wife in the stands. He frowned when he saw that she was leaning toward Jordan.

"Oh, no." Veronica sighed. "He's seen you." At once she rose to her feet, waving and beaming a smile of wifely pride. Sitting back down, she muttered, "He's so bloody suspicious."

Jordan looked at her in astonishment. "Surely he doesn't think that you and I—"

"You *are* my old chum. Naturally he wonders."

Yes, of course he does, thought Jordan. Any man married to Veronica would probably spend his lifetime in a perpetual state of doubt.

The ball was tossed. The thunder of hoofbeats, the whack of a mallet announced the resumption of play.

Veronica leaned close to Jordan. "Did you bring them?" she whispered.

"As requested." He reached into his jacket and withdrew the bundle of letters.

At once she snatched them out of his hand. "You didn't read them, did you?"

"Of course not."

"Such a gentleman!" Playfully she reached up and pinched his cheek. "You promise you won't tell anyone?"

"Not a soul. But this is absolutely the last time, Veronica. From now on, be discreet. Or better yet, honor those marriage vows."

"Oh, I will, I will!" she declared fervently. She stood and moved toward the aisle.

"Where are you going?" he called.

"To flush these down the loo, of course!" She gave him a gay wave of farewell. "I'll call you, Jordie!" As she turned to make her way up the aisle, she brushed past a broad-shouldered man. At once she halted, her gaze slanting up with interest at this new specimen of masculinity.

Jordan shook his head in disgust and turned his attention back to the polo game. Men and horses thundered past, chasing that ridiculous rubber ball across the field. Back and forth they flew, mallets swinging, a tangle of sweating men and horseflesh. Jordan had never been much of a polo fan. The few times he'd played the game he'd come away with more than his share of bruises. He didn't trust horses and horses didn't trust him and in the inevitable struggle for authority, the beasts had a seven-hundred-pound advantage.

There were still four chukkers left to go, but Jordan had had his fill. He left the viewing stands and headed for the refreshment tent.

In the shade of green-and-white-striped awning, he strolled over to the wine bar and ordered a glass of soda water. With so much celebrating this past week, he'd been waking up every morning feeling a bit pickled.

Sipping his glass of soda, Jordan wandered about looking for an unoccupied table. He spotted one off in a corner. As he approached it, he recognized the occupant of the neighboring table. It was Guy Delancey. Seated across from Delancey, her back to Jordan, was a woman with a magnificent mane of red hair. The couple seemed to be intently engaged in intimate conversation. Jordan thought it best not to disturb them. He walked straight past them and was just sitting down at the neighboring table when he caught a snatch of their dialogue.

"Just the spot to forget one's troubles," Guy was saying. "Sun. Sugary beaches. Waiters catering to your every whim. Do consider joining me there."

The woman laughed. The sound had a throaty, hauntingly familiar ring to it. "It's rather a leap, don't you think, Guy?" she said. "I mean, we've only just met. To run off with you to the Caribbean…"

Slowly Jordan turned in his chair and stared at the woman. Lustrous cinnamon red hair framed her face, softening its angles. She had fair, almost translucent skin with a hint of rouge. Though she was not precisely beautiful, there was a hypnotic quality to those dark eyes, which slanted like a cat's above finely carved cheekbones. *Cat's eyes,* he thought. *Panther's eyes.*

It was her. It had to be her.

As though aware that someone was watching her, she raised her head and looked at Jordan. The instant their gazes met she froze. Even the rouge couldn't conceal the sudden blanching of her skin. He sat staring at her, and she at him, both of them caught in the same shock of mutual recognition.

What now? wondered Jordan. Should he warn Guy Delancey? Confront the woman on the spot? And what would he say? *Guy, old chap, this is the woman I bumped into while burgling your bedroom....*

Guy Delancey swiveled around and said cheerily, "Why, hello, Jordan! Didn't know you were right behind me."

"I...didn't want to intrude." Jordan glanced in the woman's direction. Still white-faced, she reached for her drink and took a desperate swallow.

Guy noted the direction of Jordan's gaze. "Have you two met?" he asked.

Their answer came out in a simultaneous rush.

"Yes," said Jordan.

"No," said the woman.

Guy frowned. "Aren't you two sure?"

"What he means," the woman cut in before Jordan could say a word, "is that we've *seen* each other before. Last week's auction at Sotheby's, wasn't it? But we've never actually been introduced." She looked Jordan straight in the eye, silently daring him to contradict her.

What a brazen hussy, he thought.

"Let me properly introduce you two," said Guy. "This is Lord Lovat's nephew, Jordan Tavistock. And this—" Guy swept his hand proudly toward the woman "—is Diana Lamb."

The woman extended a slender hand across the table as Jordan turned his chair to join them. "Delighted to make your acquaintance, Mr. Tavistock."

"So you two met at Sotheby's," said Guy.

"Yes. Terribly disappointing collection," she said. "The St. Augustine estate. One would think there'd be *something* worth bidding on, but no. I didn't make a single offer." Again she looked straight at Jordan. "Did you?"

He saw the challenge in her gaze. He saw something else as well: a warning. *You spill the beans,* said those cheerful brown eyes, *and so will I.*

"Well, did you, Jordie?" asked Guy.

"No," muttered Jordan, staring fiercely at the woman. "Not a one."

At his capitulation, the woman's smile broadened to dazzling. He had to concede she'd beaten him this round; next round she'd not be so lucky. He'd have the right words ready, his strategy figured out….

"…dreadful shambles. Pitiful, really. Don't you agree?" said Guy.

Suddenly aware that he was being addressed, Jordan looked at Guy. "Pardon?"

"All the estates that have fallen on hard times. Did you know the Middletons have decided to open Greystones to public tours?"

"I hadn't heard," said Jordan.

"Lord, can you imagine how humiliating that must be? To have all those strangers tramping through one's house, snapping photos of your loo. I'd never sink so low."

"Sometimes one has no choice," said Jordan.

"Certainly one has the choice! You're not saying you'd ever let the tourists into Chetwynd, would you?"

"No, of course not."

"Neither would I let them into Underhill. Plus, there's the problem of security, something I'm acutely tuned in to after that robbery attempt last night. People may *claim* they're tourists. But what if they're really thieves, come to check the layout of the place?"

"I agree with you on that point," said Jordan, looking straight at the woman. "One can't be too careful."

The little thief didn't bat an eyelash. She merely smiled back, those brown eyes wide and innocent.

"One certainly can't," said Guy. "And that goes triply for you. When I think of the fortune in art hanging on your walls…"

"Fortune?" said the woman, her gaze narrowing.

"I wouldn't call it a fortune," Jordan said quickly.

"He's being modest," said Guy. "Chetwynd has a collection any museum would kill for."

"All of it under tight security," said Jordan. "And I mean, *extremely* tight."

The hussy laughed. "I believe you, Mr. Tavistock."

"I certainly hope you do."

"I'd like to see Chetwynd some day."

"Hang around with me, darling," said Guy, "and we might wangle an invitation."

With a last squeeze of the woman's hand, Guy rose to his feet. "I'll have the car sent 'round, how about it? If we leave now, we'll avoid the jam in the parking lot."

"I'll come with you," she offered.

"No, no. Do stay and finish your drink. I'll be back as soon as the car's ready." He turned and disappeared into the crowd.

The woman sat back down. No shrinking violet, this one; brazenly she faced Jordan. And she smiled.

FROM ACROSS the refreshment tent Charles Ogilvie spotted the woman. He knew it had to be her; there was no mistaking the hair color. "Cinnamon red" was precisely how one would describe that glorious mane of hers. A superb job, courtesy of Clairol. Ogilvie had found the discarded hair-color box in the bathroom rubbish can when he'd searched her hotel room this morning, had confirmed its effect when he'd pulled a few silky strands from her hairbrush. Miss Clea Rice, it appeared, had done another quick-change job. She was getting better at this. Twice she'd metamorphosed into a different woman. Twice he'd almost lost her.

But she wasn't good enough to shake him entirely. He still had the advantage of experience. And she had the disadvantage of not knowing what *he* looked like.

Casually he strolled a few feet along the tent perimeter, to get a better look at her profile, to confirm it was indeed Clea Rice. She'd gone heavy with the lipstick and rouge, but he still recognized those superb cheekbones, that ivory skin. He also had no trouble recognizing Guy Delancey, who had just risen to his feet and was now moving away through the crowd, leaving Clea at the table.

It was the other man he didn't recognize.

He was a blond chap, long and lean as a whippet, impeccably attired. The man slid into the chair where Delancey had been sitting and faced the Rice woman across the table. It was apparent, just by the intensity of their gazes, that they were not strangers to each other. This was troubling. Where did this blond man fit in? No mention of him had appeared in the woman's dossier, yet there they were, deep in conversation.

Ogilvie took the lens cap off his telephoto. Moving behind the wine bar, he found a convenient vantage point from which to shoot his photos, unobserved. He focused on the blond man's profile and clicked off a few shots, then took a few shots of Clea Rice, as well. A new partner? he wondered. My, she was resourceful. Three weeks of tailing the woman had left him with a grudging sense of admiration for her cleverness.

But was she clever enough to stay alive?

He reloaded his camera and began to shoot a second roll.

"I LIKE THE HAIR," said Jordan.

"Thank you," the woman answered.

"A bit flashy, though, don't you think? Attracts an awful lot of attention."

"That was the whole idea."

"Ah, I see. Guy Delancey."

She inclined her head. "Some men are *so* predictable."

"It's almost unfair, isn't it? The advantage you have over the poor dumb beasts."

"Why shouldn't I capitalize on my God-given talents?"

"I don't think you're putting those talents quite to the use He intended." Jordan sat back in his chair and returned her steady gaze. "There's no such company as Nimrod Associates. I've checked. Who are you? Is Diana Lamb your real name?"

"Is Jordan Tavistock yours?"

"Yes, and you didn't answer my question."

"Because I find you so much more interesting." She leaned forward, and he couldn't help but glance down at the deeply cut neckline of her flowered dress.

"So you own Chetwynd," she said.

He forced himself to focus on her face. "My uncle Hugh does."

"And that fabulous art collection? Also your uncle's?"

"The family's. Collected over the years."

"Collected?" She smiled. "Obviously I've under-estimated you, Mr. Tavistock. Not the rank amateur I thought you were."

"What?"

"Quite the professional. A thief *and* a gentleman."

"I'm nothing of the kind!" He shot forward in his chair and inhaled such an intoxicating whiff of her perfume he felt dizzy. "The art has been in my family for generations!"

"Ah. One in a long line of professionals?"

"This is absurd—"

"Or are you the first in the family?"

Gripping the table in frustration, he counted slowly to five and let out a breath. "I am not, and have never been, a thief."

"But I saw you, remember? Rooting around in the wardrobe. You took something out—papers, I believe. So you *are* a thief."

"Not in the same sense *you* are."

"If your conscience is so clear, why didn't you go to the police?"

"Perhaps I will."

"I don't think so." She flashed him that maddening grin of triumph. "I think when it comes to thievery, *you're* the more despicable one. Because you make victims of your friends."

"Whereas you make friends of your victims?"

"Guy Delancey's not a friend."

"Astonishing how I misinterpreted that scene between you two! So what's the plan, little Miss Lamb? Seduction followed by a bit of larceny?"

"Trade secrets," she answered calmly.

"And why on earth are you so fixated on Delancey? Isn't it a bit risky to stick with the same victim?"

"Who said *he's* the victim?" She lifted the glass to her lips and took a delicate sip. He found her every movement oddly fascinating. The way her lips parted, the way the liquid slid into that moist, red mouth. He found himself swallowing as well, felt his own throat suddenly go parched.

"What is it Delancey has that you want so very badly?" he asked.

"What were those papers you took?" she countered.

"It won't work, you know."

"What won't work?"

"Trying to lump me in your category. *You're* the thief."

"And you're not?"

"What I lifted from that wardrobe has no intrinsic value. It was a personal matter."

"So is this for me," she answered tightly. "A personal matter."

Jordan frowned as a thought suddenly struck him. Guy Delancey had romanced Veronica Cairncross, and then had threatened to use her letters against her. Had he done the same to other women? Was Diana Lamb, or someone close to her, also a victim of Guy's?

Or am I trying to talk myself out of the obvious? he thought. The obvious being, this woman was a garden-variety burglar, out for loot. She'd already proven herself adept at housebreaking. What else could she be?

Such a pity, he thought, eyeing that face with its alabaster cheeks and nut brown eyes. Sooner or later those intelligent eyes would be gazing out of a jail cell.

"Is there any way I can talk you out of this?" he asked.

"Why would you?"

"I just think it's a waste of your apparent… talents. Plus there's the matter of it being morally wrong, to boot."

"Right, wrong." She gave an unconcerned wave of her hand. "Sometimes it isn't clear which is which."

This woman was beyond reform! And the fact he

knew she was a thief, knew what she had planned, made him almost as guilty if she succeeded.

Which, he decided, she would not.

He said, "I won't let you, you know. While I'm not particularly fond of Guy Delancey, I won't let him be robbed blind."

"I suppose you're going to tell him how we met?" she asked. Not a flicker of anxiety was in her eyes.

"No. But I'm going to warn him."

"Based on what evidence?"

"Suspicions."

"I'd be careful if I were you." She took another sip of her drink and placidly set the glass down. "Suspicions can go in more than one direction."

She had him there, and they both knew it. He couldn't warn Delancey without implicating himself as a thief. If Delancey chose to raise a fuss about it to the police, not only would Jordan's reputation be irreparably tarnished, Veronica's, too, would suffer.

No, he'd prefer not to take that risk.

He met Diana's calm gaze with one just as steady. "An ounce of prevention is worth a pound of cure," he said, and smiled.

"Meaning what, pray tell?"

"Meaning I plan to make it bloody difficult for you to so much as lift a teaspoon from the man and get away with it."

For the first time he saw a ripple of anxiety in her eyes. Her brightly painted red lips drew tight. "You don't understand. This is not your concern—"

"Of course it is. I plan to watch you like a hawk. I'm going to follow you and Delancey everywhere. Pop up when you least expect it. Make a royal nuisance of myself. In short, Miss Lamb, I've adopted you as my crusade. And if you make one false move, I'm going to cry wolf." He sat back, smiling. "Think about it."

She *was* thinking about it, and none too happily, judging by her expression.

"You can't do this," she whispered.

"I can. I have to."

"There's too much at stake! I won't let you ruin it—"

"Ruin *what?*"

She was about to answer when a hand closed over her shoulder. She glanced up sharply at Guy Delancey, who'd just returned and now stood behind her.

"Sorry if I startled you," he said cheerily. "Is everything all right?"

"Yes. Yes, everything's fine." Though the color had drained from her face, she still managed to smile, to flash Delancey a look of coquettish promise. "Is the car ready?"

"Waiting at the gate, my lady." Guy helped her

from her chair. Then he gave Jordan a careless nod of farewell. "See you around, Jordan."

Jordan caught a last glimpse of the woman's face, looking back at him in smothered anger. Then, with shoulders squared, she followed Delancey into the crowd.

You've been warned, Diana Lamb, thought Jordan. Now he'd see if she heeded that warning. And just in case she didn't...

Jordan pulled a handkerchief out of his jacket pocket. Gingerly he picked up the woman's champagne glass by the lower stem and peered at the smudge of ruby red lipstick. He smiled. There, crystal clear on the surface of the glass, was what he'd been looking for.

Fingerprints.

OGILVIE FINISHED SHOOTING his third roll of film and clipped the lens cap back on his telephoto. He had more than enough shots of the blond man. By tonight he'd have the images transmitted to London and, with any luck, an ID would be forthcoming. The fact Clea Rice had apparently picked up an unknown associate disturbed him, if only because he'd had no inkling of it. As far as he knew, the woman traveled alone, and always had.

He'd have to find out more about the blond chap.

The woman rose from her chair and departed with Guy Delancey. Ogilvie tucked his camera in his bag and left the tent to follow them. He kept a discreet distance, far enough back so that he would blend in with the crowd. She was an easy subject to tail, with all that red hair shimmering in the sunlight. The worst possible choice for anyone trying to avoid detection. But that was Clea Rice, always doing the unexpected.

The couple headed for the gate.

Ogilvie picked up his pace. He slipped through the gates just in time to see that head of red hair duck into a waiting Bentley.

Frantically Ogilvie glanced around the parking lot and spotted his black MG socked in three rows deep. By the time he could extricate it from that sea of Jaguars and Mercedes, Delancey and the woman could be miles away.

In frustration he watched Delancey's Bentley drive off. So much for following them; he'd have to catch up with her later. No problem. He knew which hotel she was staying at, knew that she'd paid for the next three nights in advance.

He decided to shift his efforts to the blond man.

Fifteen minutes later he spotted the man leaving through the gates. By that time Ogilvie had his car ready and waiting near the parking-lot exit. He saw the man step into a champagne gold Jaguar, and he took note of the license number. The Jaguar pulled out of the parking lot.

So did Ogilvie's MG.

His quarry led him on a long and winding route through rolling fields and trees, leaves already tinted with the fiery glow of autumn. Blueblood country, thought Ogilvie, noting the sleek horses in the pasture. Whoever *was* this fellow, anyway?

The gold Jaguar finally turned off the main road, onto a private roadway flanked by towering elms. From the main road Ogilvie could just glimpse the house that lay beyond those elms. It was magnificent, a stone-and-turret manor surrounded by acres of gardens.

He glanced at the manor name. It was mounted in bronze on the stone pillars marking the roadway entrance.

Chetwynd.

"You've come up in the world, Clea Rice," murmured Ogilvie.

Then he turned the car around. It was four o'clock. He'd have just enough time to call in his report to London.

VICTOR VAN WELDON HAD HAD a bad day. The congestion in his lungs was worse, his doctors said, and it was time for the oxygen again. He thought he'd weaned himself from that green tank. But now the tank was back, hooked onto his wheelchair, and the tubes were back in his nostrils. And once again he was feeling his mortality.

What a time for Simon Trott to insist on a meeting.

Van Weldon hated to be seen in such a weak and vulnerable condition. Through the years he had prided himself on his strength. His ruthlessness. Now, to be revealed for what he was—an old and dying man—would grant Simon Trott too much of an advantage. Although Van Weldon had already named Trott his successor, he was not yet ready to hand over the company reins. *Until I draw my last breath,* he thought, *the company is mine to control.*

There was a knock on the door. Van Weldon turned his wheelchair around to face his younger associate as he walked into the room. It was apparent, by the look on Trott's face, that the news he brought was not good.

Trott, as usual, was dressed in a handsomely tailored suit that showed his athletic frame to excellent advantage. He had it all—youth, blond good looks, all the women he could possibly hope to bed. *But he does not yet have the company,* thought Van Weldon. *He is still afraid of me. Afraid of telling me this latest news.*

"What have you learned?" asked Van Weldon.

"I think I know why Clea Rice headed for England," said Trott. "There have been rumors…on the black market…" He paused and cleared his throat.

"What rumors?"

"They say an Englishman has been boasting about a secret purchase he made. He claims he recently acquired…" Trott looked down. Reluctantly he finished. "The Eye of Kashmir."

"*Our* Eye of Kashmir? That is impossible."

"That is the rumor."

"The Eye has not been placed on the market! There is no way anyone could acquire it."

"We have not inventoried the collection since it was moved. There is a possibility…"

The two men exchanged looks. And Van Weldon understood. They both understood. *We have a thief among our ranks. A traitor who has dared to go against us.*

"If Clea Rice has also heard rumors of this sale, it could be disastrous for us," said Van Weldon.

"I'm quite aware of that."

"Who is this Englishman?"

"His name is Guy Delancey. We're trying to locate his residence now."

Van Weldon nodded. He sank back in his wheelchair and for a moment let the oxygen wash through his lungs. "Find Delancey," he said softly. "I have a feeling that when you do, you will also find Clea Rice."

CHAPTER FOUR

"To NEW FRIENDS," said Guy as he handed Clea a glass brimming with champagne.

"To new friends," she murmured and took a sip. The champagne was excellent. It would go to her head if she wasn't careful, and now, more than ever, she needed to keep her head. Such a sticky situation! How on earth was she to case the joint while this slobbery Casanova was all over her? She'd planned to let him make only a few preliminary moves, but it was clear Delancey had far more than just a harmless flirtation in mind.

He sat down beside her on the flowered settee, close enough for her to get a good look at his face. For a man in his late forties, he was still reasonably attractive, his skin relatively unlined, his hair still jet black. But the watery eyes and the sagging jowls were testimony to a dissipated life.

He leaned closer, and she had to force herself not to pull back in repulsion as those eyes swam toward her. To her relief, he didn't kiss her—yet. The trick was to hold him off while she dragged as much information as she could out of him.

She smiled coyly. "I love your house."

"Thank you."

"And the art! Quite a collection. All originals, I take it?"

"Naturally." Guy waved proudly at the paintings on the walls. "I haunt the auction houses. At Sotheby's, if they see me coming, they rub their hands together in glee. Of course, this isn't the best of my collection."

"It isn't?"

"No, I keep the finer pieces in my London town house. That's where I do most of my entertaining. Plus, it has far better security."

Clea felt her heart sink. Darn, was that where he kept it, then? His London town house? Then she'd wasted the week here in Buckinghamshire.

"It's a major concern of mine these days," he murmured, leaning even closer toward her. "Security."

"Against theft, you mean?" she inquired innocently.

"I mean security in general. The wolf at the door. The chill of a lonely bed." He bent toward her and pressed his sodden lips to hers. She shuddered. "I've been searching so long for the right woman," he whispered. "A soul mate…"

Do women actually fall for this line? she wondered.

"And when I looked in your eyes today—in that tent—I thought perhaps I'd found her."

Clea fought the urge to burst out laughing and managed—barely—to return his gaze with one just as steady. Just as smoldering. "But one must be careful," she murmured.

"I agree."

"Hearts are so very fragile. Especially mine."

"Yes, yes! I know." He kissed her again, more deeply. This was more than she could bear.

She pulled back, rage making her breath come hard and fast. Guy didn't seem at all disturbed by it; if anything, he took her heavy breathing as a sign of passion.

"It's too soon, too fast," she panted.

"It's the way it was meant to be."

"I'm not ready—"

"I'll *make* you ready." Without warning he grasped her breast and began to knead it vigorously like a lump of bread dough.

Clea sprang to her feet and moved away. It was either that or slug him in the mouth. At the moment she was all in favor of the latter. In a shaky voice she said, "Please, Guy. Maybe later. When we know each other better. When I feel I know *you*. As a person, I mean."

"A person?" He shook his head in frustration. "What, exactly, do you need to know?"

"Just the small things that tell me about you. For instance…" She turned and gestured to the paintings. "I know you collect art. But all I know is what I see on these walls. I have no idea what moves you, what appeals to you. Whether you collect other things. Besides paintings, I mean." She gave him a questioning look.

He shrugged. "I collect antique weapons."

"There now, you see?" Smiling, she came toward him. "I find that fascinating! It tells me you have a masculine streak of adventure."

"It does?" He looked pleased. "Yes, I suppose it does."

"What sort of weapons?"

"Antique swords. Pistols. A few daggers."

Her heart gave an extra thump at that last word. *Daggers.* She moved closer to him. "Ancient weaponry," she murmured, "is wonderfully erotic, I think."

"You do?"

"Yes, it—it conjures up knights in armor, ladies in castle towers." She clasped her hands and gave a visible shiver of excitement. "It gives me goose bumps just to think of it."

"I had no idea it had that effect on women," he said

in wonder. With sudden enthusiasm he rose from the couch. "Come with me, my lady," he said, taking her hand. "And I'll show you a collection that'll send shivers down your spine. I've just picked up a new treasure—something I purchased on the sly from a very private source."

"You mean the black market?"

"Even more private than that."

She let him guide her into the hallway and up the stairs. *So he keeps it on the second floor,* she thought. Probably the bedroom. To think she had gotten so close to it that night.

Somewhere, a phone was ringing. Guy ignored it.

They reached the top of the stairs. He turned right, toward the east wing—the bedroom—and suddenly halted.

"Master Delancey?" called a voice. "You've a telephone call."

Guy glanced back down the stairs at the gray-haired butler who stood on the lower landing. "Take a message," he snapped.

"But it—it's—"

"Yes?"

The butler cleared his throat. "It's Lady Cairncross."

Guy winced. "What does she want?"

"She wishes to see you immediately."

"You mean *now?*"

Guy hurried down the stairs to take the receiver. From the upper landing Clea listened to the conversation below.

"Not a good time, Veronica," Guy said. "Couldn't you…look, I have other things to do right now. You're being unreasonable. No. Veronica, you mustn't! We'll talk about this some other— Hello? Hello?" He frowned at the receiver in dismay, then dropped it back in the cradle.

"Sir?" inquired the butler. "Might I be of service?"

Guy glanced up, suddenly aware of his predicament. "Yes! Yes, you'll have to see that Miss Lamb's brought home."

"Home?"

"Take her to a hotel! In the village."

"You mean—now?"

"Yes, bring the car 'round. Go!"

Guy scampered up the steps, snatched Clea by the arm and began to hustle her down to the front door. "Dreadfully sorry, darling, but something's come up. Business, you understand."

Clea planted her heels stubbornly into the carpet. "Business?"

"Yes, an emergency—client of mine—"

"Client? But I don't even know what you *do* for a living!"

"My chauffeur will find you a hotel room. I'll pick

you up at five tomorrow, how about it? We'll make it an evening."

He gave her a quick kiss, then Clea was practically pushed out the front door. The car was already waiting, the chauffeur standing beside the open door. Clea had no choice but to climb in.

"I'll call you tomorrow!" yelled Guy, and waved.

As the chauffeur drove her out through the gates, Clea clutched the leather armrest in frustration. *I was so damn close, too,* she thought. He'd been about to show her the dagger. She could have had her hands on it, were it not for the phone call from that woman.

Just who the hell *was* Veronica?

VERONICA CAIRNCROSS turned from the telephone and looked inquiringly at Jordan. "Well? Do you think that call did the trick?"

"If it didn't," he said, "then your visit will."

"Oh, must I really go see him? I told you, I want nothing to do with the man."

"It's one sure way to flush that woman out of the house before she does any damage."

"There must be some other way to stop her! We could call the police—"

"And have it all come out? My late-night foray into Guy's house? Those stolen letters?" He paused. "Your affair with Delancey?"

Veronica gave a vigorous shake of her head. "We certainly can't tell them *that*."

"That's what I thought you'd say."

Resignedly, Veronica picked up her purse and started for the door. "Oh, all right. I got you into this. I suppose I owe you the favor."

"Plus, it's your civic duty," observed Jordan. "The woman's a thief. No matter what bitter feelings you have for Guy, you can't let him be robbed blind."

"Guy?" Veronica laughed. "I don't give a damn what happens to *him*. It's your lady burglar I'm thinking of. If she gets caught and talks to the police…"

"Then my reputation is mud," admitted Jordan.

Veronica nodded. "And so, I'm afraid, is mine."

CLEA KICKED OFF her high heels, tossed her purse in a chair and flung herself with a groan across the hotel bed. What a ghastly day. She hated polo, she despised Guy Delancey and she detested this red hair. All she wanted to do was go to sleep, to forget the Eye of Kashmir, to forget everything. But whenever she closed her eyes, whenever she tried to sleep, the old nightmares would return, the sights and sounds of terror so vivid she thought she was reliving it.

She fought the memories, tried to push them aside with more pleasant images. She thought of the summer of '72, when she was eight and Tony was ten, and they'd posed together for that photo that later graced Uncle Walter's mantelpiece. They'd been dressed in identical tans and bib overalls, and Tony had draped his skinny arm over her scrawny shoulder. They'd grinned at the camera like a pair of shysters in training, which they were. They had the world's best teacher, too: Uncle Walter, con man *extraordinaire,* damn his larcenous heart of gold. How was the old fellow faring in prison these days? she wondered. Uncle Walter would be up for parole soon. Maybe— just maybe—prison had changed him, the way it had changed Tony.

The way it had changed her.

Maybe Uncle Walter would walk out of those prison gates and into a straight life, sans con games and grifters.

Maybe pigs could fly.

She jerked as the phone rang. At once she reached for the receiver. "Hello?"

"Diana, darling! It's me!"

She rolled her eyes. "Hello, Guy."

"Dreadfully sorry about what happened this afternoon. Forgive me?"

"I'm thinking about it."

"My chauffeur said you're planning to stay in the village for a few days. Perhaps you'll give me a chance to make it up to you? Tomorrow night, say?

Supper and a musicale at an old friend's house. And the rest of the evening at mine."

"I don't know."

"I'll show you my collection of antique weapons." His voice dropped to an intimate murmur. "Think of all those knights in shining armor. Damsels in distress…"

She sighed. "Oh, all right."

"I'll be by at five. Pick you up at the Village Inn."

"Right. See you at five." She hung up and realized she had a splitting headache. Ha! It was her just punishment for playing Mata Hari.

No, her *real* punishment would come if she actually had to bed that dissolute wretch.

Moaning, she rose to her feet and headed toward the bathroom to wash off the smell of polo ponies and the greasy touch of Guy Delancey.

DELANCEY WAS SCARCELY sober when he came to fetch her the next evening. She debated the wisdom of climbing into the car with him behind the wheel, but decided she had no choice—not if she wanted to see this through. All things considered, the dangers of riding with a tipsy driver seemed almost insignificant. Risk was a relative thing and this was the night for taking risks.

"Should be a jolly bunch tonight," said Guy, dodging traffic along the winding road. High hedgerows obscured the view of the road ahead; Clea could only hope that some car wasn't zooming toward them from the opposite direction. "I don't go for the music, really. It's more for the conversation afterward. The laughs."

And the drinks, she thought, clutching the armrest as they whizzed past a tree with inches to spare.

"Thought it'd be my chance to introduce you," said Guy. "Show you off to my friends."

"Will Veronica be there?"

He shot her a startled glance. "What?"

"Veronica. The one who called yesterday. You know, your client."

"Oh. Oh, *her.*" His laugh was patently forced. "No, she's not a music fan. I mean, she's fond of rock and roll, that sort of rubbish, but not classical music. No, she won't be there." He paused, then added under his breath, "Lord, I hope not, anyway."

Twenty minutes later his hopes were dashed when they walked into the Forresters' music room. Clea heard Guy suck in a startled breath and mutter, "I don't believe it" as a russet-haired woman approached them from across the room. She was dressed in a stunning gown of cream lawn, and around her neck hung a magnificent strand of pearls. But it wasn't the woman whom Clea focused on.

It was the woman's companion, a man who was now regarding Clea with a look of calm amusement.

Or was it triumph she saw in Jordan Tavistock's sherry brown eyes?

Guy cleared his throat. "Hello, Veronica," he managed to say.

"I'd heard there was a new lady in your life."

"Yes, well…" Guy managed a weak smile.

Veronica turned her gaze to Clea, and offered an outstretched hand. "I'm Veronica Cairncross."

Clea returned the handshake. "Diana Lamb."

"We're old friends, Guy and I," Veronica explained. "*Very* old friends. And yet he does manage to surprise me sometimes."

"I surprise *you?*" Guy snorted. "Since when did you become a fan of musicales?"

"Since Jordan invited me."

"Oliver is so trusting."

"Who's Oliver?" Clea ventured to ask.

Guy laughed. "Oh, no one. Just her husband. A minor inconvenience."

"You are an *ass,*" hissed Veronica, and she turned and stalked away.

"Takes one to know one!" Guy retorted and followed her out of the room.

Jordan and Clea, equally cast adrift, looked at each other.

Jordan sighed. "Isn't love grand?"

"*Are* they in love?"

"I think it's obvious they still are."

"Is that why you brought her here? To sabotage my evening?"

Jordan picked up two glasses of white wine from a passing butler and handed a glass to Clea. "As I once said to you, Miss Lamb—or is it Miss Lamb?—I've taken on your reformation as my personal crusade. I'm going to save you from a life of crime. At least, while you're in my neighborhood."

"Territorial, aren't you?"

"Very."

"What if I gave you my solemn oath not to cut into your territory? I'll let you keep your hunting grounds."

"And you'll quietly leave the area?"

"Provided you carry out your side of the bargain."

He eyed her suspiciously. "What are you proposing?"

Clea paused, studying him, wondering what made him tick. She'd thought Jordan Tavistock attractive from the very beginning. Now she realized he was far more than just a pretty face and a pair of broad shoulders. It was what she saw in his eyes that held her interest. Intelligence. Humor. And more than a touch of determination. He might be an incompetent burglar, but he had class, he had contacts and he had an insider's familiarity with this neighborhood. By the looks of him, he was an independent, not a man who'd work for someone else. But she might be able to work *with* him.

She might even enjoy it.

She glanced around at the crowded room and motioned Jordan into a quiet corner. "Here's my proposition," she said. "I help you, you help me."

"Help you do what?"

"One itty-bitty job. Nothing, really."

"Just a small burglary?" He rolled his eyes. "Where have I heard that line before?"

"What?"

"Never mind." He sighed and took a sip of wine. "What, may I ask, would I get in return?"

"What would you like?"

His gaze focused with instant clarity on hers. And she knew by the sudden ruddiness of his cheeks that the same lascivious thought had flickered in both their brains.

"I'm not going to answer that," he said.

"Actually, I was thinking of offering up my expert advice in exchange," she said. "I think you could use it."

"Private tutelage in the art of burglary? That *is* a difficult offer to turn down."

"I won't actually help you do it, of course. But I'll give you tips."

"From personal experience?"

She smiled at him blandly over the wineglass. *Time to inflate the old résumé,* she thought. While burgling had never actually been her occupation, she did have a knack for it, and she'd rubbed shoulders with the best in the business, Uncle Walter among them. "I'm good enough to make a decent living," she said simply.

"A tempting proposition. But I'll have to decline."

"I can do wonders for your career."

"I'm not in your line of work."

"Well, what line of work *are* you in?" she blurted in frustration.

There was a long silence. "I'm a gentleman," he said.

"And what else?"

"Just a gentleman."

"That's an occupation?"

"Yes." He smiled sheepishly. "Full time, as a matter of fact. Still, it leaves me enough leisure for other pursuits. Such as local crime prevention."

"All right." She sighed. "What *can* I offer you just to stay out of my way? And not pop up at inconvenient times?"

"So that you can finish the job on poor old Guy Delancey?"

"Then I'll be out of here for good. Promise."

"What does he own that's so tempting to you, anyway?"

She stared down at her wineglass, refusing to meet

his gaze. No, she wouldn't tell him. She couldn't tell him. For one thing, she didn't trust him. If he heard about the Eye of Kashmir, he might want it for himself, and then where would that leave her? No evidence, no proof. She'd be left twisting in the wind.

And Victor Van Weldon would go unpunished.

"It must be quite a valuable item," he said.

"No, its value is rather more…" She hesitated, searching for a believable note. "Sentimental."

He frowned. "I don't understand."

"Guy has something that belongs to my family. Something that's been ours for generations. It was stolen from us a month ago. We want it back."

"If it's stolen property, why not go to the police?"

"Delancey knew it was hot when he purchased it. You think he'd admit to its ownership?"

"So you're going to steal it back?"

"I haven't any choice." Meekly she met his gaze, and she saw a flicker of uncertainty in his eyes. Just a flicker. Was he actually buying this story? She was surprised how rotten that made her feel. She'd been telling a lot of lies lately, had justified each and every one of them by reminding herself this was what she had to do to stay alive. But lying to Jordan Tavistock felt somehow, well…*criminal.* Which made no sense at all, because that's exactly what *he* was. A thief and a gentleman, she thought, gazing up at him. He had the most penetrating brown eyes she'd ever seen. A face made up of intriguing angles. And a smile that could make her knees weak.

In wonder she glanced down at her drink. What was *in* this wine, anyway? The room was starting to feel warm and she was having trouble catching her breath.

The return of Guy Delancey was like an unwelcome slap of cold air. "It's starting," said Guy.

"What is?" murmured Clea.

"The music. Come on, let's sit down."

She focused at last on Guy and saw that he was looking positively grim. "What about Veronica?"

"Don't mention the name to me," he growled.

Now Veronica entered the room, and she came toward them, her gaze pointedly avoiding Guy. "Jordie, *darling,*" she purred, snatching Jordan's arm with ruthless possession. "Let's sit down, shall we?"

With a look of resignation, Jordan allowed himself to be led away to the performance room.

The musicians, a visiting string quartet from London, were already tuning up, and the audience was settled in their seats. Clea and Guy sat on the opposite end of the room from Jordan and Veronica, but the two couples might as well have been seated side by side, for all the barbed looks flying between Guy and Veronica. All during the performance Clea could almost hear the zing of arrows soaring back and forth.

Dvorak was followed by Bartok, Quartet no. 6, and then Debussy. Through it all, Clea was busy plotting out the evening, wondering how close she could get to the Eye of Kashmir. Hoping that this would be the last evening she'd have to put up with Guy Delancey, with the lies, and with this hideous red hair. She scarcely heard the music. It was only when applause broke out that she realized the program had come to an end.

Refreshments followed, an elegant display of cakes and canapés and wine. A lot of wine. Guy, who'd been barely on the edge of sobriety when he entered the house, now proceeded to drink himself into outright intoxication. It was Veronica's presence that did it. The sight of a lost love flirting with her new escort was just too much for Guy.

Clea watched him reach for yet another glass of wine and decided that things had gone far enough. But how to stop him without making a scene? He was already talking too loudly, laughing too heartily.

That's when Jordan stepped in. She hadn't asked him to, but she'd seen him frowning at Guy, counting the glasses of wine he'd consumed. Now he slipped in beside Guy and said quietly, "Perhaps you should slow down a bit, chap?"

"Slow down what?" demanded Guy.

"That's your sixth, I believe. And you'll be driving the lady home."

"I can handle it."

"Come on, Delancey," Jordan urged. "A little self-control."

"Self-*control?* Who the hell're you to be talking about self-control?" Guy's voice had risen to a bellow, and all around them, conversations ceased. "You take up with another man's wife and you point at *me?*"

"No one's taken up with anyone's wife—"

"At least when I did it, I had the decency to be discreet about it!"

Veronica gave a startled gasp of dismay and ran out of the room.

"Coward!" Guy yelled after her.

"Delancey, please," murmured Jordan. "This isn't the time or place—"

"Veronica!" Guy broke away and pushed his way toward the door. "Why don't you face the bloody music for once! Veronica!"

Jordan looked at Clea. "He's pickled. You can't drive home with him tonight."

"I'll handle him."

"Well, take his keys, at least. Insist on driving yourself."

That was exactly what she'd planned to do. But when she followed Guy outside, she found that he and Veronica were still wrangling away, and loudly, too.

Guy was so drunk he was weaving, barely able to stay on his feet. Lying bitch, he kept saying, couldn't trust her, could never trust her. She'd rip your heart in pieces, that's what she'd do, damn her, and he didn't need that. He could find another woman with just the snap of his fingers.

"Then why don't you?" Veronica lashed back.

"I will! I have." Guy swiveled around and focused, bleary-eyed, on Clea. He grabbed her hand. "Come on, let's go!"

"Not in your condition," Clea said, pulling back.

"There's nothing wrong with my condition!"

"Give me the car keys, Guy."

"I can drive."

"No, you can't." She pulled out of his grasp. "Give me the keys."

In disgust he waved her off. "Go on, then. Find your own way home! To hell with both of you! To hell with women!" He stumbled away to his car. With difficulty he managed to open the door and climb in.

"Bloody idiot," muttered Veronica. "He's going to get himself killed."

She's right, thought Clea. She ran to Guy's car and yanked open the door. "Come on, get out."

"Go away."

"You're not driving. I am."

"Go away!"

Clea grabbed his arm. "I'll take you home. You get into the back seat and lie down."

"I don't take orders from any bloody *woman!*" he roared and viciously shoved her away.

Tottering on high heels, Clea stumbled backward and landed in the shrubbery. Stupid man, he was too damn drunk to listen to reason. Even as she struggled to disentangle her necklace from the branches, she could hear him cranking the engine, could hear him muttering about parasitic women. He cursed and slapped the steering wheel as the motor died. Again he cranked the ignition. Just as Clea managed to free her necklace from the shrub, just as she started to sit up, the car's engine roared to life. Without even a farewell glance at her, Guy pulled away.

Idiot, she thought, and rose to her feet.

The explosion slammed her backward. She flew clear over the shrub and landed flat on her back under a tree. She was too stunned to feel the pain of the impact. What she registered first were the sounds: the screams and shouts, the clatter of flying metal hitting the road and then the crackle of flames. Still she felt no pain, just a vague awareness that it was surely to come. She got to her knees and began to crawl like a baby—toward what, she didn't know. Just away from the tree, from the damn bushes. Her brain was starting to work now and it was telling her things she didn't want to know. Her head was starting to hurt, too. Pain and awareness in a simultaneous rush. She thought she was crying, but she wasn't sure; she couldn't even hear her own voice through the roar of noises. She couldn't tell if the warmth streaming down her cheek was blood or tears or both. She kept crawling, thinking, *I'm dead if I don't get away. I'm dead.*

A pair of shoes stood in her way. She looked up and saw a man staring down at her. A man who seemed vaguely familiar, only she couldn't quite figure out why.

He smiled and said, "Let me get you to a hospital."

"No—"

"Come on, you're hurt." He grabbed her arm. "You need to see a doctor."

"No!"

Suddenly the man's hand evaporated and he was gone.

Clea huddled on the ground, the night twirling around her in a carousel of flames and darkness. She heard another voice now—this one familiar. Hands grasped her by the shoulders.

"Diana? *Diana?*"

Why was he calling her that? It wasn't her name. She squinted up into the face of Jordan Tavistock.

And she fainted.

CHAPTER FIVE

THE DOCTOR switched off the ophthalmoscope and turned on the hospital room light. "Everything appears neurologically intact. But she has had a concussion, and that brief loss of consciousness concerns me. I recommend at least one night in hospital. For observation."

Jordan looked at the pitiful creature lying in bed. Her red hair was tangled with grass and leaves, and her face was caked with dried blood. He said, "I wholeheartedly agree, Doctor."

"Very good. I don't expect there'll be any problems, but we'll watch for danger signs. In the meantime, we'll keep her comfortable and—"

"I can't stay," the woman said.

"Of course you're staying," said Jordan.

"No, I have to get out of here!" She sat up and swung her legs over the side of the bed.

Jordan quickly moved to restrain her. "What the blazes are you doing, Diana?"

"Have to... Have to..." She paused, obviously dizzy, and gave her head a shake.

"You can't leave. Not after a concussion. Now then, let's get back into bed, all right?" Gently but firmly he urged her back under the covers. That attempt to sit up had drained all the color from her face. She seemed as fragile as tissue paper, and so insubstantial she might float away without the weight of the blankets to hold her down. Yet her eyes were bright and alive and feverish with...what? Fear? Grief? Surely she didn't harbor any real feelings for Guy Delancey?

"I'll have a nurse in to help you straightaway," said the doctor. "You just rest, Miss Lamb. Everything will be fine."

Jordan gave her hand a squeeze. It felt like a lump of ice in his grasp. Then, reluctantly, he followed the doctor out of the room.

Down the hall, out of the woman's earshot, Jordan asked, "What about Mr. Delancey? Do you know his condition?"

"Still in surgery. You'd have to inquire upstairs. I'm afraid it doesn't sound hopeful."

"I'm surprised he's alive at all, considering the force of that blast."

"You really think it was a bomb?"

"I'm sure it was."

The doctor glanced at the nurses' station, where a policeman stood waiting for a chance to question the woman. Two cops had grilled her already, and they hadn't been very considerate of her condition. The doctor shook his head. "God, what's the world coming to? Terrorist bombs going off in *our* corner of the world…."

Terrorists? thought Jordan. Yes, of course it *would* be blamed on some shadowy villain, some ill-defined evil. Who but a terrorist would plant a bomb in a gentleman's car? It was a miracle that only one person had been seriously hurt tonight. A half dozen other musicale guests had suffered minor injuries— glass cuts, abrasions—and the police were calling this a lucky escape.

For everyone but Delancey.

Jordan rode the lift upstairs to the surgical floor. The waiting room was aswarm with police, none of whom would tell him a thing. He hung around for a while, hoping to hear some news, any news, but all he could learn was that Delancey was still alive and on the operating table. As for whether he would live, that was a matter for God and the surgeons.

He returned to the woman's floor. The policeman was still standing in the nurses' station, sipping coffee and chatting up the pretty clerk. Jordan walked right past them and opened the door to Diana's room.

Her bed was empty.

At once he felt a flicker of alarm. He crossed to the bathroom door and knocked. "Diana?" he called. There was no answer. Cautiously he opened the door and peeked inside.

She wasn't there, either, but her hospital gown was. It lay in a heap on the linoleum.

He yanked open the closet door. The shelves were empty; the woman's street clothes and purse had vanished.

What the hell are you thinking? he wondered. Why would she crawl out of her hospital bed, get dressed and steal away like a thief into the night?

Because she is a thief, you bloody fool.

He ran out of the room and glanced up and down the hall. No sign of her. The idiot cop was still flirting with the clerk and was oblivious to anything but the buzz of his own hormones. Jordan hurried down the hall, toward the emergency stairs. If the woman was running from the police, then she'd probably avoid the lift, which opened into the lobby. She'd go for the side exit, which led straight to the parking lot.

He pushed into the stairwell. He was on the third floor. When last he'd seen Diana, she'd looked scarcely strong enough to stand, much less run down two flights of stairs. Could she make it? Was she even now lying in a dead faint on some lower landing?

Terrified of what he might find, Jordan started down the stairs.

HER HEAD WAS POUNDING mercilessly, the high heels were killing her, but she kept marching like a good soldier down the road. That was how she managed to keep going, left-right-left, some inner drill sergeant screaming commands in her brain. Don't stop, don't stop. The enemy approaches. March or die.

And so she marched, stumbling along on her high heels, her head aching so badly she could scream. Twice she heard a car approaching and had to scramble off the road to hide in the bushes. Both times the cars passed without seeing her, and she crawled back to the road and resumed her painful march. She had only a vague plan of what came next. The nearest village couldn't be more than a few miles away. If she could just get to a train station, she could get out of Buckinghamshire. Out of England.

And then where do I go?

No, she couldn't think that far ahead. All she knew was that she'd failed miserably, that there'd be no more chances and that she was at the very top of Van Weldon's hit list. With new desperation she pushed on, but her feet didn't seem to be working, and the road was weaving before her eyes. *Can't stop,* she thought. *Have to keep going.* But shadows were puddling her vision now, creeping in from the sides. Suddenly nauseated, she dropped to her knees and lowered her head, waiting for the dizziness to pass. Crouching there in the darkness, she vaguely sensed the vibrations through the asphalt. Little by little the sound penetrated the fog clouding her brain.

It was a car, approaching from behind.

Her gaze shot back up the road and she saw the headlights gliding toward her. With a spurt of panic she stumbled to her feet, ready to dash into the bushes, but the dizziness at once assailed her. The headlights danced, blurred into a haze. She discovered she was on her knees, and that the asphalt was biting into her palms. The slam of a car door, the hurried crunch of shoes over gravel told her it was too late. She'd been spotted.

"No," she said as arms closed around her body. "Please, no!"

"It's all right—"

"No!" she screamed. Or thought she had. Her face was wedged against someone's chest, and her cry came out no louder than a strangled whisper. She began to flail at her captor, her fists connecting with his back, his shoulders. The arms only closed in tighter.

"Stop it, Diana! I won't hurt you. *Stop it!*"

Sobbing, she raised her head, and through a mist

of tears and confusion she saw Jordan gazing down at her. Her fists melted as her hands reached out to clutch at his jacket. The wool felt so warm, so substantial. Like the man. They stared at each other, her face upturned to his, her body feeling numb and weightless in his arms.

All at once his mouth was on hers, and the numbness gave way to a flood of glorious sensations. With that one kiss he offered his warmth, his strength, and she drank from it, felt its nourishment revive her battered soul. She wanted more, more, and she returned his kiss with the desperate need of a woman who's finally found, in a man's arms, what she'd long been seeking. Not desire, not passion, but comfort. Protection. She clung to him, relinquishing all control of her fate to the only man who'd ever made her feel safe.

Neither of them heard the sound of the approaching car.

It was the distant glare of headlights that forced them to pull apart. Clea turned to look up the road and registered the twin lights burning closer. Instantly she panicked. She jerked out of Jordan's arms and plunged headlong into the bushes.

"Wait!" called Jordan. "Diana?"

Blindly she thrashed through the branches, desperate to flee, but her legs still weren't working right.

She heard Jordan right behind her, his footsteps snapping across twigs as he ran to catch up. He snagged her arm.

"Diana—"

"They'll see me!"

"Who?"

"Let me go!"

On the road, the car braked to a stop. They heard the door swing open. At once Clea dropped to the ground and cowered in the shadows.

"Halloa!" called a man's voice. "Everything all right?"

Please, Jordan, Clea prayed. *Cover for me! Don't tell him I'm here....*

There was a pause, then she heard Jordan call back, "Everything's fine!"

"Saw your car had pulled off. Just wanted to check," said the man.

"I'm, er..." Jordan gave a convincingly sheepish laugh. "Answering the call of nature."

"Oh. Well. Carry on, then." The car door slammed shut, and the taillights glided away down the road.

Clea, still shaking, gave a sob of relief. "Thank you," she whispered.

For a moment he stood watching her in silence. Then he reached down and pulled her to her feet. She swayed unsteadily against him.

"Come on," he said gently. "I'll take you back to the hospital."

"No."

"Now see here, Diana. You're in no condition to be wandering around at night."

"I can't go back."

"What are you afraid of, anyway? The police?"

"Just let me *go!*"

"They won't arrest you. You haven't done anything." He paused. Softly he asked, "Have you?"

She wrenched herself free. That one effort cost her what little strength she had left. Suddenly her head was swimming and the darkness seemed to whirl around her like black water. She didn't remember sinking to the ground, didn't remember how she got into his arms, but suddenly she was there, and he was carrying her to the car. She was too tired to struggle, too weak to care anymore what happened to her. She was thrust into the front seat, where she sagged with her head against the door, trying not to faint, fighting the nausea that was beginning to roil her stomach again. *Can't throw up in this nice car,* she thought. *What a shame it would be to ruin his leather upholstery.* She vaguely registered the fact that he was sitting beside her, that the car was now moving. That was enough to nudge fear back into her addled brain.

She reached for his arm, her fingers clutching at his jacket sleeve. "Please," she begged. "Don't take me back to the hospital."

"Relax. I won't force you to go back."

She struggled to focus. Through the darkness of the car, she saw his profile, lean and tense as he stared ahead at the road.

"If you insist, I'll take you to your hotel," he offered. "But you need someone to look after you."

"I can't go there, either."

He frowned at her. Her fear, her desperation, must have registered on her face. "All right, Diana." He sighed. "Just tell me where you want to go."

"The train station."

He shook his head. "You're in no condition to travel."

"I can do it."

"You can scarcely stand up on your own two feet!"

"I have no choice!" she cried. Then, with a desperate sob, she whispered, "I have no choice."

He studied her in silence. "You're not getting on the train," he said at last. "I won't allow it."

"Won't *allow* it?" Sudden rage made her raise her head in defiance. "You have no right. You don't have any idea what I'm facing—"

"Listen to me! I'm taking you to a safe place. You have to trust me on this." He looked at her, a gaze so direct it defied her not to believe him. How simple it would be to hand over her fate to this man, and hope for the best. She wanted to trust him. She *did* trust him. Which meant it was all over for her, because no one who made a mistake that stupid would live long enough to regret it.

I don't have a choice, she thought as another wave of dizziness sent her head lolling to her knees. She might as well wave the white flag. Her future was now out of her hands.

And firmly in the grasp of Jordan Tavistock.

"HOW IS SHE DOING?" asked Richard.

Drained and exhausted, Jordan joined Richard in the library and poured himself a generous shot of brandy. "Obviously scared out of her wits," he said. "But otherwise she seems all right. Beryl's putting her to bed now. Maybe we'll get more out of her in the morning." He drained the brandy in a few gulps, then proceeded to pour himself a well-deserved second shot. He could feel Richard's doubtful gaze on him as he took another sip and sank into the easy chair by the fireplace. Sobriety was normally one of Jordan's virtues. It was unlike him to guzzle a triple brandy in one sitting.

It was certainly not like him to drag home stray females.

Yet that's exactly what he had upstairs at this

moment, bundled away in the guest bedroom. Thank God Beryl hadn't bombarded him right off with questions. His sister was good that way; in a crisis she simply did what needed to be done. For the moment the bruised little waif would be well taken care of.

Questions, however, were sure to follow, and Jordan didn't know how to answer them because he himself didn't have the answers. He didn't even know why he'd brought Diana home. All he knew was that she was terrified, and that he couldn't turn his back on her. For some insane reason he felt responsible for the woman.

Even more insane, he *wanted* to feel responsible for her.

He leaned back and rubbed his face with both hands. "What a night," he groaned.

"You've been a very busy fellow," Richard observed. "Car bombs. Runaway females. Why didn't you tell us all this was cooking?"

"I had no idea bombs *would* be going off! I thought all I was dealing with was a cat burglar. Or is it burglaress?" He gave his head a shake to clear away the pleasant fog of brandy. "Theft is one thing. But she never mentioned anything about mad bombers."

Richard moved closer. "My question is," he said quietly, "who was the intended victim?"

"What?" Jordan looked up. He had great respect

for his future brother-in-law. Years of working in the intelligence business had taught Richard that one should never accept evidence at face value. One had to examine around it, under it, looking for the twists and turns that might lead to completely different conclusions. Richard was doing that now.

"The bomb was planted in Guy Delancey's car," said Richard. "It could have been a random attack. It could have been aimed specifically at Delancey. Or…"

Jordan frowned at Richard. He saw that they were both considering the same possibility. "Or the target wasn't Delancey at all," Jordan finished softly.

"She was supposed to be riding in the car with him," said Richard. "She would have been killed, as well."

"There's no doubt Diana's terrified. But she hasn't told me what she's afraid of."

"What *do* you know about the woman?"

Jordan shook his head. "All I know is her name is Diana Lamb. Other than that I can't tell you much. I'm not even sure what her real hair color is! One day she's blond, then the next day she transforms into a redhead."

"What about the fingerprints? The ones you got off her glass?"

"I had Uncle Hugh's friend run them through the Scotland Yard computer. No match. Not a surprise, really. Since I'm sure she's a Yank."

"You *have* been busy, haven't you? Why the hell

didn't you let me in on this earlier? I could've sent the fingerprints off to American authorities by now."

"I wasn't at liberty to say a thing. I'd promised Veronica, you see."

Richard laughed. "And a gentleman always keeps his promises."

"Well, yes. Except under certain circumstances. Such as car bombs." Jordan stared at his empty brandy snifter and considered pouring another. No, better not. Just look at what drink had done to Guy Delancey. Drink and women—the sole purpose of Delancey's life. And now he lay deprived of both.

Jordan set down the glass. "Motive," he said. "That's what I don't know. Why would someone kill Diana?"

"Or Delancey."

"That," said Jordan, "isn't too difficult to answer. God only knows how many women he's gone through in the past year. Add to that a few angry husbands, and you've probably got a slew of people who'd love to knock him off."

"Including your friend Veronica and her husband."

That possibility made Jordan pause. "I hardly think either one of them would ever—"

"Nevertheless, we have to consider them. Everyone's a suspect."

The sound of footsteps made both men turn. Beryl

walked into the library and frowned at her brother and her fiancé. "Who's a suspect?" she demanded.

"Richard wants to include anyone who's had an affair with Guy Delancey," said Jordan.

Beryl laughed. "It'd be easier to start off with who *hasn't* had an affair with the man." She caught Richard's inquiring glance and she snapped, "No, I never have."

"Did I say anything?" asked Richard.

"I saw the look in your eye."

"On that note," cut in Jordan, rising to his feet, "I think I'll make my escape. Good night all."

"Jordan!" called Beryl. "What about Diana?"

"What about her?"

"Aren't you going to tell me what's going on?"

"No."

"Why not?"

"Because," he said wearily, "I haven't the faintest idea." He walked out of the library. He knew he owed Beryl an explanation, but he was too exhausted to repeat the story a second time. Richard would fill her in on the details.

Jordan climbed the stairs and started up the hall toward his bedroom. Halfway there, he stopped. Some compulsion made him turn around and walk, instead, to the bedroom where Diana was staying. He lingered outside the closed door, debating whether he should walk away.

He couldn't help himself; he tapped on the door. "Diana?" he called.

There was no answer. Quietly he entered the room.

A corner lamp had been left on, and the glow spilled softly over the bed, illuminating its sleeping occupant. She lay curled up on her side, her arms wrapped protectively around her chest, her hair rippling in red-gold waves across the pillow. The linen nightgown she wore was Beryl's, and a few sizes too big; the billowing sleeves almost engulfed her hands. He knew he should leave, but he found himself sinking into the chair beside the bed. There he watched her sleep and thought how very small she looked, how defenseless she truly was.

"My little thief," he murmured.

A sigh suddenly escaped her throat and she stirred awake. She looked at him with unfocused eyes, then slowly seemed to comprehend where she was.

"I'm sorry," he said, and rose from the chair. "I didn't mean to wake you. Go back to sleep." He turned to leave.

"Jordan?"

He glanced back at her. She seemed to be lost in a sea of white sheets and goose-down pillows and puffy nightgown linen, and he had the ridiculous urge to pull her out of there before she drowned.

"I…have to tell you something," she whispered.

"It can wait till tomorrow."

"No, I have to tell you now. It's not fair of me, pulling you into this. When you could get hurt."

Frowning, he moved back to the bed. "The bomb. In the car. *Was* it meant for Guy?"

"I don't know." She blinked, and he saw the sparkle of tears on her lashes. "Maybe. Or maybe it was meant for me. I can't be sure. That—that's what makes this so confusing. Not knowing if I'm the one who was supposed to die. I keep thinking…" She looked at him, her eyes full of torment. "I keep thinking it's my fault, what happened to Guy. He never really did anything wrong. I mean, not *seriously* wrong. He just got caught up in a bit of greed. But he didn't deserve…" She swallowed and looked down at the sheets. "He didn't deserve to die," she whispered.

"There's a chance he might live."

"You saw the explosion! Do you really think anyone could survive it?"

After a pause Jordan admitted, "No. To be honest, I don't think he'll survive."

They fell silent for a moment. *Had she cared at all for Delancey?* he wondered. *Or are her tears purely from guilt?* He couldn't help but feel a little guilty himself. After all, he'd invaded the man's house. He'd never really liked Delancey, had thought him laughable. But now the man was at death's door. No one, not even Guy Delancey, deserved such a terrible end.

"Why do you think *you* might have been the target?" he asked.

"Because…" She let out a deep breath. "Because it's happened before."

"Bombs?"

"No. Other things. Accidents."

"When?"

"A few weeks ago, in London, I was almost run down by a taxi."

"In London," he noted dryly, "that could happen to anyone."

"It wasn't the only time."

"You mean there was another accident?"

She nodded. "In the Underground. I was standing on the train platform. And someone pushed me."

He stared at her skeptically. "Are you positive, Diana? Isn't it more likely that someone just bumped into you?"

"Do you think I'm *stupid?*" she cried. "Wouldn't I know it if someone *pushed* me?" With a sob of frustration she buried her face in her hands.

Her unexpected outburst left him stunned. For a

moment he could think of nothing to say. Then, gently, he reached for her shoulder. With that one touch, something seemed to leap between them. A longing. Through the flimsy nightgown fabric he felt the warmth of her skin, and with sudden vividness he remembered the taste of her mouth, the sweetness of her kisses earlier that night.

Ruthlessly he suppressed all those inconvenient urges now threatening to overwhelm his sense of reason. He sat beside her on the bed. "Tell me," he said. "Tell me again what happened in the Underground."

"You won't believe me."

"Give me a chance. Please."

She raised her head and looked at him, her gaze moist and uncertain. "I—I fell onto the tracks. The train was just pulling in. If it hadn't been for a man who saw me…"

"A man? Then someone pulled you out?"

She nodded. "I never even learned his name. All I remember is that he reached down and yanked me back onto the platform. I tried to thank him, but he just—just told me to be more careful. And then he was gone." She shook her head in bewilderment. "My guardian angel."

He looked into those glistening brown eyes and wondered if any of this was possible. Wondered how anyone could be cold-blooded enough to push this woman under a train.

"Why would anyone want you dead?" he asked. "Is it something you've done?"

Instantly she stiffened, as though he'd struck her. "What do you mean, is it something I've done?"

"I'm just trying to understand—"

"Do you think I deserve this somehow? That I must be guilty of something?"

"Diana, I'm not accusing you of anything. It's just that murder—attempted murder—generally involves a motive. And you haven't told me what it is."

He waited for an answer, but he realized that he'd somehow lost her. She was huddled in a self-protective embrace, as though to ward off any further attacks he might launch against her.

"Diana," he said gently, "you have to trust me."

"I don't have to trust anyone."

"It would make it easier. If I'm to help you at all—"

"You've already helped me. I can't really ask you for anything more."

"The least you can do is tell me what I've gotten involved in. If bombs are going to be blowing up around here, I'd like to know why."

She sat stubbornly huddled, not responding. In frustration he rose from the bed, paced to the door, then paced back. Damn it all, she *was* going to tell him. Even if he had to use the threat of last resort.

"If you don't tell me," he said, "I really shall have to call the police."

She looked up in astonishment and gave a disbelieving laugh. "The *police?* I'd think they're the last people you'd want to call. Considering."

"Considering what?"

"Delancey's bedroom. The minor matter of a little burglary."

Sighing, he clawed his hair back. "The time has come to set you straight on that. The truth is, I broke into Guy's house as a favor to a lady."

"What favor?"

"She'd written a few…indiscreet letters to him. She wanted the letters back."

"You're saying it was all a gentleman's errand?"

"You could call it that."

"You didn't mention any lady before."

"That's because I'd promised her I'd stay silent. For the sake of her rather tenuous marriage. But now Delancey's been hurt and bombs are exploding. I think it's time to start telling the truth." He gave her a pointed look. "Don't you agree?"

She thought it over for a moment. Then her gaze slid away from his and she said, "All right. I guess it's confession time." She took a deep breath. "I'm not a thief, either."

"Why were you in Delancey's bedroom?"

"I was doing my job. We're trying to collect evidence. An insurance fraud case."

This time Jordan burst out laughing. "You're claiming to be with the police?"

Red faced, she looked up defiantly. "Why is that funny?"

"Which branch do you work for? The local constabulary? Scotland Yard? Interpol, perhaps?"

"I…I work for a private investigator. Not the police."

"Which investigator?"

"You wouldn't know the company."

"I see. And who, may I ask, is the subject of your investigation?"

"He's not English. His name's not important to you."

"How does Guy Delancey fit in?"

Wearily she ran her hand through her hair. In a voice drained of emotion, she said, "A few weeks ago Guy purchased an antique dagger known as the Eye of Kashmir. It was one of several art pieces reportedly carried aboard the *Max Havelaar* last month. That ship later sank off the coast of Spain. Nothing was recovered. The man who owned the vessel—a Belgian—filed a thirty-two-million-dollar insurance claim for the loss of the ship. And for the artwork. He owned it all."

Jordan frowned. "But you say Delancey recently acquired this dagger. When?"

"Three weeks ago. *After* the boat sank."

"Then…the dagger was never aboard the vessel."

"Obviously not. Since Delancey was able to buy it from some private seller."

"And that's the case you're trying to build? Against the owner of the boat? This Belgian fellow?"

She nodded. "He gets reimbursed by the insurance company for the losses. And he keeps the art to resell. It works out as a sort of double indemnity."

"How did you know Delancey'd acquired the dagger?"

Drained, she sank back against the pillows. "People brag." She sighed. "Delancey did, anyway. He told friends about a seventeenth-century dagger he'd bought from a private source. A dagger with a star corundum—a sapphire—mounted in the hilt. Word got around in the antiques community. From the description, we knew it was the Eye of Kashmir."

"And that's what you were trying to steal from Delancey?"

"Not steal. Confirm its whereabouts. So it can later be confiscated as evidence."

Silently he mulled over this rush of new information. Or was it new fabrication? "You told me earlier tonight that you were stealing something once owned by your family."

She gave a regretful shrug. "I lied."

"Really?"

"I didn't know if I could trust you."

"And you trust me now?"

"You've given me no reason not to." She studied his face, as though looking for some betraying sign that he was not to be trusted, that she'd made a fatal mistake. Slowly she smiled. A coy, almost seductive smile. "And you've been so awfully kind to me. A true gentleman."

Kind? he thought with a silent groan. Was there anything that could dash a man's hopes more brutally than to be called *kind?*

"I *can* trust you," she asked, "can't I?"

He began to pace again, feeling irritated at her, at himself, at how much he wanted to believe this latest outlandish story. He'd been gazing too long into those doe eyes of hers. It was turning his brain into gullible mush. "Why not trust me?" he muttered in exasperation. "Since I've been so awfully *kind.*"

"Why are you angry? Is it because I lied to you before?"

"Shouldn't I be angry?"

"Well, yes. I suppose so. But now that I've come clean—"

"Have you?"

Her jaw squared. It made her even prettier, damn

it. He could kick himself for being so susceptible to this creature.

"Yes," she said, her gaze steady. "The Belgian, the *Max Havelaar,* the dagger—it's all *completely* on the level." She paused, then added quietly, "So is the danger."

The bomb is proof enough of that, he thought.

That, and the sight of her curled up in that bed, gazing at him with those liquid brown eyes, was enough to make him accept everything she'd told him. Which meant he was either going out of his mind or he was too exhausted to think straight.

They both needed to sleep.

He knew he should simply say good-night and walk out of the room. But some irresistible compulsion made him lean down and place a kiss on her forehead. The scent of her hair, the sweetness of soap, was intoxicating.

At once he backed away. "You'll be absolutely safe here," he said.

"I believe you," she said. "And I don't know why I should."

"Of course you should. It's the solemn word of a gentleman." Smiling, he turned off the lamp and left the room.

An hour later he still lay awake in bed, thinking about what she'd told him. All that babbling about insurance fraud and undercover investigations was rubbish and he knew it. But he did believe she was in danger. That much he could see in her eyes: the fear.

He considered just how safe she was here. He knew the house was up-to-date when it came to locks and alarm systems. During the years Uncle Hugh had worked with British Intelligence, security had been a priority here at Chetwynd. The grounds had been monitored, the personnel screened, the rooms regularly swept for listening devices. But since his uncle's retirement a few months ago, those precautions had gradually fallen by the wayside. Civilians, after all, did not need the trappings of a fortress. While Chetwynd was still fairly secure, anyone determined to break in could probably find a way.

But first they'd have to learn that the woman was here.

That last thought eased Jordan's fears. No one outside this house could possibly know the woman's location. As long as that fact remained a secret, she was safe.

CHAPTER SIX

CLEA WAITED until the house had fallen completely silent before she climbed out of bed. Her head still pounded, and the floor seemed to wobble under her bare feet, but she forced herself to cross the room and crack open the door.

The hallway was deserted. At the far end a small lamp burned, casting its glow across the carpet runner. Next to the lamp was a telephone.

Noiselessly Clea crept down the hall and picked up the receiver. Shaking off a twinge of guilt, she punched in Tony's number in Brussels. All right, so it was a long-distance call. This was an emergency, and the Tavistocks could surely afford the phone bill.

Four rings and Tony answered. "Clea?"

"I'm in trouble," she whispered. "Somehow they've tracked me down."

"Where are you?"

"Safe for the moment. Tony, Delancey's been hurt. He's in a hospital, not expected to live."

"What? How…"

"A bomb went off in his car. Look, I don't think I can reach the Eye. Not for a while. There'll be hordes of police watching his house."

He didn't answer. She thought for a moment the call had been cut off. Then Tony said, "What do you plan to do?"

"I don't know." She glanced around at the sound of a creak, but saw no one. Just old house noises, she thought, her heart still hammering. She said softly, "If they found me, they could find you, too. Get out of Brussels. Go somewhere else."

"Clea, there's something I have to tell you—"

She spun around at another noise. It came from one of the bedrooms. Someone was awake! She hung up the phone and scurried away up the hall.

Back in her room she stood by the door, listening. To her relief, she heard nothing more. At least she'd had a chance to warn Tony. Now it was time to think about herself. She locked the door and wedged a chair against it for good measure. Then she climbed back into bed.

Her headache was starting to fade; perhaps by morning she'd be as good as new. In which case she'd leave Chetwynd and get the hell away before Van Weldon's people tracked her down again. She'd been lucky up till now, but luck couldn't hold, not against the sort of people she was facing. Another change of appearance was called for. A haircut and a reincarnation as a brunette. Glasses. Yes, that might do it, might allow her to slip unnoticed into the London crowd. Once she got out of England, Van Weldon might lose interest in her. She might have a chance of surviving to a ripe old age.

Might.

TONY DROPPED THE RECEIVER back in the cradle. "She hung up on me," he said, and turned to the other man. "I couldn't keep her on the line."

"It may have been long enough."

"Christ, she sounded scared out of her wits. Can't you people call this off?"

"Not yet. We don't have enough. But we're getting close."

"How do you know?"

"Because Van Weldon's getting close to her. He'll be making another move soon."

Tony watched the other man pull out a cigarette and tap it against his lighter. *Why do people do that, tap their cigarettes?* Just another annoying habit of this fellow. In the past week Tony had gotten to know Archie MacLeod's every tic, every quirk, and he was well-nigh sick of the man. If only there was some other way.

But there wasn't. MacLeod knew all about Tony's

past, knew about the years he'd spent in prison. If Tony didn't cooperate, MacLeod and Interpol would have that information broadcast to every antiques buyer in Europe. They'd ruin him. Tony had no choice but to go along with this crazy scheme. And pray that Clea didn't get killed in the process.

"You let Van Weldon get too close this time," Tony observed. "Clea could've been blown up in that car."

"But she wasn't."

"Your man slipped up. Admit it!"

MacLeod exhaled a puff of cigarette smoke. "All right, so we were taken by surprise. But your cousin's alive, isn't she? We're keeping an eye on her."

Tony laughed. "You don't even know where she is!"

MacLeod's cellular phone rang. He picked it up, listened a moment, then hung up. He looked at Tony. "We know exactly where she is."

"The phone call?"

"Traced to a private residence. A Hugh Tavistock in Buckinghamshire."

Tony shook his head. "Who's that?"

"We're running the check now. In the meantime, she'll be safe. Our field man's been notified of her whereabouts."

Tony sat on the bed and clutched his head. "When Clea finds out about this, she's bloody well going to kill me."

"From what we've seen of your cousin," said MacLeod with a laugh, "she very likely will."

"THEY HAVE LOST HER," said Simon Trott.

Victor Van Weldon allowed no trace of alarm to show on his face as he received the news, but he could feel the rage tightening its grip on his chest. In a moment it would pass. In a moment he'd let his displeasure be known. But he must not lose control, not in front of Simon Trott.

"How did it happen?" asked Van Weldon, his voice icy calm.

"It happened at the hospital. She was taken there after the bombing. Somehow she slipped away from our man."

"She was injured?"

"A concussion."

"Then she can't have gotten very far. Track her down."

"They're trying to. They're afraid, though, that…"

"What?"

"She may have enlisted the help of authorities."

Again, that giant fist seemed to close around Van Weldon's chest. He paused for a moment, struggling for air, counting the seconds for the spell to pass. This was a bad one, he thought, and all because of that woman. She'd be the death of him. He took out his bottle of nitroglycerin and slipped two tablets under his tongue. Slowly the discomfort began to fade. *I'm not ready to die,* he thought. *Not yet.*

He looked at Trott. "Have we any proof she's contacted the authorities?"

"She's escaped too many times. She must be getting help. From the police. Or Interpol."

"Not Clea Rice. She'd never trust the police." He slipped the nitroglycerin bottle back in his pocket and took a deep breath. The pain was gone.

"She has been lucky, that's all," said Van Weldon. He gave a careless wave of his hand. "Her luck will run out."

SHE HAD NOT MEANT to sleep so late, but the concussion had left her groggy and the bed was so comfortable and she felt safe in this house—the safest she'd felt in weeks. By the time she finally crawled out of bed, the sun was shining straight through her window and her headache had faded to only a dull soreness.

I'm still alive, she thought in wonder.

From various parts of the house came the sounds of morning stirrings: creaking floorboards, water running through the pipes. Too late to make an escape unnoticed. She would simply have to play the guest for a few hours. Later she'd slip away, make it on foot to the village train station. How far was it, a few miles? She could do it. After all, she'd once trudged ten miles along the Spanish coast. And that was in the dead of night, while sopping wet. But then, she hadn't been wearing high heels.

She surveyed her clothes. Her dress, torn and dirt stained, was draped over a chair. Her stockings were in shreds. Her shoes, those wretched instruments of torture, sat mocking her with their three-inch spike heels. No, she'd rather go barefoot. Or perhaps in bedroom slippers? She spied a pair by the dresser, comfy-looking pink slippers edged with fluff. Wouldn't *that* blend in with the crowd?

She pulled on a silk bathrobe she found in the closet, slid her feet into the pink slippers and pulled away the chair she'd wedged against the door. Then she ventured out of the room.

The rest of the household was already up and about. She went downstairs and spied them through the French doors. They were outside, assembled around a breakfast table on the terrace. It looked like a photo straight from the pages of some stylish magazine, the iron railings traced by climbing roses, the dew-kissed autumn garden, the table with its linen and china. And the people sitting around that table! There was Beryl with her model's cheekbones and glossy black hair. There was Richard Wolf, lean and relaxed, his arm slung possessively around Beryl's shoulders.

And there was Jordan.

If last night had been a trial for him, it certainly didn't show this morning. He was looking unruffled and elegant as ever, his fair hair almost silvery in the morning light, his tweed jacket perfectly molded to his shoulders. As Clea watched them through the glass, she thought how perfect they looked, like thoroughbreds reared on bluegrass. It wasn't envy she felt, but a sense of wonder, as though she were observing some alien species. She could move among them, could even act the part, but the wrong blood would always run in her veins. Tainted blood. Like Uncle Walter's blood.

Too timid to intrude on that perfect tableau, she turned to retreat upstairs. But as she backed away from the French doors she heard Jordan call her name and she knew she'd been spotted. He was waving to her, beckoning her to join them. No chance of escape now; she'd simply have to brazen it out.

She smoothed out the silk robe, ran her fingers through her hair and stepped out onto the terrace. Only then did she remember the pink slippers. The soles made painfully distinct scuffing sounds across the flagstones.

Jordan rose and pulled out a chair for her. "I was about to check on you. Feeling better this morning?"

Uneasily she tugged the edges of the robe together.

"I'm really not dressed for breakfast. My clothes are a mess and I didn't know what else—"

"Don't give it a thought. We're a casual bunch here."

Clea glanced at Beryl, flawlessly pulled together in cashmere and jodhpurs, at Jordan in his wool tweed. A casual bunch. Right. Resignedly she sat down in the offered chair and felt like some sort of zoo specimen with fluffy pink feet. While Jordan poured her coffee and dished out a serving of eggs and sausages, she found herself focusing on his hands, on his long fingers, on the golden hairs glittering on the backs of his wrists. An aristocrat's hands, she thought, and remembered with sudden clarity the gentle strength with which those hands had reached for her in the road last night.

"Don't you care for eggs?"

She blinked at her plate. Eggs. Yes. Automatically she picked up the fork and felt all eyes watching her as she took her first bite.

"I did try to leave you some fresh clothes this morning," Beryl explained. "But I couldn't seem to get in your door."

"I had a chair in front of it," said Clea.

"Oh." Beryl gave a sheepish smile, as though to say, *Well, of course. Doesn't everybody barricade their door?*

No one seemed to know how to respond, so they

simply watched Clea eat. Their gazes were not un-friendly, merely…puzzled.

"It's just a habit I picked up," Clea said as she poured cream in her coffee. "I don't trust locks, you see. It's so easy to get past them."

"Is it?" said Beryl.

"Especially bedroom doors. One can bypass your typical bedroom lock in five seconds. Even the newer ones with the disk tumblers."

"How very useful to know that," Beryl murmured.

Clea looked up and saw that everyone was watching her with fascination. Face flushing, she quickly dropped her gaze back to the eggs. *I'm babbling like an idiot,* she thought.

She flinched when Jordan reached for her hand.

"Diana, I've told them."

She stared at him. "Told them? You mean… about…"

"Everything. The way we met. The attempts on your life. I *had* to tell them. If they're to help you, then they need to know it all."

"Believe me, we *do* want to help," said Beryl. "You can trust us. Every bit as much as you trust Jordie."

Clea's hands were unsteady. She dropped them to her lap. *They're asking me to trust them,* she thought in misery. *But I'm the one who hasn't been telling the truth.*

"We have resources that might prove useful," said Jordan. "Connections with Intelligence. And Richard's firm specializes in security. If you need any help at all…"

The offer was almost too tempting to resist. For weeks she'd been on her own, had hopscotched from hotel to hotel, never sure whom she could trust, or where she would go next. She was so very tired of running.

And yet she wasn't ready to put her life in anyone's hands. Not even Jordan's.

"The only favor I ask," she said quietly, "is a ride to the train station. And perhaps…" She glanced down at the pink slippers and gave a laugh. "A change of clothes?"

Beryl rose to her feet. "That I can certainly arrange." She tugged on her fiancé's arm. "Come on, Richard. Let's go rummage around in my closet."

Clea was left sitting alone with Jordan. For a moment they sat in silence. Up in the trees, doves cooed a lament to the passing of summer. The clouds drifted across the sun, tarnishing the morning to gray.

"Then you'll be leaving us," said Jordan.

"Yes." She folded her napkin and carefully laid it on the table. Though she remained focused on that small square of cream linen, she couldn't shut out her awareness of the man. She could almost feel the warmth of his gaze. All her senses were conspiring against her efforts at indifference. Last night, with that first kiss, they'd crossed some invisible threshold, had wandered into territory with no boundaries, where the possibilities seemed limitless.

That's all they are, she reminded herself. *Possibilities.* Fantasies winking in the murk of half-truths. She had told him so many lies, had changed her story so many times. She still hadn't told him the worst truth of all. Who she was, what she was.

What she had been.

Better to leave him with the fantasy, she thought. Let him assume the best about me. And not know the worst.

She looked up and found he was watching her with a gaze both puzzled and thoughtful. "Where will you go next?" he asked.

"London. It's clear I can't handle this alone. My…associates at the agency will carry on the investigation."

"And what will you do?"

She gave a shrug, a smile. "Take an easier case. Something that doesn't involve exploding cars."

"Diana, if you ever need my help—anything at all—"

Their gazes met and she saw in his eyes the offer of more than just assistance. She had to fight off the temptation to confess everything, to draw him into this dangerous mess.

She shook her head. "I have some very capable

colleagues. They'll see I'm taken care of. But thanks for the offer."

He gave a curt nod of the head and said no more about it.

SEATED ON A BENCH on the train platform, a gray-suited man read his newspapers and watched the passengers gather for the twelve-fifteen to London. It was the fourth train of the day, and so far he hadn't spotted Clea Rice. The bench was occupied by three other women and a bouncy child who kept knocking at the newspaper, and the man was ready to give the brat a whack out of frustration. He'd been so sure Clea Rice would choose the train; now it looked as if she'd managed to sneak out of town some other way. Yes, she was definitely getting better at the game—a quick study at doing the unexpected. He still didn't know how she'd managed to slip away from the hospital last night. That would have been a far easier place to finish it, a private room, the patient under sedation. He had passed for a doctor once before, on a previous job. He certainly could have repeated the ruse.

A pity she hadn't cooperated.

Now he'd have to track her down again, before she vanished into the teeming masses of London.

"Other people 'ere could use the bench, y'know," said a woman.

He looked sideways and saw a steel-haired lady toting a shopping bag. "It's occupied," he said, and snapped his newspaper taut.

"Decent man'd leave it to folks wi' difficulties," said the woman.

He kept reading his newspaper, his fingers suddenly itching for the automatic in his shoulder holster. A hole right between the old biddy's eyes, that's what he'd like to do, just to shut her up. She was nattering on and on now about the dearth of gentlemen in this world, saying it to no one in particular, but loudly enough to draw the attention of people standing nearby. This was not good.

He stood, shot a poisonous look at the old hag, and surrendered his spot on the bench. She claimed it with a grunt of satisfaction. Folding up his newspaper, he wandered to the other end of the platform.

That's when he spotted Clea Rice.

She'd just emerged from the loo. She was wearing a houndstooth skirt and jacket, both a few sizes too large. Her hair was almost completely concealed by a scarf, but a few tendrils of red bangs peeked out. That, plus the way she moved—her gaze darting around, her circuitous route keeping her well away from the platform's edge—told him it was her.

This was not the place to do it.

He decided he'd let her board and would follow

her onto the train. There he could keep an eye on her. Perhaps when she got off again…

He had his ticket ready. He stepped forward and joined the crowd of passengers waiting to board.

SO CLEA RICE WAS TAKING the twelve-fifteen to London. Not the wisest move she could make, thought Charles Ogilvie as he stood in line behind her at the ticket office. He'd had no trouble tailing her from Chetwynd. Jordan Tavistock's champagne gold Jaguar wasn't exactly easy to miss. If he had been able to stay on their trail, surely someone else could do it, as well.

And now the woman was about to board a train in broad daylight.

Ogilvie reached the head of the line and quickly purchased his ticket. Then he followed the woman onto the platform. She vanished into the women's loo. He waited. Only as the train approached the station did she reemerge. There were about two dozen people standing on the platform, a mingling of business types and housewives, any one of whom could prove lethal. Ogilvie allowed his gaze to drift casually across the faces, trying to match one of them with a face he might have seen before.

At the far edge of the crowd he spotted someone who seemed familiar, a man in a gray suit and carrying a newspaper. His face, while not in any way distinctive, still struck a memory chord. Where had he seen him before?

The hospital. Last night, in the lobby. The man had been buying a paper from the hall newsstand.

Now he was boarding the twelve fifteen to London. Right behind Clea Rice.

A surge of adrenaline pumped through Ogilvie's veins. If something was going to happen, it'd be soon. Perhaps not here in the crowd, but on the train, or at the next stop. All it took was a gun barrel to the back of the head. Clea Rice would never see it coming.

The man in the gray suit was edging closer to the woman.

Ogilvie pushed forward. Already he had his jacket unbuttoned, his shoulder holster within easy reach. His gaze stayed focused on Mr. Gray Suit. At the first sign of attack, he'd bloody well better be ready. He was Clea Rice's only lifeline.

And there'd be no second chances.

ALMOST THERE. Almost there.

Clea clutched the ticket like a good-luck charm as she waited for the train to glide to a stop. She hung back a bit, allowing everyone else to press forward first. The memory of that incident in the London Underground was still too fresh; never again would she stand at any platform edge while a train pulled in.

All it took was one push from behind. No, it was better to hang back where she could see trouble coming.

The train had pulled to a stop. Passengers were starting to board.

Clea eased into the gathering. Her headache had come throbbing back with a vengeance, and she longed for the relative privacy of a train compartment. A few more steps, and she'd be on her way back to London. To anonymity. It was the best choice, after all—to simply drop out of sight. She'd been insane to think she could match wits with Van Weldon, an opponent who'd met her every thrust with a deadlier parry, who had every reason, and every resource, to crush her. Call it surrender, but she was ready to yield. Anything to stay alive.

She was so focused on getting aboard that she didn't notice the disturbance behind her. Just as she climbed onto the first step, a hand gripped her by the arm and tugged her back onto the platform.

She spun around, every nerve instantly wired for attack, her fingers arcing to claw across her assailant's face. An instant before striking flesh, she froze.

"Jordan?" she said in astonishment.

He grabbed her wrist. "Let's get out of here."

"What are you doing?"

"I'll explain later. Come on."

"But I'm leaving—"

He tugged her away, out of the line of passengers. She tried to yank free but he caught her by the shoulders and pulled her close to him. "Listen to me," he whispered. "Someone's followed us here, from Chetwynd. You can't get on the train."

Instantly she stiffened. His breath felt hot in her hair, and her awareness of his scent, his warmth, had never been more acute. Even through the tweed jacket she could feel the thudding of his heart, the tension in his arms. Without a word she nodded, and the arms encircling her relaxed their hold. Together they turned away from the train and took a step back up the platform.

A man seemed to appear from nowhere. He materialized directly in their path, a man in a gray suit. His face was scarcely worth noting; it was the gun in his hand that drew Clea's stunned gaze.

She was already pivoting away to the left when the first shot rang out. Something slammed into her shoulder, shoving her away. Jordan. In what seemed like slow motion she caught a flash of Jordan's tweed jacket as he lunged against her, and then she was stumbling sideways, falling to her knees onto the platform. The impact of the pavement sent a shock wave straight up her spine. The pain in her head was almost blinding.

Screams erupted all around her. She scrambled

back to her feet, at the same time twisting around to locate the attacker. The platform was a melee of panicked bodies scattering in every direction. Jordan still shielded her from a clear view, but over his shoulder she caught a glimpse of the gunman.

Just as he caught a glimpse of her. He raised his pistol.

The shot was like a thunderclap. Clea flinched, but she felt no pain, no impact, nothing but astonishment that she was still alive.

On the gunman's face was registered equal astonishment. He stared down at his chest, where the crimson stain of blood was rapidly blossoming across his shirt. He wobbled, dropped to his knees.

"Get out of here!" barked a voice somewhere off to the side.

Clea turned and saw a second man with a gun standing a few yards away. Frantically he waved at her to get moving.

The man in the gray suit was crawling on hands and knees now, gurgling, cursing, still refusing to drop his pistol. It took a firm push from Jordan to propel Clea forward. Suddenly her legs were working again. She began to run along the edge of the platform, every pounding footstep like another nail being driven into her aching head. She could hear Jordan right behind her, could hear the shouts of confusion echoing in their wake. They reached the rear of the train, leapt off onto the tracks and dashed across to the opposite platform.

Clea scrambled up first. Jordan seemed to be lagging behind. She paused to grab his hand and haul him up from the tracks.

"Don't wait for me," he gasped as they sprinted for the steps. "Just go—the parking lot—"

"I have to wait for you! You have the bloody car keys!"

The Jaguar was double-parked near the station gate. Jordan tossed Clea his keys. "You'd better drive," he said.

She didn't stop to argue. She slid in behind the wheel and threw the car into gear. They screeched out of the lot.

Farther up the road the sound of sirens drew close. The police were headed for the station, thought Clea; they weren't interested in *her.*

She was right. Two police cars sped right past them and kept going.

Clea glanced in the rearview mirror and saw that the road behind them was empty. "No one seems to be following us. I think we're all right."

"For now."

"You said we were tailed from Chetwynd. How did you know?"

"I wasn't sure at first. I kept seeing a black MG on

the road behind us. Then it dropped out of sight. That's why I didn't mention it. I thought it was gone."

"But you came back to get me."

"On the way out of the gate I saw the MG again. It was pulling in to a parking space. That's when I realized…" Grimacing, he shifted in his seat. "Are you going to tell me what the hell's going on?"

"Someone just tried to kill us."

"That I think I knew. Who was the gunman?"

"You mean his name?" She shook her head. Just that movement brought the throbbing back to her skull. "No idea."

"And the other man? The one who just saved our lives?"

"I don't know his name, either. But…" She paused. "I think I've seen him before. In London. The Underground."

"Your guardian angel?"

"But this time *you* saw him. So I guess he's not an angel at all." She glanced in the mirror. Still no one following them. Breathing more easily, she thought ahead to what came next. Chetwynd?

As if he'd read her mind, he said, "We can't go back to Chetwynd. They'll be expecting that."

"*You* could go back."

"I'm not so sure."

"You're not the one they want."

"Are you going to tell me who *they* are?"

"The same people who blew up Guy Delancey's car."

"These people—are they connected with this mysterious Belgian? Or was that just another fable?"

"It's the truth. Sort of."

He groaned. "Sort of?"

She glanced sideways and she noticed that his jaw was tightly squared. *He must be as terrified as I am,* she thought.

"I think I have the right to know the whole truth," he said.

"Later. When I've carved us out some breathing space." She nudged the accelerator. The Jaguar responded with a quiet purr and a burst of speed. "Right now, I just want to get the hell out of this county. When we hit London—"

"London?" He shook his head. "You think it'll be that easy? Just cruise down the highway? If they're as dangerous as you say, they'll have the main roads covered."

And a pale gold Jaguar wasn't a car they'd be likely to miss, she realized. She'd have to ditch the Jag. And maybe the man, as well. He'd be better off without her. Trouble seemed to attach itself to her like iron filings to a magnet, and when the next crisis hit, she didn't want Jordan caught in the cross fire. She owed him that much.

"There's a turnoff coming up," he said. "Take it."

"Where does it go?"

"Back road."

"To London?"

"No. It'll take us to an inn. I know the proprietors. There's a barn where we can hide the car."

"And how do I get to London?"

"We don't. We stay put for a while and get our bearings. Then we figure out our next move."

"I say our next move is to keep going! On foot if we have to! I won't hang around this neighborhood any longer than—"

"But I'm afraid I'll have to," he murmured.

She glanced sideways again. What she saw almost made her swerve off the road in horror.

He had pulled back the edge of his jacket and was staring down at his shirt. Bright splotches of blood stained the fine linen.

CHAPTER SEVEN

"Oh, my God," said Clea. "Why didn't you tell me?"

"It's not serious."

"How the hell can you tell?"

"I'm still breathing, aren't I?"

"Oh, that's just *wonderful*." She spun the wheel and sent the Jag in a dizzying U-turn. "We're going to a hospital."

"No." He reached over and grabbed her hand. "They'd be on you in a flash."

"What am I supposed to do? Let you bleed to death?"

"I'm all right. I think it's stopped." He looked down again at his shirt. The stains didn't seem to be spreading. "What's the cliché? 'It's only a flesh wound'?"

"What if it isn't? What if you're bleeding internally?"

"I'll be the first to beg for help. Believe me," he added with a pained smile, "I'm truly a coward at heart."

A coward? she thought. Not this man. He was the least cowardly man she knew.

"Go to the inn," he insisted. "If this is really serious, I can call for help."

Reluctantly she made another U-turn and headed back the way they'd been going. The turnoff brought them onto a narrow road lined by hedgerows. Through gaps in the foliage she spied a patchwork of fields and stone walls. The hedgerows gave way to a graveled driveway, and they pulled up at last in front of the Munstead Inn. A cottage garden, its blossoms fading into autumn, lined the front walk.

Clea scrambled out of the car to help Jordan to his feet.

"Let me walk on my own," he said. "Best to pretend nothing's wrong."

"You might faint."

"I'd never do anything so embarrassing." Grunting, he managed to slide out of the car and stand without her assistance. He made it on his own power through the garden and up the front steps.

Their knock on the door was answered by an elderly gentleman whose peat-colored trousers hung limp on his bony frame. He peered at them through bifocals, then exclaimed in pleasure, "Why, if it isn't young Mr. Tavistock!"

Jordan smiled. "Hello, Munstead. Any rooms available?"

"For friends o' yours, anytime!" The old man stepped

aside and waved them into the front hall. "Chetwynd's full up, then?" he asked. "No room for guests?"

"Actually, this room would be for me and the lady."

"You and…" Munstead turned and regarded Jordan with surprise. A sly grin spread across his face. "Ah, it's a bit of a hush thing, is it?"

"Just between us."

Munstead winked. "Gotcha, sir."

Clea didn't know how Jordan managed to hold up his end of the banter. As the old man rummaged for a key, Jordan politely inquired as to Mrs. Munstead's health, asked how the garden was this summer and were the children coming to visit at Christmas? At last they were led upstairs to the second floor. Under better circumstances Clea might have appreciated the romantic touches to the place, the flocked wallpaper, the lace curtains. Now her only focus was to get Jordan into a bed and his wound checked.

When they were safely behind closed doors, Clea practically forced Jordan down onto the mattress. He sat there, his face screwed up in discomfort, as she pulled off the tweed jacket. The droplets of blood staining his shirt led a trail under his right arm.

She unbuttoned the shirt. The blood had dried, adhering the fabric to his skin. Slowly, gently she peeled the shirt off, revealing a broad chest with tawny hair, some of it caked with blood. What she saw looked more like a slash than a bullet wound, as though a knife blade had caught him just in front of the armpit and sliced straight back along his right side.

She gave a sigh of relief. "It looks like just a graze. Caught you in passing. It could just as easily have gone straight through your chest. You're lucky."

He stared down at his wound and frowned. "Maybe it's more a case of divine intervention than luck."

"What?"

"Hand me my coat."

Perplexed, she passed him the tweed jacket. The bullet's entry was easy to locate. It cut a hole through the fabric over the right chest. Jordan reached inside the inner pocket and pulled out a handsome watch attached to a chain. Clearly stamped on the gold watch cover was an ugly dent.

"A helping hand from beyond the grave," he said, and handed Clea the watch.

She flipped open the dented cover. Inside was engraved the name Bernard Tavistock.

"My father's," said Jordan. "I inherited it on his death. It seems he's still watching out for me."

"Then you'd better keep it close by," she said, handing it back. "So it can ward off the next bullet."

"I sincerely hope there won't *be* a next bullet. This one's bloody uncomfortable as it is."

She went into the bathroom, soaked a towel in warm

water and wrung it out. When she came back to the bed, he was looking almost sheepish about all the fuss. As she bent to clean the wound, their heads brushed, and she inhaled a disturbingly primal mingling of scents. Blood and sweat and after-shave. His breath warmed her hair, and that warmth seemed to seep into her cheeks. Desperately trying to ignore his effect on her, she kept her gaze focused on his wound.

"I had no idea you'd been hurt," she said softly.

"It was the first shot. I sort of stumbled into it."

"Stumbled, hell! You pushed me away, you idiot."

He laughed. "Chivalry goes unappreciated."

Without warning she planted both hands on either side of his face and lowered her mouth to his in a fierce kiss. She knew at once it was a mistake. Her stomach seemed to drop away inside her. She felt his lips press hard against hers, heard his growl of both longing and satisfaction. Before he could tug her against him, she pulled away.

"You see, you're wrong," she whispered. "Chivalry is most definitely appreciated."

"If that's my reward, I may just do it again."

"Well, don't. Once is chivalry. Twice is stupidity."

Breathing hard, she focused her attention back on his wound. She could feel him watching her, could still taste the tang of his lips on hers, but she stubbornly refused to meet his gaze. If she did, they'd only kiss again.

She wiped up the last dried flecks of blood and straightened. "How are we going to dress it?"

"I've a first aid kit in the car. Bandages and such."

"I'll get it."

"Park the car in the barn, while you're at it. Get it out of sight."

With almost a sense of relief, she fled the room and hurried down the stairs. Once outside, she felt she could breathe again, felt she was back in control.

She walked deliberately to the Jaguar, started the engine and parked it inside the barn. After fetching the first aid kit out of the trunk, she stood by the car for a moment, taking deep, calming breaths of hay-scented air. At last her headache was all but gone and she could think clearly again. *Must concentrate,* she thought. *Remember what it is I'm facing. I can't afford to be distracted. Even by someone as distracting as Jordan.*

With first aid kit in hand, she returned to the room. The instant she stepped inside she felt her hard-won composure begin to crack around the edges. Jordan was standing at the window, his broad back turned to her, his gaze focused somewhere on the garden outside. She suppressed the impulse to go to him, to slide her hands down that expanse of naked skin.

"I hid the car," she said.

She thought he nodded, but he didn't answer.

After a pause she asked, "Is something wrong?"

He turned to look at her. "I called Chetwynd."

She frowned, trying to understand why, with that one call, his whole demeanor should change. "You called? Why?"

"To tell them what's happened. We're going to need help."

"It's better if they don't know. Safer if we don't—"

"Safer for whom?"

"For everyone. They might talk to the wrong people. Reveal things they shouldn't—"

She couldn't read his expression against the glare of the window. But she could hear the anger in his voice. "If I can't count on my own family, who *can* I count on?"

Stung by his tone, she sat on the bed and stared dully at the first aid kit in her lap. "I envy you your blind faith," she said softly. She opened the kit. Inside were bandages, adhesive tape, a bottle of antiseptic. "Come here. I'd better dress that wound."

He came to the bed and sat beside her. Neither of them spoke as she opened packets of gauze and snipped off lengths of tape. She heard him suck in a startled gasp of air when she dabbed on the antiseptic, but he said nothing. His silence frightened her. Something had changed between them since she'd left the room, something about that phone call to Chetwynd. She was afraid to ask about it, afraid to cut what few threads of connection still remained between them. So she said nothing, but simply finished the task, the whole time fighting off a sense of panic that she'd lost him. Or even worse, that he'd turned against her.

Her worst suspicions seemed confirmed when he said, as she was pressing the last strip of tape to his chest, "Richard's on his way."

She sat back and stared at him. "You told him where we are?"

"I had to."

"Couldn't you just say you're alive and well? Leave it at that?"

"He has something to tell me."

"He could have said everything over the phone."

"It has to be face-to-face." Jordan paused, then he added quietly, "It has to do with you."

She sat clutching the roll of tape, her gaze frozen on his face. *He knows,* she thought. She felt sick to her stomach, sick of herself and her sorry past. Whatever attraction Jordan had felt for her was obviously gone now, destroyed by some revelation gleaned from a phone call.

She swallowed and looked away. "What did he tell you?"

"Only that you haven't been entirely honest about who you are."

"And…" She cleared her throat. "How did he find out?"

"Your fingerprints."

"What fingerprints?"

"The polo field. You left them on your glass in the refreshment tent."

It took her a moment for the implications to sink in. "Then you—*you're* the one who—"

He nodded. "I picked up your glass. Your fingerprints weren't on record at Scotland Yard. So I asked Richard to check with American authorities. And they had the prints on file."

She shot to her feet and backed away from the bed. "I trusted you!"

"I never meant to hurt you."

"No, you just prowled around behind my back."

"I knew you weren't being straight with me. How else could I find out? I had to know."

"Why? What difference would it make to you?" she cried.

"I wanted to believe you. I wanted to be absolutely sure of you."

"So you set out to prove I'm a fraud."

"Is that what I've proved?"

She shook her head and laughed. "What else would I be but a fraud? It's what you looked for. It's what you expected to find."

"I don't know what I expected to find."

"Maybe that I'd be some—some princess in disguise? Instead you learn the truth. A frog instead of a princess. Oh, but you must be *so* disappointed! *I* find it disappointing that I can't ever outrun my past. No matter how hard I try, it follows me around like one of those little cartoon rain clouds over my head." She looked down at the flowered rug. For a moment she studied the pattern of its weave. Then, wearily, she sighed. "Well, I do thank you for your help. You've been more of a gentleman than any man has ever been to me. I wish…I'd hoped…" She shook her head and turned to the door.

"Where are you going?"

"It's a long walk to London. I think I'll get started."

In an instant he was on his feet and crossing toward her. "You can't go."

"I have a life to get on with."

"And how long will it last? What happens at the next train station?"

"Are you volunteering to take another bullet?"

He caught her arm and pulled her against him. As she collided with his chest, she felt her whole body turn liquid against his heat.

"I'm not sure what I'm volunteering for," he murmured. "But I think I've already signed up…"

The kiss caught them both off-balance. The instant

their lips met, Clea felt herself swaying, tilting. He pressed her to the wall, his lips on hers, his body a warm and breathing barrier to escape. Their breaths were coming so loud and fast, their sighs so needy, that she didn't hear the footsteps creaking on the stairs, didn't hear them approach their room.

The knock on the door made them both jerk apart. They stared at each other, faces flushed with passion, hair equally tousled.

"Who is it?" Jordan called.

"It's me."

Jordan opened the door.

Richard Wolf stood in the hall. He glanced at Clea's reddened cheeks, then looked at Jordan's bare chest. Without comment he stepped into the room and locked the door behind him. Clea noticed he had a file folder stuffed with papers.

"You weren't followed?" asked Jordan.

"No." Richard looked at Clea, and she almost felt like slinking away, so cool was that gaze of his. *So now the truth will be spilled. He knows all, of course.* That must be what he had in that folder—the proof of her identity. Who and what she'd been. He would lay it all out for Jordan, and she wouldn't be able to deny it. And how would Jordan react? With anger, disgust?

Feeling defeated beyond words, she went to the bed and sat down. She wouldn't look at either one of the men; she didn't want to see their faces as they shared the facts about Clea Rice. She would just sit here and passively confirm it all. Then she would leave. Surely Jordan wouldn't bother to stop her this time. Surely he'd be happy to see her go.

She waited on the bed and listened as the truth was finally told.

"Her name isn't Diana Lamb," said Richard. "It's Clea Rice."

Jordan looked at the woman, half expecting a protest, a denial, *some* sort of response, but she said nothing. She only sat with her shoulders hunched forward, her head drooping with what looked like profound weariness. It was almost painful to look at her. This was not at all the brash Diana—correction, Clea—he knew. But then, he'd never really known her, had he?

Richard handed the folder to Jordan. "That was faxed to me just an hour ago from Washington."

"From Niki?"

Richard nodded. Nikolai Sakaroff was his partner in Sakaroff and Wolf, Security Consultants. Formerly a colonel with the KGB and now an enthusiastic advocate of capitalism, Sakaroff had turned his talents for intelligence gathering to more profitable uses. If anyone could dig up obscure information, it was Niki.

"Her fingerprints were on file with the Massachusetts police," said Richard. "Once that fact was established, the rest of it came easy."

Jordan opened the folder. The first page he saw was a grainy reproduction of a mug shot, a frontal and two profiles. The faxing process had blurred the details, but he could still tell it was a younger version of Clea. The subject gazed unsmiling at the camera, her dark eyes wide and bewildered, her lips pressed tightly together. Her hair, free flowing about her shoulders, appeared to be blond. Jordan glanced once again at the live woman. She hadn't moved.

He turned to the next page.

"Three years ago she was convicted of harboring a felon and destruction of evidence," said Richard. "She served ten months in the Massachusetts State Penitentiary, with time off for good behavior."

Jordan turned to Clea. "Is this true?"

She gave a low and bitter laugh. "Yes. In prison I was *very* well behaved."

"And the rest of it? The conviction? The ten months served?"

"You have it all there. Why are you asking me?"

"Because I want to know if it's true."

"It's true," she whispered, and her head seemed to droop even lower. She seemed in no mood to elaborate, so Jordan turned back to Richard. "Who was the felon? The one she aided?"

"His name's Walter Rice. He's still serving time in Massachusetts."

"Rice? Is he a relative?"

"He's my uncle Walter," said Clea dully.

"What crime did this uncle Walter commit?"

"Burglary. Fraud. Trafficking in stolen goods." She shrugged. "Take your pick. Uncle Walter had a long and varied career."

"Of which Clea was a part," said Richard.

Clea's chin shot up. It was the first spark of anger she'd displayed. "That's not true!"

"No? What about your juvenile record?"

"Those were supposed to be sealed!"

"Sealed doesn't mean nonexistent. At age twelve, you were caught trying to pawn stolen jewelry. At age fourteen, you and your cousin burglarized half a dozen homes on Beacon Hill."

"I was only a child! I didn't know what I was doing!"

"What did you *think* you were doing?"

"Whatever Uncle Walter told us to do!"

"Did Uncle Walter have such power over you that you didn't know right from wrong?"

She looked away. "Uncle Walter was…he was the one I looked up to. You see, I grew up in his house. It was just the three of us. My cousin Tony and my uncle and me. I know what we did was wrong. But the burglaries—they didn't seem real to me, you know. It was more of a...a game. Uncle Walter used to dare us. He'd say, 'Who's clever enough to beat *that* house?' And we'd feel cowardly if we didn't take him up on the dare. It wasn't the money. It was never the money." She looked up. "It was the challenge."

"And what about that issue of right and wrong?"

"That's why I stopped. I was eighteen when I moved out of Uncle Walter's house. For eight years I stayed on the straight and narrow. I swear it."

"In the meantime, your uncle went right on robbing houses. The police say he was responsible for dozens of burglaries in Boston's wealthiest neighborhoods. Luckily, no one was ever hurt."

"He'd never hurt anyone! Uncle Walter didn't even own a gun."

"No, he was just a virtuous thief."

"He swore he never took from people who couldn't afford it."

"Of course not. He went where the money was. Like any smart burglar."

She stared down again at her knotted hands. A convicted criminal, thought Jordan. She hardly looked the part. But she had managed to deceive him from the start, and he knew now he couldn't trust his own eyes, his own instincts. Not where she was concerned.

He refocused his attention on the file. There were

a few pages of notes written in Niki Sakaroff's precise hand, dates of arrest, conviction, imprisonment. There was a copy of a news article about the career of Walter Rice, whose exploits had earned legendary status in the Boston area. As Clea had said, old Walter never actually hurt anyone. He just robbed and he did it with style. He was known as the Red Rose Thief, for his habit of always leaving behind his calling card: a single rose, his gesture of apology to the victims.

Even the most skillful thief, however, eventually meets with bad luck. In Walter's case it took the form of an alert homeowner with a loaded pistol. Caught in the act, with a bullet in his arm, Walter found himself scrambling out the window for his life.

Two days later he was arrested in his niece's apartment, where he'd sought refuge and first aid.

No wonder she did such a good job of dressing my wound, thought Jordan. *She's had practice.*

"It seems to be a Rice family trait," observed Richard. "Trouble with the law."

Clea didn't refute the statement.

"What about this cousin Tony?" asked Jordan.

"He served six years. Burglary," said Richard. "Niki hears through the grapevine that Tony Rice is somewhere in Europe, working as a fence in black market antiques. Am I right, Miss Rice?"

Clea looked up. "Leave Tony out of this. He's clean now."

"Is he the one you're working with?"

"I'm not working with anyone."

"Then how were you planning to fence the loot?"

"What loot?"

"The items you planned to steal from Guy Delancey?"

She reacted with a look of hopeless frustration. "Why do I bother to answer your questions?" she said. "You've already tried and convicted me. There's nothing left to say."

"There's plenty left for you to say," said Jordan. "Who's trying to kill you? And maybe pop me off in the process?"

"He won't bother with you, once I'm gone."

"*Who* won't?"

"The man I told you about." She sighed. "The Belgian."

"You mean that part of the story was true?"

"Yes. Absolutely true. So was the part about the *Max Havelaar.*"

"What Belgian?" asked Richard.

"His name is Van Weldon," said Clea. "He has people working for him everywhere. Guy was just an accidental victim. *I'm* the one Van Weldon wants dead."

There was a long silence. Richard said slowly, "Victor Van Weldon?"

A glint of fear suddenly appeared in Clea's eyes. She was staring at Richard. "You...know him?"

"No. I just heard the name. A short time ago, in fact." He was frowning at Clea, as though seeing some new aspect to her face. "I spoke to one of the constables about the man shot at the railway station."

"The one who tried to kill us?" said Jordan.

Richard nodded. "He's been identified as a George Fraser. English, with a London address. They tried to track down his next of kin, but all they came up with was the name of his employer. He's a service rep for the Van Weldon Shipping Company."

At the mention of the company's name, Jordan saw Clea give an involuntary shudder, as though she'd just been touched by the chill hand of evil. Nervously she rose to her feet and went to the window, where she stood hugging herself, staring out at the afternoon sunlight.

"What about the other gunman?" asked Jordan.

"No sign of him. It seems he managed to slip away."

"My guardian angel," murmured Clea. "Why?"

"You tell us," said Richard.

"I know why someone's trying to kill me. But not why anyone wants to keep me *alive*."

"Let's start with what you do know," said Jordan.

He went to her, placed his hand gently on her shoulder. She felt so small, so insubstantial to his touch. "Why does Victor Van Weldon want you dead?"

"Because I know what happened to the *Max Havelaar.*"

"Why it sank, you mean?"

She nodded. "There was nothing valuable aboard that boat. Those insurance claims were false. And the crew was considered expendable."

"How do you know all this?"

"Because I was there." She turned and looked at him, her eyes haunted by some vision of horror only she could see. "I was aboard the *Max Havelaar* the night it went down."

CHAPTER EIGHT

"It was my first trip to Naples," she said. "My first year ever in Europe. I was desperate to escape all those bad memories from prison. So when Tony wrote, inviting me to Brussels, I leapt at the chance."

"That's your cousin?" asked Richard.

Clea nodded. "He's been in a wheelchair since his accident on the autobahn last year. He needed someone he could trust to serve as his business representative. Someone who'd round up buyers for the antiques he sells. It's a completely legitimate business. Tony's no longer dealing in the black market."

"And that's why you were in Naples? On your cousin's behalf?"

"Yes. And that's where I met my two Italian sailors." She looked away again, out the window. "Carlo and Giovanni…"

They were the first mate and navigator aboard a boat docked in the harbor. Both men had liquid brown eyes and ridiculously long lashes and a penchant for innocent mischief. Both adored blondes. And although they'd flirted and made eyes at her, Clea had known on some instinctive level that they were absolutely harmless. Besides, Giovanni was a good friend of Tony's, and in Italy the bond of trust between male friends overrode even the Italian's finely honed mating instinct. Much as they might be tempted, neither man would dream of crossing the line with Clea.

"We spent seven evenings together, the three of us," murmured Clea. "Eating in cafés. Splashing in fountains. They were so sweet to me. So polite." She gave a soft laugh. "I thought of them as younger brothers. And when they came up with this wild idea of taking me to Brussels aboard their ship, I never thought to be afraid."

"You mean as a passenger?" asked Jordan.

"More as an honored stowaway. It was a little escapade we hatched over Campari and pasta. Their ship was sailing in a few days, and they thought, wouldn't it be fun if I came along? Their captain had no objections, as long as I stayed below and out of sight until they left the harbor. He didn't want any flack from the ship's owner. I could come out on deck once we were at sea. And in Brussels they'd sneak me off again."

"You trusted them?"

"Yes. It sounds crazy now, but I did. They were

so…harmless." Clea smiled at the memory. "Maybe it was all that Campari. Maybe I was just hungry for a bit of adventure. We had it all planned out, you see. The wine we'd bring aboard. The meals I'd whip up for everyone. They told me it was a large boat, and the only cargo was a few crates of artwork bound for an auction house in Brussels. There'd be plenty of room for a crew of eight. And me.

"So that night I was brought aboard. While the men got ready to leave, I waited below in the cargo hold. Giovanni brought me hot tea and chocolate biscuits. He was such a nice boy…."

"It was the *Max Havelaar* you boarded?" asked Richard softly.

She swallowed. "Yes. It was the *Max Havelaar.*" She took a deep breath, mustering the strength to continue. "She was an old boat. Everything was rusted. Everything seemed to creak. I thought it odd that a vessel that large would carry as its only cargo a few crates of artwork.

"I saw a manifest sheet hanging on one of the crates in the hold. I looked it over. And that's when I realized there was a fortune's worth of antique art in those crates."

"Was the owner listed?"

"Yes. It was the Van Weldon company. They were the shipping agent, as well."

"What did you do then?"

"I was curious, of course. I wanted to take a peek, but all the crates were nailed shut. I looked around for a bit, and finally found a knothole in one of the boards. It was big enough to shine a penlight through. What I saw inside didn't make sense."

"What was there?"

"Stones. The bottom of the crate was lined with stones."

She turned from the window. The two men were staring at her in bewilderment. No wonder. She, too, had been just as bewildered.

"Did you speak to the crew about this?" asked Richard.

"I waited until we'd left the dock. Then I found Giovanni. I asked him if he realized they were carrying crates of rocks. He only laughed. Said I must be seeing things. He'd been told the crates were valuable. He'd seen them loaded aboard himself."

"Who loaded them?"

"The Van Weldon company. They came in a truck directly from their warehouse."

"What did you do then?"

"I insisted we speak to Vicenzo. The captain. He laughed at me, too. Why would a company ship rocks, he kept asking me. And he had other concerns at the time. The southern coast of Sardinia was coming up, and he had to keep a watch out for other ships. He told me he'd check the cargo later.

"It wasn't until we'd passed Sardinia that I was able to drag them below decks to look. They finally pried open one of the crates. There was a layer of wood shavings on top. Typical packing material. I told them to keep digging. They went through the shavings, then through a layer of newspapers. They kept going deeper and deeper, expecting to find the artwork that was on the manifest. All they found were stones."

"The captain must have believed you then?"

"Of course. He had no choice. He decided to radio Naples, to find out what was going on. So we climbed up the steps to the bridge. Just as we got there, the engine room exploded."

Richard and Jordan said nothing. They only watched her in grim silence as she told them about the last moments of the *Max Havelaar.*

In the panic that followed the explosion, as Giovanni radioed his last SOS, as the crew—what remained of the crew—scrambled to lower the lifeboat, the rocks in the cargo hold were forgotten. Survival was all that mattered. The flames were spreading rapidly; the *Max Havelaar* would be a floating inferno.

They lowered the lifeboat onto the swells. There was no time to climb down the ladder; with the flames licking at their backs, they leapt into the dark Mediterranean.

"The water was so cold," she said. "When I surfaced, I could see the *Havelaar* was all in flames. The lifeboat was drifting about a dozen yards away. Carlo and the second mate had already managed to crawl in, and they were leaning over the gunwale, trying to haul aboard Vicenzo. Giovanni was still in the water, struggling just to keep his head up.

"I've always been a strong swimmer. I can stay afloat for hours if I have to. So I yelled to the men that they should get the others to climb aboard first. And I treaded water…." She'd felt strangely calm, she remembered. Almost detached from the crisis. Perhaps it was the rhythmic motion of her limbs stroking the liquid darkness. Perhaps it was the sense of dreamlike unreality. She hadn't been afraid. Not yet.

"I knew the Spanish coast was only two miles or so to the north. By morning we could've paddled the lifeboat to land. Finally, all the men were hauled aboard. I was the only one left in the water. I swam over to the lifeboat and had just reached up for a hand when we all heard the sound of an engine."

"Another boat?" asked Jordan.

"Yes. A speedboat of some kind. Suddenly the men all were shouting, waving like crazy. The lifeboat was rocking back and forth. I was behind the gunwale and couldn't see the other boat as it came toward us. They had a searchlight. And I heard a voice calling to us in English. Some sort of accent—I'm not sure what kind. He identified their boat as the *Cosima*.

"Giovanni reached down to help me climb aboard. He'd just grabbed my hand when…" She paused. "When the *Cosima* began to fire on us."

"On the *lifeboat?*" asked Jordan, appalled.

"At first I didn't understand what was happening. I could hear the men crying out. And my hand slid away from Giovanni's. I saw that he was crumpled against the gunwale, staring down at me. I didn't understand that the sound was gunfire. Until a body fell into the water. It was Vicenzo's," she whispered, and looked away.

"How did you escape?" asked Jordan, gently.

Clea took an unsteady breath. "I dove," she said softly. "I swam underwater as far as my lungs would carry me. As fast as I could stroke away from that searchlight. I came up for air, then dove again and kept swimming. I thought I heard bullets hitting the water around me, but *Cosima* didn't chase after me. I just kept swimming and swimming. All night. Until I reached the coast of Spain."

She stood for a moment with bowed head. Neither man spoke. Neither man broke the silence.

"They killed them all," she whispered. "Giovanni.

The captain. Six helpless men in a lifeboat. They never knew there was a witness."

Jordan and Richard stood watching her. They were both too shocked by her story to say a word. She didn't know if they believed any of it; all she knew was that it felt good to finally tell it, to share the burden of horror.

"I reached the coast around dawn," she continued. "I was cold. Exhausted. But mostly I was desperate to reach the police." She shook her head. "That was my mistake, of course. Going to the police."

"Why?" asked Jordan gently.

"I ended up in some village police station, trying to explain what had happened. They made me wait in a back room while they checked the story. It turns out they called the Van Weldon company, to confirm their boat was missing. It made sense, I suppose. I can't blame the police for checking. So I waited three hours in that room for some representative from Van Weldon to arrive. Finally he did. I heard his voice through the door. I recognized it." She trembled at the memory. "It was the voice from the *Cosima*."

"You mean the killers were working for Van Weldon?" said Jordan.

Clea nodded. "I was climbing out that window so fast I must have left scorch marks. I've been running ever since. I found out later that *Cosima*'s registered owner is the Van Weldon Shipping Company. They sabotaged the *Havelaar*. They murdered its crew."

"And then claimed it as a giant loss," said Richard. "Artwork and all."

"Only there *wasn't* any artwork aboard," said Clea. "It was a dummy shipment, meant to go down on a boat they didn't need anymore. The real art's being stored somewhere. I'm sure it will be sold, piece by piece, on the black market. A double profit, counting the insurance."

"Who carried the policy?"

"Lloyd's of London."

"Have you contacted them?"

"Yes. They were skeptical of my story. Kept asking me what I wanted out of this, whether I had a grudge against the Van Weldon company. Then they learned about my prison record. After that, they didn't believe anything I said." Sighing, she went to the bed and sat down. "I told my cousin Tony to drop out of sight— he's the obvious person they'd use to track me down. He's in a wheelchair. Vulnerable. He's hiding out somewhere in Brussels. I can't really expect much help from him. So I'm floundering around on my own."

A long silence passed. When at last she found the courage to look up, she saw that Jordan was frowning at the wall, and that Richard Wolf was obviously not convinced of her story.

"You don't believe me, do you, Mr. Wolf?" she said.

"I'll reserve judgment for later. When I've had a chance to check the facts." He turned to Jordan. "Can we talk outside?"

Jordan nodded and followed Richard out of the room.

From the window Clea watched the two men standing in the garden below. She couldn't hear what they were saying, but she could read their body language—the nods, the grim set of Jordan's face. After a few moments Richard climbed in his car and drove away. Jordan reentered the building.

Clea stood waiting for him. She was afraid to face him, afraid to confront his skepticism. Why should he believe her? She was an ex-con. In the past month she had told so many lies she could scarcely keep them all straight. It was too much to ask that he would take her word for it this time.

The door opened and Jordan entered, his expression unreadable. He studied her for a moment, as though not certain just what to do with her. Then he let out a deep breath.

"You certainly know how to throw a fellow for a loop," he said.

"I'm sorry" was all she could think of saying.

"Sorry?"

"I never meant to drag you into this. Or your family either. It would be easier all around if you just go home. Somehow I'll get to London."

"It's a little late in the game, isn't it? To be casting me off?"

"You'll have no problems. Van Weldon isn't interested in *you*."

"But he is."

"What?"

"That's what Richard wanted to tell me. On his way to meet us, he was followed. Someone's watching Chetwynd, monitoring everyone's comings and goings."

Clea stiffened with alarm. "They followed him here?"

"No, he lost them."

"How can he be sure?"

"Believe me, Richard's an old hand at this. He'd know if he was followed."

Heart racing, she began to pace the room. She didn't care how skilled Richard Wolf might be—the chances were, he would underestimate Van Weldon's power, his resources. She'd spent the past month fighting for her life. She'd made it her business to learn everything she could about Van Weldon, and she knew, better than anyone, how far his tentacles reached. He had already discovered the link between her and the Tavistocks. It was just a matter of time before he used that knowledge to track her down.

She stopped pacing and looked at Jordan. "What next? What does your Mr. Wolf have in mind?"

"A fact-finding mission. Some discreet inquiries, a chat with Lloyd's of London."

"What do we do in the meantime?"

"We sit tight and wait right here. He'll call us in the morning."

She nodded and turned away. *In the morning,* she thought, *I'll be gone.*

VICTOR VAN WELDON WAS having another attack, and this was a severe one, judging by the pallor of his face and the tinge of blue around his lips. Van Weldon was not long for this world, thought Simon Trott—a few months at the most. And then he'd be gone and the path would be clear for his appointed successor—Trott himself.

If Van Weldon didn't sack him first, a possibility that was beginning to seem likely since the latest news had broken.

"How can this be?" Van Weldon wheezed. "You said it was under control. You said the woman was ours."

"A third party stepped in at the last moment. He ruined everything. And we lost a man."

"What about this family you mentioned—the Tavistocks?"

"The Tavistocks are a distraction, nothing more. It's not them I'm worried about."

"Who, then?"

Trott paused, reluctant to broach the possibility. "Interpol," he said at last. "It seems the woman has attracted their attention."

Van Weldon reacted with a violent spasm of coughing. When at last he'd caught his breath again, he turned his malevolent gaze to Trott. "You have brought us to disaster."

"I'm sure it can be remedied."

"You left the task to fools. And so," he added ironically, "did I."

"The police have nothing. Our man is dead. He can't talk."

"Clea Rice can."

"We'll find her again."

"How? Every day she grows more and more clever. Every day we seem to grow more and more stupid."

"Eventually we'll have a lead. Our contact in Buckinghamshire—"

Van Weldon gave a snort. "That contact is a liability! I want the connection severed. And there must be a consequence. I will not tolerate such treachery."

Trott nodded. Consequences. Penalties. Yes, he understood their necessity.

He only hoped that he would not someday be on the receiving end.

IT WAS WELL AFTER DARK when Richard Wolf finally drove in through the gates of Chetwynd. As he passed between the stone pillars his gaze swept the road, searching for a telltale silhouette, a movement in the bushes. He knew he was being watched, just as he knew he'd been followed earlier today. Even if he didn't quite believe Clea Rice's story, he did believe that she was in real danger. Her fear had infected him as well, had notched up his alertness to the point he was watching every shadow. He was glad Beryl had gone off to London for a few days. He'd call her later and suggest she stay longer—anything to keep her well away from this Clea Rice mess.

A car he didn't recognize was parked in the driveway.

Richard pulled up beside it. Cautiously he got out and circled around the Saab, glanced through the window at the interior. Inside were a few folded newspapers, nothing to identify the driver.

He went up the steps to the house.

Davis greeted him at the front door and helped him off with his raincoat. "You have a visitor, Mr. Wolf."

"So I've noticed. Who is it?"

"A Mr. Archibald MacLeod. He's in the library."

"Did he mention the purpose of his visit?"

"Some sort of police business."

At once Richard crossed the hall to the library. A man—brown haired, short but athletic build—stood beside the far bookcase, examining a leather-bound volume. He looked up as Richard entered.

"Mr. MacLeod? I'm Richard Wolf."

"Yes, I know. I've made inquiries. I've just spoken to an old colleague of yours—Claude Daumier, French Intelligence. He assures me I can have complete confidence in you." MacLeod closed the book and slid it back on the shelf. "I'm from Interpol."

"And I'm afraid I'm quite in the dark."

"We believe you and Mr. Tavistock have stumbled into a somewhat hazardous situation. I'm anxious to see that no one gets hurt. That's why I'm here to ask for your cooperation."

"In what matter?"

"Tell me where I can find Clea Rice."

Richard hoped his alarm didn't show on his face. "Clea Rice?" he asked blankly.

"I know you're familiar with the name. Since you requested an ID of her fingerprints. And a copy of her criminal record. The American authorities alerted us to that fact."

The man really must be with the police, Richard

concluded. Nevertheless, he decided to proceed cautiously. Just because MacLeod was a cop didn't mean he could be trusted.

Richard crossed to the fireplace and sat down. "Before I tell you anything," he said, "I'd like to hear the facts."

"You mean about Clea Rice?"

"No. About Victor Van Weldon."

"Then will you tell me how to find Miss Rice?"

"Why do you want her?"

"We've decided it's time to move on her. As soon as possible."

Richard frowned. "You mean—you're arresting her?"

"Not at all." MacLeod faced him squarely. "We've used Miss Rice long enough. It's time to bring her into protective custody."

A SOFT DRIZZLE WAS falling as Clea stepped out the front door of the Munstead Inn. It was past midnight and all was dark inside, the other occupants having long since retired. For a full hour she had lain awake beside Jordan, waiting until she was certain he was asleep. Since the revelations of that afternoon, mistrust seemed to loom between them, and they had staked out opposite sides of the bed. They'd scarcely spoken to each other, much less touched.

Now she was leaving, and it was all for the better. The break was cleaner this way—no sloppy emotions, no uneasy farewells. He was the gentleman. She was the ex-con. Never the twain could meet.

The back gate squealed as she opened it. She froze, listening, but all she heard was the whisper of drizzle on tree leaves and, in the distance, the barking of a dog. She pulled her jacket tightly against the moist chill and began to trudge down the road.

It would be an all-night walk; by daybreak she could be miles from here. If her feet held out. If she wasn't spotted by the enemy.

Ahead stretched the twin hedgerows lining both sides of the road. She debated whether or not to walk on the far side of the hedge, where she would be hidden from the road, but after a few steps in the mud she decided the pavement was worth the risk. She wouldn't get far in this sucking mire. Chances were, no one would be driving this late at night, anyway. She slogged back around the hedge and clambered onto the road. There she froze.

The silhouette of a man was standing before her.

"You could have told me you were leaving," said Jordan.

Relieved it was him, she found her breath again. "I could have."

"Why didn't you?"

"You would have stopped me. And I can't afford any more delays. Not when I know they're one step behind."

"You'll be safer with me than without me."

"No, I'm safer on my own. I'm getting good at this, you know. I may actually survive to see the ripe old age of thirty-one."

"As what, a fugitive? What kind of life is that?"

"At least it's a life."

"What about Van Weldon? He gets off with murder?"

"I can't do anything about that. I've tried. All it's earned me is a bunch of thugs on my tail and a head of peroxide-damaged hair. I give up, okay? He wins. And I'm out of here." She turned and began to walk away, down the road.

"Why did you come to England, anyway? Was it really the dagger you were after?"

"Yes. I thought, if I could steal it back, I'd have my evidence. I could prove to everyone that Van Weldon was lying. That he'd filed a false claim. And maybe— maybe someone would believe me."

"If what you're saying is true—"

"*If* it's true?" She turned in disgust and continued walking up the road. Away from him. "I suppose I made up the guy with the gun, too."

He followed her. "You can't keep running. You're the only witness to what happened to the *Havelaar*. The only one who can nail Van Weldon in court."

"If he doesn't nail me first."

"The police need your testimony."

"They don't believe me. And they won't without solid evidence. I wouldn't trust the police, anyway. You think Van Weldon got rich playing by the rules? Hell, no. I've checked into him. He has a hundred lawyers who'll pull strings to get him off. And probably a hundred cops in his pocket. He owns a dozen ships, fourteen hotels and three casinos in Monaco. Okay, so last year he didn't do so well. He got overextended and lost a bundle. That's why he ditched the *Havelaar,* to— pardon the pun—keep his head above water. He's a little desperate and a little paranoid. And he'll squash anyone who gets in his way."

"I'll get you help, Clea."

"You have a nice mansion and a CIA-in-law. That's not enough."

"My uncle worked for MI6. British Intelligence."

"I suppose your uncle's chummy with a few members of Parliament?"

"Yes, he is."

"So is Van Weldon. He makes friends everywhere. Or he buys them."

He grabbed her arm and pulled her around to face him. "Clea, eight men died on the *Havelaar.* You saw it happen. How can you walk away from that?"

"You think it's easy?" she cried. "I try to sleep at

night, and all I see is poor Giovanni slumping over the lifeboat. I hear gunfire. And Vicenzo moaning. And I hear the voice of that man. The one on the *Cosima*. The one who ordered them all killed...." She swallowed back an unexpected swell of tears. Angrily she wiped them away. "So, no, it ain't easy. But it's what I have to do if I want—"

Jordan cut her off with a sharp tug on her arm. Only at that instant did Clea notice the flicker of light reflected in his face. She spun around to face the road.

In the distance a car was approaching. As it rounded a curve, its headlights flitted through the hedgerow branches.

At once Jordan and Clea were dashing back the way they'd come. The hedges were too high and thick to cross; their only escape route was along the road. Rain had left the pavement slippery, and Clea's every step was bogged down by the mud still clinging to her shoes. Any second they'd be spotted.

Jordan yanked her sideways, through a gap in the hedge.

They tumbled through and landed together in a bed of wet grass. Seconds later the car drove past and continued on, toward the Munstead Inn. Through the stillness of the night they heard the engine's growl fade away. Then there was nothing. No car doors slamming, no voices.

"Do you think they've gone on?" whispered Clea.

"No. It's a dead-end road. There's only the inn."

"Then what are they doing?"

"Watching. Waiting for something."

For us, she thought.

Suddenly she was frantic to get away, to escape the threat of that car and its faceless occupants. This time she didn't dare use the road. Instead she headed across the field, not knowing where she was going, knowing only that she had to get as far away from the Munstead Inn as she could. The mud sucked at her shoes, slowing every step, making her stumble again and again, until she felt as if she was trapped in that familiar nightmare of pursuit, her legs refusing to work. She was panting so hard she didn't hear Jordan following at her heels. Only when she fell to her knees and he reached down for her did she realize he was right beside her.

He pulled her back to her feet. She stood swaying, her legs shaky, her breath coming in gasps. Around them stretched the dark vastness of the field. Overhead the sky was silvery with mist and rain.

"We're all right," he panted, struggling to catch his breath, as well. "They're not following us."

"How did they know where to look for us?"

"It couldn't have been the Munsteads."

"Then it was Richard Wolf."

"No," said Jordan firmly. "It wasn't Richard."

"They could've followed him—"

"He said he wasn't followed."

"Then he was wrong!" She pulled away. "I should never have trusted you. Any of you. Now it's going to get me killed." She turned and struggled on through the mire.

"Clea, wait."

"Go home, Jordan. Go back to being a gentleman."

"Can you keep on running?"

"Damn right I can! I'm getting as far away as possible. I yanked on the tiger's tail. I was lucky to live through it."

"You think Van Weldon will let you go? He'll hunt you down, Clea. Wherever you run, you'll be looking over your shoulder. You're a constant threat to him. The one person who could destroy him. Unless he destroys you first."

She turned. In the darkness of the field his face was a black oval against the silver of the night clouds. "What do you want me to do? Fight back? Surrender?" She gave a sob of desperation. "Either way, Jordan, I'm lost. And I'm scared." She hugged herself in the rain. "And I'm freezing to death."

At once his arms came around her, pulling her into his embrace. They were both damp and shivering, yet even through their soaked clothes she felt his warmth seep toward her. He took her face in his hands, and the kiss he pressed to her lips was enough to sweep away, just for a moment, her discomfort. Her fear. As the rain began to beat down on the fields and the clouds swept across the moon, she was aware only of him, the salty heat of his mouth, the way his body molded itself around hers.

When at last she'd caught her breath again, and they stood gazing at each other in the darkness, she found she was no longer shaking from fear, but from longing.

For him.

He said softly, "I know a place we can go tonight. It's a long walk. But it will be warm there, and dry."

"And safe?"

"And safe." Again he framed her face in his hands and kissed her. "Trust me."

I have no choice, she thought. *I'm too tired to think of what I should do. Where I should go.*

He took her hand. "We cross this field, then follow the roads," he said. "On pavement, so they won't be able to track our footprints."

"And then?"

"It's a three-, four-mile walk. Think you can make it?"

She thought about the men in the car, waiting outside the Munstead Inn. She wondered if somewhere, in the cylinder of one of their guns, there lurked a bullet with her name on it.

"I can make it," she said, her pace quickening. "I'll do anything," she added under her breath, "to stay alive."

CHAPTER NINE

A FEW TAPS of a rock and the window shattered.

Jordan broke away the jagged edges and climbed in. A moment later he reappeared at the cottage's front door and motioned for Clea to enter.

She stepped inside and found herself standing in a quaint room furnished with rough-hewn antiques and pewter lamps. Massive ceiling beams, centuries old, ran the length of the room, and all around her, burnished wainscoting gleamed against the white-washed walls. It would have been a cozy room were it not so cold and drafty. The English, thought Clea, must have thermally insulated hides.

Jordan, soaked as he was, looked scarcely discomfited as he moved about the room, closing shutters. "I'll have to make it up to old Monty, that broken window. He'll understand. Doesn't much use this cottage except in the summer. In fact, I believe he's in Moritz at the moment. Trying to land the next Mrs. Montgomery Dearborn."

How many Mrs. Dearborns are there? Clea wanted to ask, but she couldn't get out the question; her teeth were chattering too hard. What feeling she had left in her limbs was quickly fading to numbness. She knew she should strip off her wet clothes, should try to start a fire in the hearth, but she couldn't seem to make her body move. She could only stand there, water dripping from her clothes onto the wood floor.

Jordan turned on a lamp. By the light's glow he caught his first real look at her. "Good Lord," he said, touching her face. "You're like an ice cube."

"Fire," she whispered. "Please, start a fire."

"That'll take too long. You need to get warmed up now." He pulled her down a hall and into the bathroom. Quickly he turned on the shower spigot. As water hissed out in a sputtering stream he began to peel off her sopping wool jacket.

"Electric coil heater," said Jordan. "It'll warm up in a minute." He tossed her jacket aside and unzipped her skirt. She was too cold to care about anything so trivial as modesty; she let him pull her skirt off, let the fabric drop in a pile on the floor. The water was steaming now; he tested the temperature, then thrust her, underwear and all, into the shower.

Even with hot water streaming over her body, it seemed to take forever for her to stop shaking. She huddled, dazed, under the spigot. Slowly the heat penetrated her numbness and she could feel her blood start to circulate again, could feel the flush of warmth at last seeping toward her core.

"Clea?" she heard Jordan say.

She didn't answer. She was too caught up in the pleasure of being warm again. Sighing, she shifted around to let the stream roll down her back. Vaguely, through the rattle of water, she heard Jordan call.

"Are you all right?"

Before she could answer, the shower curtain was abruptly pushed aside. She found herself gazing up at Jordan's face.

As he was gazing at hers.

For a moment they said nothing. The only sound was the pounding of the shower. And the pulsing of her heartbeat in her ears. Though she was barely clothed, though her transparent undergarments clung to her skin, Jordan's gaze never wavered from her face. He seemed mesmerized by what he saw there. Drawn by the longing he surely recognized in her eyes.

She reached out and touched his face. His cheek felt rough and chilled under her hot fingertips. Just that one contact, that brush of her skin against his, seemed to melt all the barriers between them. She felt another kind of heat ignite within her. She pulled his face down to hers and met his lips in a kiss.

At once they were both clinging to each other.

Whimpering. Hot water streamed across their shoulders, hers bare, his still clothed in the shirt. Through the curls of steam, she saw in his face the long-suppressed desire that had been throbbing between them since the night they'd met.

She pressed even more eagerly against him and gave a soft sigh of pleasure, of triumph, at the burgeoning response of his body.

"Your clothes," she murmured, and reached up feverishly to pull off his shirt. He shrugged it off onto the bathroom floor, baring his chest, so recently bandaged. The golden hairs were damp and matted from the shower. They were both breathing in gasps now, both working frantically at his belt.

Somehow they got the water shut off. Somehow they managed to find their way out of the shower, out of the bathroom with its obstacle course of wet clothes littering the tiles. They left a trail of still more wet clothes, lying where they'd dropped, his trousers near the bathroom door, her bra in the hallway, his undershorts at the threshold of the bedroom. By the time they reached the bed, there were no more clothes to shed. There was only damp flesh and murmurs and the yearning to be joined.

The bedroom was cold and they slid, shivering, beneath the goose-down duvet. As they lay with limbs intertwined, mouths exploring, tasting, the heat of their bodies warmed the bed. Her shivering ceased. The room's chill was forgotten in the rush of sensations now flooding through her, the sweet ache between her thighs, the sharp darts of pleasure as his mouth found her breasts, drawing her nipples to almost agonizing tautness.

She rose above him and returned the torment with a vengeance. Her mouth traced down the plane of his chest, grazed his belly, seeking ever more sensitive flesh. Groaning, he gripped her shoulders, and his body twisted off the mattress, rolling her onto the pillow. Suddenly she was lying beneath him, his body hard atop hers, his hands cupping her face.

Their gazes met, held. They never stopped looking at each other, even as he slid inside her, filled her. Even as she cried out with the pleasure of his penetration.

He moved slowly, gently. Their gazes held.

His breaths came faster, his hands clutching more tightly at her face. Still they looked at each other, joined in a bond that went deeper than flesh.

Only when she felt that exquisite ache build to the first ripples of release did she close her eyes and surrender to the sensations flooding through her. A soft cry floated from her throat, a sound both foreign and wonderful. It was matched, seconds later, by his groan. Through the ebbing waves of her own pleasure she felt his last frantic thrusts, and then he pulsed deep within her. With a shuddering sigh his spent body came to rest and fell still.

She cradled his head against her shoulder. As she pressed a kiss to his damp hair, she felt a wave of tenderness so overpowering it frightened her.

We made love. What does it mean?

They'd enjoyed each other's bodies. They'd given each other satisfaction and, for a few moments, even happiness.

But what does it mean?

She pressed another kiss to the damp tendrils and felt again that twinge of affection, so intense this time it brought tears to her eyes. Blinking them away, she turned her face from him, only to feel his hand cradle her cheek and nudge her gaze back to his.

"You are the most surprising woman I've ever met," he said.

She swallowed. And laughed. "That's me. Full of surprises."

"And delights. I never know what to expect from you. And it's starting to drive me quite mad." He lowered his mouth and tenderly brushed his lips against hers, tasting, nibbling. Enjoying. Already she could feel the rekindling of his arousal, could feel his heaviness stirring against her thigh.

She slid her hand between their hips and with a few

silken strokes she had him hard and throbbing again. "You're full of surprises yourself," she murmured.

"No, I'm quite…" he gave a sigh of delight "—conventional."

"Are you?" She lowered her mouth to his nipple and traced a circle of wetness with her tongue.

"Some would even call me—" he dropped his head back and groaned "—damned predictable."

"Sometimes," she whispered, "predictable is good."

With her tongue she began to trace a wet line across his chest to his other nipple. He was breathing hard, struggling to check his rising tide of passion.

"Wait. Clea…" He caught her face. Gently he tilted it up toward him and looked at her. "I have to know. Why were you crying?"

"I wasn't."

"You were. A moment ago."

She studied him, hungrily devouring every detail. The way the light played on his ruffled hair. The crescent shadows cast by his eyelashes. The way he looked at *her,* so quietly, intently. As though she was some strange, unknowable creature.

"I was thinking," she said, "how different you are from any man I've known."

"Ah. No wonder you were crying."

She laughed and gave him a playful slap. "No, silly. What I meant was, the men I've known were always…after something. Wanting something. Planning the next take."

"You mean, like your uncle Walter?"

"Yes. Like my uncle Walter."

The mention of her past, her flawed childhood, suddenly dampened her desire. She pulled away from him. Sitting up, she hugged her knees. If only she could make that part of her life drop away. If only she could be born anew. Without shame.

"I'm embarrassed to admit he's my relative," she said.

He laughed. "I'm embarrassed by my relatives all the time."

"But none of yours are in prison…are they?"

"Not as of this moment, no."

"Uncle Walter is. So was my cousin Tony." She paused and added softly, "So was I."

He reached for her hand. He didn't say anything. He just watched her, and listened.

"It was so ironic, really. For eight years I went perfectly straight. And suddenly Uncle Walter pops up outside my apartment. Bleeding all over my front porch. I couldn't turn him in. And he wouldn't let me take him to the hospital. So there I was, stuck with him. I burned his clothes. Tossed his lock picks in a Dumpster across town. And then the police showed up." She gave a shrug, as though that last detail was scarcely worth mentioning. "The funny thing is," she said, "I don't hate him for it. Not a bit. You can't hate Uncle Walter. He's so damn…" She gave a sheepish shrug. "Lovable."

Laughing, he pressed her palm to his lips. "You have a most unique take on life. Like no other woman I've known."

"How many ex-cons have you slept with?"

"You, I must admit, are my first."

"Yes, I imagine you'd normally prefer a proper lady."

He frowned at her. "What's this rubbish about *proper* ladies, anyway?"

"Well, I don't exactly qualify."

"*Proper* is dull. And you, my dear Miss Rice, are not dull."

She tossed her head back and laughed. "Thank you, Mr. Tavistock, for the compliment."

He tugged her toward him. "And as for your notorious uncle Walter," he whispered, pulling her down on top of him, "if he's related to you, he must have some redeeming features."

She smiled down at him. "He *is* charming."

He cupped her face and kissed her. "I'm sure."

"And clever."

"I can imagine."

"And the ladies say he's quite irresistible…."

Again Jordan's mouth found hers. His kiss,

deeper, harder, swept all thoughts of Uncle Walter from her mind.

"Quite irresistible," murmured Jordan, and he slid his hand between her thighs.

At once she was lost, needing him, crying out for him. She bared her warmth and he took it tenderly. And when it was over, when exhaustion finally claimed him, he fell asleep with his head on her breast.

She smiled down at his tousled hair. "You will remember me fondly some day, won't you, Jordan?" she whispered.

And she knew it was the best she could hope for.

It was all she dared hope for.

HE AWAKENED to the subtle perfume of a woman's scent, to the tickle of hair against his face. He opened his eyes and by the gray light slanting in through the shutters he saw Clea asleep beside him. Without a trace of makeup, and her hair lushly tangled across the pillow, she looked like some fairy princess over whom a spell of deathless repose had been cast. Unarousable, untouchable. Not altogether real.

How real she'd felt to him last night! Not a princess at all, but a temptress, full of sweet mischief and even sweeter fire.

Even now he couldn't resist her. He reached for her and kissed her on the mouth.

Her reaction was abrupt and startling. She gave a shudder of alarm and jerked up from the pillow.

"It's all right," he soothed. "It's only me."

She stared for a moment, as though not recognizing him. Then she gave a soft gasp and shook her head. "I—I haven't been sleeping very well. Needless to say."

He watched her huddle beneath the duvet and wondered how she had maintained her sanity through these weeks of running and hiding. He couldn't help but feel a rush of pity for her. It was mingled with admiration for her strength. Her will to live.

She glanced at the window and saw daylight gleaming through the closed shutters. "They'll be searching for us. We can't stay here much longer."

"We can't exactly stroll away, either. Not without help."

"Oh, no. No more calling on friends and family. I'm sure that's how they found us last night. Your Richard Wolf must have told someone."

"He'd never do that."

"Then they followed him. Or they've tapped your phone. Something." Abruptly she climbed out of bed and snatched up her underwear. Finding it still damp, she tossed it in disgust onto a chair. "I'm going to have to leave naked."

"Then you'll most certainly catch someone's eye."

"You're not much help. Can't you get out of bed, at least?"

"I'm thinking. I think best in bed."

"Bed is where most men don't think at all." She picked up her bra. It, too, was damp. She looped it over the doorknob and glanced around the room in frustration. "You say the man who owns this place is a bachelor?"

"In between states of wedded bliss."

"Does he have any women's clothes?"

"I've never thought to ask Monty such a personal question."

"You know what I mean."

He rose from the bed and went to open the wardrobe door. Inside hung two summer suits, a raincoat and a few neatly pressed shirts. On Jordan they'd all fit nicely. On Clea they'd look ridiculous. He took out a bathrobe and tossed it to her.

"Unless we can turn you into a six-foot man," he said, "this wardrobe won't work. And even if we did find women's clothes in here, there's still the matter of your hair. That flaming red isn't the most subtle color."

She snatched a lock of her hair and frowned at it. "I hate it, anyway. Let's cut it off."

He eyed those lustrous waves and was forced to give a regretful nod. "Monty always keeps a bottle of hair dye around to touch up his graying temples. We could darken what's left of your hair."

"I'll find some scissors."

"Wait. Clea," he said. "We have to talk."

She turned to him, her jaw set with the determination of what had to be done. "About what?"

"Even if we do change your appearance, running may not be your best option."

"I think it's my only option."

"There's still the authorities."

"They didn't believe me before. Why should they believe me now? My word's nothing against Van Weldon's."

"The Eye of Kashmir would change that."

"I don't have it."

"Delancey does."

She shook her head. "By now, Van Weldon must have realized what a mistake it was to sell the Eye so soon. His people will be trying to get it back."

"What if they haven't? It may still be in Delancey's house, waiting to be snatched. By us."

She went very still. "Us?" she asked quietly.

"Yes, us." He smiled at her, a smile that did not seem to inspire much confidence, judging by her expression. "Congratulations. Meet your new partner in crime," he said.

"That's supposed to make me feel better?"

"Doesn't it?"

"I'm just thinking about your last burglary attempt. And how close you came to getting us both handcuffed."

"That was inexperience. I'm now fully seasoned."

"Right. And ready for the frying pan."

"What is this, a crisis of confidence? You told me you used to burglarize houses just for the challenge of it."

"I didn't know better then. I was a kid."

"And now you're experienced. Better at the art."

Letting out a breath, she began to pace a line back and forth in the carpet. "I know I could break in again. I'm *sure* I could. But I don't know where to look. The dagger could be anywhere upstairs. The bedroom, the guest rooms. I'd need time."

"Together, we could do it in half the time."

"Or get caught twice as fast," she muttered. And she left the room.

He followed her into the kitchen, where he found her rummaging through drawers for the scissors. "There's always the other option," he said. "The logical one. The reasonable one. We go to the police."

"Where they'll laugh in my face, the way they did before. And Van Weldon will know exactly where to find me."

"You'll be under protection. I promise."

"The safest place for me, Jordan, is out where I can

run. A moving target's not so easy to hit." She found the scissors and handed them to him. "Especially when the target keeps changing its appearance. Go ahead, do it."

He looked down at the scissors, then looked at that beautiful mane of hair. The task was almost too painful, but he had no choice. Regretfully he took a handful of cinnamon red hair. Just the scent of those silky strands was enough to reawaken all the memories of last night. The way her body had fitted against his. The way she'd moved beneath him, not a docile release but the joyous shudders of a wild creature.

That's what she was. A wild thing. Sensuous. Unpredictable. In time she would drive him crazy.

Already he was losing his long-practiced sense of self-control. All it took was a few whiffs of her hair, the touch of silk in his palm, and he was ready to drag her back to bed.

He gave his head a shake to clear away those inconvenient images. Then he lifted the scissors and calmly, deliberately, began to snip off her hair.

BY THE GRAY MORNING LIGHT, they followed the footprints in the mud—a pair of them, one large set, one smaller set, veering away from the road. The prints headed west across the field. It had rained heavily last night, and the tracks were easy to follow for about three hundred yards or so, until they connected up with another road. Then, after a few muddy imprints on the pavement, the footprints faded.

They could be anywhere by now.

Archie MacLeod gazed out over the field and cursed. "I should've known she'd do this. Probably got one inkling we were on her trail and off she goes. Like a bloody she-fox, that one."

"You can hardly blame her," said Richard. "Of course she'd expect the worst. How did your people fumble this one? They were supposed to bring her into custody. Instead they managed to chase her underground."

"Their orders were to do it quietly. Somehow she got wind of them."

"Or Jordan did," said Richard. "I should have contacted him last night. Told him what was coming down. Now he'll wonder."

"You don't think he doubts *you?*"

"No. But he'll be cautious now. He'll assume Van Weldon's got me covered, that it won't be safe to contact me. That's what I'd assume in his place."

"So how do we find them now?"

"We don't." Richard turned to his car and slid in behind the wheel. "And we hope Van Weldon doesn't, either."

"I'm not so confident of that."

"Jordan's clever. So is Clea Rice. Together they may do all right."

MacLeod leaned in the car window. "Guy Delancey died this morning."

"I know," said Richard.

"And we've just heard rumors that Victor Van Weldon's upped the price on Clea Rice to two million. Within twenty-four hours this area will be swarming with contract men. If they get anywhere near Clea Rice, she won't stand a chance. Neither will Tavistock."

Richard stared at him. "Why the hell did you wait so long to bring her into custody? You should have locked her under guard weeks ago."

"We didn't know whether to believe her."

"So you waited for Van Weldon to make a move, was that the strategy? If he tried to kill her, she must be telling the truth?"

MacLeod slapped the car door in frustration. "I'm not defending what we've done. I'm just saying we're now convinced she's told the truth." He leaned forward. "Jordan Tavistock is your friend. You must have an idea where he'd go."

"I'm not even sure he's the one calling the shots right now. It might be the woman."

"You let me know if you come up with any ideas. Anything at all about where they might go next."

Richard started the car. "I know where *I'd* go if I were them. I'd get away from here. I'd run as fast as I could. And I'd damn well get lost in a crowd."

"London?"

Richard nodded. "Can you think of a better place to hide?"

"THAT WOMAN MUST HAVE nine lives. And she's used up only three of them," said Victor Van Weldon. He was wheezing again. His breathing, which was normally labored even on the best of days, had the moist rattle of hopelessly congested lungs.

Soon, thought Simon Trott. Victor was a dying man. What a relief it would be when it was over. No more of these distasteful audiences, these grotesque scenes of a virtual corpse fighting to hang on. If only the old man would just get it over with and die. Until then, he'd have to stay in the old man's good graces. And for that, he'd have to take care of this Clea Rice problem.

"You should have seen to this yourself," said Victor. "Now we've lost our chance."

"We'll find her again. We know she's still with Tavistock."

"Has he surfaced yet?"

"No. But eventually he'll turn to his family. And we'll be ready."

Van Weldon exhaled a deep sigh. His breathing seemed clearer, as though the assurances had eased the congestion in his lungs. "I want you to see to it personally."

Trott nodded. "I'll leave for London this evening."

CROUCHED BEHIND THE YEW hedge of Guy Delancey's yard, Jordan and Clea waited in the darkness for the house lights to go out. Whitmore's nightly habit was as it had always been, the checking of the windows and doors at nine o'clock, the pause in the kitchen to brew a pot of tea, then the retreat upstairs to his room in the servants' wing. *How many years has the fellow clung to that petrified routine of his?* Clea wondered. What a shock it must be to him, to know that all would soon change.

Clea and Jordan had heard it on the radio that morning: Guy Delancey was dead.

Soon others would come to claim this house. And old Whitmore, a relic from the dinosaur age, would be forced to evolve.

The lights in the servants' wing went out.

"Give him half an hour," whispered Jordan. "Just to make sure he's asleep."

Half an hour, thought Clea, shivering. She'd freeze by then. She was dressed in Monty's black turtleneck and a baggy pair of jeans, which she'd shortened with a few snips of the scissors. It wasn't enough protection against this chill autumn night.

"Which way do we enter?" asked Jordan.

Clea scanned the house. The French door leading from the terrace was how she'd broken in the last time. No doubt that particular lock had since been replaced. So, undoubtedly, had the locks on all the ground-floor doors and windows.

"The second floor," she said. "Balcony off the master bedroom."

"That's how I got in the last time."

"And if *you* managed to do it," she said dryly, "it must have been a piece of cake."

"Oh, right, insult your partner. See where it gets you."

She glanced at him. His blond hair was concealed under a watch cap, and his face was blackened with grease. In the darkness only the white arc of his teeth showed in a Cheshire-cat grin.

"You're sure you're up to this?" she asked. "It could get sticky in there."

"Clea, if things do go wrong, promise me."

"Promise you what?"

"You'll run. Don't wait for me. And don't look back."

"Trying to be chivalrous again? Something silly like that?"

"I just want to get things straight now. Before things go awry."

"Don't say that. It's bad luck."

"Then this is for good luck." He took her arm, pulled her against him and kissed her. She floundered in his embrace, torn between wanting desperately to get kissed again, and wanting to stay focused on the task that lay ahead. When he finally released her, they stared at each other for a moment. Only the gleam of his eyes and teeth were visible in the darkness.

That was a farewell kiss, she realized. In case things went wrong. In case they got separated and never saw each other again. A chill wind blew and the trees creaked overhead. As the moments passed, and the night grew colder, she tried to commit every detail to memory. Because she knew, as he did, that every step they took could end in disaster. She had not counted on this complication, had not wanted this attraction. But here it was, shimmering between them. The fact it couldn't last, that any feelings they had for each other were doomed by who she was, and who he was, only made those feelings all the sweeter. *Will you miss me someday, Jordan Tavistock?* she wondered. *As much as I'll miss you?*

At last he turned and looked at the house. "I think it's time," he said softly.

She, too, turned to face the house. The wind swept

the lawn, bringing with it the smell of dead leaves and chill earth. The scent of autumn, she thought. Too soon, winter would be upon them....

She eased away from the hedge and began to move through the shadows. Jordan was right behind her.

They crossed the lawn, their shoes sinking into wet grass. Beneath the bedroom balcony they crouched to reassess the situation. They heard only the wind and the rustle of leaves.

"I'll go first," he said.

Before she could protest, he was scrambling up the wisteria vine. She winced at the rattle of branches, expecting at any moment that the balcony doors would fly open, that Whitmore would appear waving a shotgun. Lucky for them, old Whitmore still seemed to be a sound sleeper. Jordan made it all the way up without a hitch.

Clea followed and dropped noiselessly onto the balcony.

"Locked," said Jordan, trying the doorknob.

"Expected as much," she whispered. "Move away."

He stepped aside and watched in respectful silence as she shone a penlight on the lock. "This should be even easier than the one downstairs," she whispered and gently inserted the makeshift L-pick she'd fashioned that afternoon using a wire hanger and a pair of pliers. "Circa 1920. Probably came with the house.

Let's hope it's not so rusty that it bends my…" She gave a soft chuckle of satisfaction as the lock clicked open. Glancing at Jordan she said wryly, "There's nothing like a good stiff tool."

He answered, just as wryly, "I'll remember to keep one on me."

The room was as she'd remembered it, the medieval curtained bed, the wardrobe and antique dresser, the desk and tea table near the balcony doors. She'd searched the desk and dresser before; now she'd take up where she had left off.

"You search the wardrobe," she whispered. "I'll do the nightstands."

They set to work. By the thin beam of her penlight she examined the contents of the first nightstand. In the drawers she found magazines, cigarettes and various other items that told her Guy Delancey had used this bed for activities beyond mere sleeping. A flicker of movement overhead made her aim the penlight at the ceiling. There was a mirror mounted above the bed. To think she had actually considered a romp in this bachelor playpen! Turning her attention back to the nightstand, she saw that the magazines featured naked ladies galore, and not very attractive ones. Entertainment, no doubt, for the nights Guy couldn't find female companionship.

She searched the second nightstand and found a

similar collection of reading material. So intent was she on poking for hidden drawers, she didn't notice the creak of floorboards in the hallway. Her only warning was a sharp hiss from Jordan, and then the bedroom door flew open.

The lights sprang on overhead.

Clea, caught in midcrouch beside the bed, could only blink in surprise at the shotgun barrel pointed at her head.

CHAPTER TEN

THE GUN WAS wavering ominously in Whitmore's unsteady grasp. The old butler looked most undignified in his ratty pajamas, but there was no mistaking the glint of triumph in his eyes.

"Gotcha!" he barked. "Thinkin' to rob a dead man, are you? Think you can get away with it again? Well, I'm not such an old fool!"

"Apparently not," said Clea. She didn't dare glance in Jordan's direction, but off in her peripheral field of vision she spied him crouched beside the wardrobe, out of Whitmore's view. The old man hadn't yet realized there were two burglars in the room.

"Come on, come on! Out from behind that bed! Where I can see you!" ordered Whitmore.

Slowly Clea rose to her feet, praying that the man's trigger finger wasn't as unsteady as his grip. As she straightened to her full height, Whitmore's gaze widened. He focused on her chest, on the unmistakable swell of breasts.

"Ye're only a woman," he marveled.

"Only?" She gave him a wounded look. "How insulting."

At the sound of her voice, his eyes narrowed. He scanned her grease-blackened face. "You sound familiar. Do I know you?"

She shook her head.

"Of course! You come to the house with poor Master Delancey! One of his lady friends!" The grip on the shotgun steadied. "Come 'ere, then! Away from the bed, you!"

"You're not going to shoot me, are you?"

"We're going to wait for the police. They'll be here any minute."

The police. There wasn't much time. Somehow they had to get that gun away from the old fool.

She caught a glimpse of Jordan, signaling to her, urging her to shift the butler's gaze toward the left.

"Come on, move out from behind the bed!" ordered Whitmore. "Out where I can get a clear shot if I have to!"

Obediently she crawled across the mattress and climbed off. Then she took a sideways step, causing Whitmore to turn leftward. His back was now squarely turned to Jordan.

"I'm not what you think," she said.

"Denying you're a common thief, are you?"

"Certainly not a *common* one, anyway."

Jordan was approaching from the rear. Clea forced herself not to stare at him, not to give Whitmore any clue of what was about to happen….

What *was* about to happen? Surely Jordan wouldn't bop the old codger on the head? It might kill him.

Jordan raised his arms. He was clutching a pair of Guy Delancey's boxer shorts, was going to pull them like a hood over old Whitmore's head. Somehow Clea had to get that gun pointed in another direction. If startled, Whitmore might automatically let fly a round.

She gave a pitiful sob and fell to her knees on the floor. "You can't let them arrest me!" she wailed. "I'm afraid of prison!"

"Should've thought of that before you broke in," said Whitmore.

"I was desperate! I had to feed my children. There was no other way…." She began to sob wretchedly.

Whitmore was staring down at her, astonished by this bizarre display. The shotgun barrel was no longer pointed at her head.

That's when Jordan yanked the boxer shorts over Whitmore's face.

Clea dived sideways, just as the gun exploded. Pellets whizzed past. She scrambled frantically back to her feet and saw that Jordan already had Whitmore's arms restrained, and that the gun had fallen from the old man's grasp. Clea scooped it up and shoved it in the wardrobe.

"Don't hurt me!" pleaded Whitmore, his voice muffled by the makeshift hood. The boxer shorts had little red hearts. Had Delancey really pranced around in little red hearts? "Please!" moaned Whitmore.

"We're just going to keep you out of trouble," said Clea. Quickly she bound the butler's hands and feet with Delancey's silk ties and left him trussed on the bed. "Now you lie there and be a good boy."

"I promise!"

"And maybe we'll let you live."

There was a pause. Then Whitmore asked fearfully, "What do you mean by *maybe?*"

"Tell us where Delancey keeps his weapons collection."

"What weapons?"

"Antique swords. Knives. Where are they?"

"There's not much time!" hissed Jordan. "Let's get out of here."

Clea ignored him. *"Where are they?"* she repeated.

The butler whimpered. "Under the bed. That's where he keeps them!"

Clea and Jordan dropped to their knees. They saw nothing beneath the rosewood frame but carpet and a few dust balls.

Somewhere in the night, a siren was wailing.

"Time to go," muttered Jordan.

"No. Wait!" Clea focused on an almost imperceptible crack running the length of the bed frame. A seam in the wood. She reached underneath and tugged.

A hidden drawer glided out.

At her first glimpse of the contents, she gave an involuntary gasp of wonder. Jewels glittered in hammered-gold scabbards. Sword blades of finely tempered Spanish steel lay in gleaming display. In the deepest corner were stored the daggers. There were six of them, all exquisitely crafted. She knew at once which dagger was the Eye of Kashmir. The star sapphire mounted in the hilt gave it away.

"They were his pride and joy," moaned Whitmore. "And now you're stealing them."

"I'm only taking one," said Clea, snatching up the Eye of Kashmir. "And it didn't belong to him, anyway."

The siren was louder now and closing in.

"Let's *go!*" said Jordan.

Clea jumped to her feet and started toward the balcony. "Cheerio!" she called over her shoulder. "No hard feelings, right?"

"Bloody unlikely!" came the growl from under the boxer shorts.

She and Jordan scrambled down the wisteria vine and took off across the lawn, headed at a mad dash for the woods fringing the property. Just as they reached the cover of trees, a police car careened around the bend, siren screaming. Any second now the police would find Whitmore tied up on the bed and then all hell would break loose. The threat of pursuit was enough to send Jordan and Clea scrambling deep into the woods. Replay of the night we met, thought Clea. Hanging around Jordan Tavistock must be bad luck; it always seemed to bring the police on her tail.

The sting of branches whipping her face, the ache of her muscles, didn't slow her pace. She kept running, listening for sounds of pursuit. A moment later she heard distant shouting, and she knew the chase had begun.

"Damn," she muttered, stumbling over a tree root.

"Can you make it?"

"Do I have a choice?"

He glanced back toward the house, toward their pursuers. "I have an idea." He grabbed her hand and tugged her through a thinning copse of trees. They stumbled into a clearing. Just ahead, they could see the lights of a cottage.

"Let's hope they don't keep any dogs about," he said and started toward the cottage.

"What are you doing?" she whispered.

"Just a small theft. Which, I'm sorry to say, seems to be getting routine for me."

"What are you stealing? A car?"

"Not exactly." Through the darkness his teeth gleamed at her in a smile. "Bicycles."

IN THE LAUGHING MAN PUB, Simon Trott stood alone at the bar, nursing a mug of Guinness. No one bothered him, and he bothered no one, and that was the way he liked it. None of the usual poking and prodding of a stranger by the curious locals. The villagers here, it seemed, valued a man's privacy, which was all to the better, as Trott had no tolerance tonight for even minor annoyances. He was not in a good mood. That meant he was dangerous.

He took another sip of stout and glanced at his watch. Almost midnight. The pub owner, anxious to close up, was already stacking up glasses and darting impatient looks at his customers. Trott was about to call it a night when the pub door opened.

A young policeman walked in. He sauntered to the bar where Trott stood and called for an ale. A few moments went by, no one saying a word. Then the policeman spoke.

"Been some excitement around 'ere tonight," he said to no one in particular.

"What sort?" asked the bartender.

"'Nother robbery, over at Under'ill. Guy Delancey's."

"Thieves gettin' bloody cheeky these days, if you ask me," the bartender said. "Goin' for the same 'ouse twice."

"Aren't they, though?" The policeman shook his head. "Makes you wonder what's become of society these days." He drained his mug. "Well, I best be gettin' 'ome. 'Fore the missus gets to worryin'." He paid the tab and walked out of the pub.

Trott left, as well.

Outside, in the road, the two men met. They walked across the village green, stepping in and out of shadows.

"Anything stolen from Underhill tonight?" asked Trott.

"The butler says just one item was taken. Antique weapon of some sort."

Trott's head lifted in sudden interest. "A dagger?"

"That's right. Part of a collection. Other things weren't touched."

"And the thieves?"

"There were two of them. Butler only saw the woman."

"What did she look like?"

"Couldn't really tell us. Had some sort of black grease on 'er face. No fingerprints, either."

"Where were they last seen?"

"Escaped through the trees. Could've gone in any direction. I'm afraid we lost 'em."

Then Clea Rice had not left Buckinghamshire, thought Trott. Perhaps she was right now in this very village.

"If I 'ear more, I'll let you know," said the policeman.

Their conversation had come to an end. Trott reached into his jacket and produced an envelope stuffed with five-pound notes. Not a lot of money, but enough to help keep a young cop's family clothed and fed.

The policeman took the envelope with an odd reluctance. "It's only information you'll be wantin', right? You won't be expecting more?"

"Only information," Trott reassured him.

"Times are...difficult, you see. Still, there are things I don't—won't—do."

"I understand." And Trott did. He understood that even upright cops could be tempted. And that for this one, the downhill slide had already begun.

After the two men parted, Trott returned to his room in the inn and called Victor Van Weldon.

"As of a few hours ago, they were still in the area," said Trott. "They broke into Delancey's house."

"Did they get the dagger?"

"Yes. Which means they've no reason to hang around here any longer. They'll probably be heading for London next."

Even now, he thought, Clea Rice must be wending her way along the back roads to the city. She'll be feeling a touch of triumph tonight. Perhaps she's thinking her ordeal will soon end. She'll sense hope, even victory whenever she looks at that dagger. The dagger she calls the Eye of Kashmir.

How wrong she will be.

THE SOUNDS OF LONDON traffic awakened Clea from a sleep so heavy she felt drugged. She rolled onto her back and peered through slitted lids at the daylight shining in through the ratty curtains. How long had they slept? Judging by her grogginess it might have been days.

They'd checked in to this seedy hotel around six in the morning. Both of them had stripped off their clothes and collapsed on the bed, and that was the last she remembered. Now, as her brain began to function again, the events of last night came back to her. The endless wait at the station for the 4:00 a.m. train out of Wolverton. The fear that, lurking among the shadows on the platform, was someone who'd been watching for them. And then, during the train ride to London, the anxiety that they'd be robbed, that they'd lose their precious cargo.

She reached under the bed and felt the wrapped bundle. The Eye of Kashmir was still there. With a sigh of relief she settled back on the bed, next to Jordan.

He was asleep. He lay with his face turned toward her, his bare shoulder tanned a warm gold against the linen, his wheat-colored hair boyishly tousled. Even in sleep he looked every inch the aristocrat. Smiling, she stroked his hair. *My darling gentleman,* she thought. *How lucky I am to have known you. Someday, when you're married to some proper young lady, when your life has settled in according to plan, will you still remember your Clea Rice?*

Sitting up, she stared at her own reflection in the dresser mirror. Right, she thought.

Suddenly depressed, she left the bed and went to take a shower. Later, as she inspected her latest hair color—this time a nut brown, courtesy of Monty's bottle of hair dye—she felt resentment knot up in her stomach. She was not a lady, nor was she proper, but she damn well had her assets. She was bright, she could think fast on her feet and, most important, she could take care of herself. What possible use did *she* have for a gentleman? He'd be a nuisance, really, dragging her off all the time to soirees. Whatever those were. She'd never fit into his world. He'd never fit into hers.

But here, in this room with the mangy carpet and mildewed towels, they could share a temporary world. A world of their own making. She was going to enjoy it while it lasted.

She went back to the bed and climbed in next to Jordan.

At the touch of her damp body, he stirred and murmured, "Is this my wake-up call?"

She answered his question by sliding her hand under the covers and stroking slowly down the length of his torso. He sucked in a startled gasp as she found exquisitely tender flesh and evoked the hoped-for response.

"If that was my wake-up call," he groaned, "I think it worked."

"Maybe now you'll get up, sleepyhead," she said, laughing, and rolled away.

He caught her arm and hauled her right back. "What about this?"

"What about what?"

"This."

Her gaze traveled to the distinct bulge under the sheets. "Shall I take care of that for you?" she whispered.

"Seeing as you're the reason it's there in the first place…"

She rolled on top of him, fitting her hips to his. He was at her mercy now, and she intended to make him beg for his pleasure. But as their bodies moved together, as she felt him grasp her hips in both hands and pull her down against him, it was she who was at his mercy, she who was begging for release. He gave it to her, in wave after glorious wave, and through the roar of her pulse in her ears she heard him say her name aloud. Once, twice, in a murmur of delight.

Yes, I'm the one he's making love to, she thought. *Me. Only me.*

For these few sweet moments, it was enough.

ANTHONY VAUXHALL WAS a starched little prig of a man with a nose that always seemed to be tilted up in distaste of mere mortals. Jordan had met him several times before, on matters relating to his late parents' estate. Their conversations had been cordial, and he hadn't formed much of an opinion of the man either way.

He was forming an opinion of Anthony Vauxhall now, and it wasn't a good one.

It was nearly 4:00 p.m., and they were seated in Vauxhall's office in the Lloyd's of London building on Leadenhall Street. In the past hour and a half Jordan and Clea had managed to purchase decent clothes, grab a bite to eat and scurry downtown to Lloyd's before the offices closed. Now it appeared that their efforts might prove futile. Vauxhall's response to Clea's story was one of obvious skepticism.

"You must understand, Miss Rice," said Vauxhall, "Van Weldon Shipping is one of our most distin-guished clients. One of our oldest clients. Our relationship goes back three generations. For us to accuse Mr. Van Weldon of fraud is, well…" He cleared his throat.

"Perhaps you weren't listening to Miss Rice's story," said Jordan. "She was *there*. She was a witness. The loss of the *Max Havelaar* wasn't an accidental sinking. It was sabotage."

"Even so, how can we assume Van Weldon is responsible? It could have been another party. Pirates of some kind."

"Doesn't a multimillion-dollar claim concern your firm?"

"Well, naturally."

"Wouldn't your underwriters want to know if they've paid out to a company that staged its own losses?"

"Of course, but—"

"Then why aren't you taking these accusations seriously?"

"Because—" Vauxhall took a deep breath. "I spoke to Colin Hammersmith about this very matter. Right after I got your call earlier today. He's in charge of our investigations branch. He'd heard this rumor a few weeks back and his advice was, well…" Vauxhall shifted uneasily. "To consider the source," he said at last.

The source. Meaning Clea Rice, ex-con.

Jordan didn't need to look at her; he could feel her pain, as surely as if the blow had landed on his own shoulders. But when he did look at her, he was impressed by how well she was taking it, her chin held high, her expression calm and focused.

Ever since that long red hair had been cut away, her face had seemed even more striking to him, her sculpted cheeks feathered by wisps of brown hair, the dark eyes wide and gamine. He had known Clea Rice as a blonde, then a redhead and now a brunette. Though he'd found each and every version of her fascinating, of all her incarnations, this one he liked the best. Perhaps it was the fact he could actually focus on her face now, without the distraction of all that hair. Perhaps it matched her personality, those elfin tendrils wisping around her forehead.

Perhaps he was beyond caring about details as inconsequential as hair because he was falling in love with her.

That's why this insult by Vauxhall so enraged him.

He said, none too civilly, "Are you questioning Miss Rice's integrity?"

"Not…not exactly," said Vauxhall. "That is—"

"What *are* you questioning, then?"

Vauxhall looked miserable. "The story, it just appears— Oh, let's be frank, Mr. Tavistock. A slaughter at sea? Sabotage of one's own vessel? It's so shocking as to be—"

"Unbelievable."

"Yes. And when the accused is Victor Van Weldon, the story seems even more farfetched."

"But I saw it," insisted Clea. "I was there. Why won't you believe me?"

"We've already looked into it. Or rather, Mr. Hammersmith's department did. They spoke to the Spanish police, who assert that it was most probably an accident. An engine explosion. No bodies were ever found. Nor did they find evidence of murder."

"They wouldn't," said Clea. "Van Weldon's people are too clever."

"And as for the wreckage of the *Havelaar*, it went down in deep water. It's not easily salvageable. So we have nothing on which to base an accusation of sabotage."

Throughout Vauxhall's almost disdainful rebuttal, Clea had maintained her composure. She had regarded the man with almost regal calm. Jordan had watched in fascination as she took it all without batting an eyelash. Now he recognized the glimmer of triumph in her eyes. She was going to unveil the evidence.

Clea reached into her purse and withdrew the cloth-wrapped bundle that she'd so carefully guarded for the past sixteen hours. "You may find it difficult to take my word," she said, laying the bundle on his desk. "I understand that. After all, who am I to walk in off the street and tell you some fantastic tale? But perhaps this will change your mind."

Vauxhall frowned at the bundle. "What is that?"

"Evidence." Clea removed the cloth wrapping. As the last layer fell away, Vauxhall sucked in an audible gasp of wonder. A jeweled scabbard lay gleaming in its undistinguished bed of muslin cloth.

Clea slid the dagger out of the scabbard and laid it down, razor tip pointed toward Vauxhall. "It's called the Eye of Kashmir. Seventeenth century. The jewel in the hilt is a blue star sapphire from India. You'll find a description of it in your files. It was part of Victor Van Weldon's collection, insured by your company. A month ago it was being transported from Naples to Brussels aboard a vessel which, coincidentally, was also insured by your company. The *Max Havelaar*."

Vauxhall glanced at Jordan, then back at Clea. "But that would mean…"

"This dagger should be on the ocean floor right now. But it isn't. Because it was never aboard the *Havelaar*. It was kept safely in storage somewhere, then sold on the black market to an Englishman."

"How did *you* get it?"

"I stole it."

Vauxhall stared at her for a moment, as though not certain she was being serious. Slowly he reached for his intercom button. "Miss Barrows," he murmured, "could you ring Mr. Jacobs, down in appraisals? Tell him to come up to my office. And have him bring his loupe or whatever it is he uses to examine gems."

"I'll ring him at once."

"Also, could you fetch the Van Weldon company's file for me? I want the papers for an antique dagger known as the Eye of Kashmir." Vauxhall sat back in his chair and regarded Clea with a troubled look. "This puts a new complexion on things. Mr. Van Weldon's claims, if I recall correctly, were in the neighborhood of fifteen million pounds for the art collection alone. This—" he waved at the dagger "—would call his claims into question."

Jordan looked at Clea and recognized her look of relief. *It's over,* he read in her eyes. *This nightmare is finally over.*

He took her hand. It was clammy, shaking, as though in fear. Of all the frightening events this past week, this moment must have been one of the most harrowing, because she had traveled so long and hard to reach it. She was too tense to smile at him, but he felt her fingers tighten around his. When this is over, he thought, well and truly over, we're going to celebrate. We're going to check in to a hotel suite and have all our meals delivered. And we're going to make love day and night until we're too exhausted to move. Then we'll sleep and start all over again….

They continued to cast knowing looks back and forth even as Vauxhall's secretary entered to deliver Van Weldon's files, even as Mr. Jacobs arrived from appraisals to examine the dagger. He was a distinguished-looking gentleman with a full mane of silver hair. He studied the Eye for what seemed like an eternity. At last he looked up and said to Vauxhall, "May I see the policy appraisal?"

Vauxhall handed it over. "There's a photo, as well. It seems to be identical."

"Yes. It does." Mr. Jacobs squinted at the photo, then regarded the dagger again. This time he focused his attention on the star sapphire. "Quite excellent work," he murmured, peering through the jeweler's loupe. "Exquisite craftsmanship."

"Don't you think it's time to call the authorities?" asked Jordan.

Vauxhall nodded and reached for the telephone. "Even Victor Van Weldon can't argue away the Eye of Kashmir, can he?"

Mr. Jacobs looked up. "But this isn't the Eye of Kashmir," he said.

The room went absolutely silent. Three pairs of eyes stared at the elderly appraiser.

"What do you mean, it's not?" demanded Vauxhall.

"It's a reproduction. A synthetic corundum. An excellent one, probably made using the Verneuil method. But as you'll see, the star is rather more pronounced than you'd find in a natural stone. It's worth perhaps two, three hundred pounds, so it's not entirely without value. But it's not a true star sapphire, either." Mr. Jacobs regarded them with a calm, bespectacled gaze. "This is not the Eye of Kashmir."

Clea's face had drained of color. She sat staring at the dagger. "I don't...don't understand...."

"Couldn't you be mistaken?" asked Jordan.

"No," said Mr. Jacobs. "I assure you, it's a reproduction."

"I demand a second opinion."

"Certainly. I'll recommend a number of gemologists—"

"No, we'll make our own arrangements," said Jordan.

Mr. Jacobs reacted with a look of injured dignity. He slid the dagger to Jordan. "Take it to whomever you wish," he said, and rose to leave.

"Mr. Jacobs?" called Vauxhall. "We hold the policy on the Eye of Kashmir. Shouldn't we retain this dagger until this matter is cleared up?"

"I see no reason to," snapped Mr. Jacobs. "Let them keep the thing. After all, it's nothing but a fake."

CHAPTER ELEVEN

NOTHING BUT A FAKE.

Clea clutched the wrapped bundle in both hands as she and Jordan rode the elevator to the first floor. They walked out into the fading sunlight of late afternoon.

Nothing but a fake.

How could she have been so wrong?

She tried to reason out the possibilities, but her brain wouldn't function. She was operating on auto-pilot, her feet moving mechanically, her body numb. She had no evidence now, nothing to back up her story. And Van Weldon was still in pursuit. She could change her name a hundred times, dye her hair a hundred different shades, and still she'd be looking over her shoulder, wondering who might be moving in for the kill.

Victor Van Weldon had won.

It would almost be easier just to walk into his office, meet him face-to-face and tell him, "I give up. Just get it over with quick." She wouldn't last much longer, anyway. Even now she was scarcely aware of the faces on the street, much less able to watch for signs of danger. Only the firm guidance of Jordan's hand kept her moving in any sort of purposeful direction.

He pulled her into a taxi and directed the driver to Brook Street.

Gazing out dully at the passing traffic, she asked, "Where are we going?"

"To get that second opinion. There's a chap I know, has a shop in the area. He's done some appraisals for Uncle Hugh in the past."

"Do you think Mr. Jacobs could be wrong?"

"Wrong. Or lying. At this point, I don't trust anyone."

Does he trust me? she wondered. *The dagger's a fake. Maybe he thinks I am, as well.*

The taxi dropped them off at a shop in the heart of Mayfair. From the exterior it did not look like the sort of establishment any family as lofty as the Tavistocks would patronize. A sign in the window said, Clocks and Jewellery—Bought and Sold. Behind the dusty plate glass was arranged a selection of rings and necklaces that were obviously paste.

"This is the place?" asked Clea.

"Don't be fooled by appearances. If I want a straight answer, this is the man I ask."

They stepped inside, into a dark little cave of a room. On the walls were hung dozens of wooden cuckoo clocks, all of them ticking away. The counter was deserted.

"Hello?" called Jordan. "Herr Schuster?"

A door creaked open and an elderly gnome of a man shuffled out from a back room. At his first glimpse of Jordan, the man gave a cackle of delight.

"It's young Mr. Tavistock! How many years has it been?"

"A few," admitted Jordan as he shook the man's hand. "You're looking very well."

"Me? Bah! I am twenty years on borrowed time. To be alive is enough. And your uncle, he is retired now?"

"As of a few months ago. He's enjoying it immensely." Jordan slid an arm around Clea's shoulders. "I'd like you to meet Miss Clea Rice. A good friend of mine. We've come to ask you for some help."

Herr Schuster shot a sly glance at Clea. "Would this perhaps be for an engagement ring?"

Jordan cleared his throat. "It's rather…your expert opinion we need at the moment."

"On what matter?"

"This," said Clea. She unwrapped the bundle and handed him the dagger.

"The star sapphire in the hilt," said Jordan. "Is it natural or man-made?"

Gingerly Herr Schuster took the dagger and weighed it in his hands, as though trying to divine the answer by its touch. He said, "This will require some time."

"We'll wait," said Jordan.

The old jeweler retreated into the back room and shut the door behind him.

Clea looked doubtfully at Jordan. "Can we trust his opinion?"

"Absolutely."

"You're that sure of him?"

"He used to be the leading authority on gemstones in East Berlin. In the days before the wall came down. He also happened to work as a double agent for MI6. You'd be amazed how much one can learn from chats with the wives of high Communist officials. When things got dangerous, Uncle Hugh helped him cross over."

"So that's why you trust him."

"It's a debt he owes my uncle." Jordan glanced at the door to the back room. "Old Schuster's been keeping a low profile here in London ever since. Touch of paranoia, I suspect."

"Paranoia," said Clea softly. "Yes, I know exactly how he's lived." She turned to the window and stared out through the dusty glass at Brook Street. A bus rumbled past, spewing exhaust. It was early evening now, and the afternoon crowd had thinned out to a few shop girls straggling home for the night and a man waiting at the bus stop.

"If it is a fake," she said, "will you…still believe me, Jordan?"

He didn't answer at first. That brief silence was enough to send despair knifing through her. He said at last, "Too much has happened for me *not* to believe you."

"But you have doubts."

"I have questions."

She laughed softly. Bitterly. "That makes two of us."

"Why, for instance, would Delancey have bought a replica? He certainly had the money to spend. He would have insisted on the genuine item."

"He might have been misled. Believed it was the real Eye of Kashmir."

"No, Guy was a discerning collector. He'd get an expert's advice before he bought it. You saw how easily Mr. Jacobs identified that stone as man-made. Guy would have learned that fact just as easily."

She gave a sigh of frustration. "You're right, of course. He would have had it looked at. Which means whoever appraised it was either crooked or incompetent or…" Suddenly she turned to him. "Or he was right on the money."

"I told you, Guy would never buy a reproduction."

"Of course he wouldn't. He bought the real Eye of Kashmir."

"Then how did he wind up with a fake?"

"Someone switched it for the real one. *After* Guy bought it." She was moving around the room now, her mind racing. "Think about it, Jordan. Before you buy a painting or antique, aren't you very careful to confirm it's genuine?"

"Naturally."

"But after you've bought it—say, a painting—and you've had it hanging on your wall for a while, you don't bother to have it reauthenticated."

Slowly Jordan nodded. "I think I'm beginning to understand. The dagger was replaced sometime after Guy bought it."

"And he didn't realize! He has so many collectibles in that house. He'd never notice that one little dagger wasn't quite the same."

"All right, time for a reality check here. You're saying that our theoretical thief commissioned an exact replica. And then he managed to switch daggers without Guy's knowledge? That would require a hell of a lot of inside knowledge. Remember how much trouble we had, locating the Eye? Without Whitmore's help, we never would've found that hiding place."

"You're right, of course," she admitted with a sigh.

"A thief would have to know exactly where it was hidden. Which means it had to be someone very close to Delancey."

"And that would eliminate an outside thug. Van Weldon's or otherwise." He shook his head. "I don't want to say 'the butler did it.' But I think the list of suspects is rather short."

"What about Guy's family?"

"Estranged. None of them even live in the neighborhood."

"One of his lovers, then?"

"He did have a few." He aimed an inquiring glance her way.

"I wasn't one of them," she snapped. "So who *has* Guy romanced in the last month?"

"Only one woman I'm aware of. Veronica Cairncross."

There was a long silence. "You're the one who knows her, Jordan," said Clea. "You two are friends…."

He frowned, troubled by the possibilities. "I've always considered her a bit wild. Impulsive. And not altogether moral. But a thief…"

"She's someone to consider. There's the household staff, as well. Come to think of it, anyone could've slipped into that bedroom. I got in. So did you. If it hadn't been for old Whitmore, we would have slipped out without anyone being the wiser."

Jordan went very still. "Whitmore," he said.

"What about him?"

"I'm thinking."

She watched in bewilderment as he muttered the name again, more softly. With sudden comprehension he looked at her. "Yes, Whitmore's the key."

She laughed. "You're not back to saying the butler did it?"

"No, it's the fact he was *home* that night! Veronica assured me it was Whitmore's night off. That the house would be empty. But when I broke in, he was right there. All this time I assumed she'd made a mistake. But what if it wasn't a mistake? What if she *wanted* the butler home?"

"Why on earth would she?"

"To raise the alarm. And notify the police."

"What would be the point?"

"There'd be an official record of a break-in. If Guy ever discovered the real Eye of Kashmir was gone, he'd assume the theft occurred that night. The night Whitmore raised the alarm."

"A night Veronica had an airtight alibi. Your sister's engagement party."

Jordan nodded. "It'd never occur to him that the switch was made earlier. *Before* that night. By an acquaintance so intimate she knew exactly where the Eye was hidden. An acquaintance who'd been in and out of that bedroom." Jordan slapped his temple in frustration. "All this time I thought *she* was the thick one. *I'm* the idiot."

Clea shook her head. "You're giving Veronica an awful lot of credit. How would she manage to commission such an accurate replica? It would take time. The forger would need to work from the original. I hardly think Guy would let her borrow it for a week. So where would this replica come from?"

"There's always the previous owner," said Jordan.

Clea's mouth went dry. *Van Weldon. The previous owner was Van Weldon.*

She went to stand beside him, close enough to lean her cheek against the fine wool of his jacket. Softly she said, "Veronica. Van Weldon. Could there be a link?"

"I don't know. She's never mentioned Van Weldon's name."

"He has connections everywhere. People who owe him. People who are afraid of him."

"It seems unlikely."

"But how well do you really *know* her, Jordan? How well do we really know anyone?"

He said nothing. He stood very still, not reaching for her, not even looking at her. Aching, she thought, *Oh, Jordan. How well do I really know you? And what little you know of me is the very worst....*

They stood just inches apart, yet she felt cold and alone as they both gazed out at that street where the shadows crept toward dusk. She reached out to him. His shoulder was rigid. Unresponsive to her touch.

"Clea," he said softly. "I want you to go into the back room. Ask Herr Schuster if there's a rear door."

"What?"

"There's a man standing at the bus stop. See him?"

She focused on the street. And on the man standing there. He wore a brown suit and carried a black umbrella, and every so often he glanced at his watch, as though late for some appointment. No wonder. He'd been waiting for his bus a long time now.

Slowly Clea backed away from the window.

Jordan didn't move, but continued to gaze out calmly at the street. "He's let two go past now," he said. "I don't think he's waiting for a bus."

She fought the impulse to run headlong through that rear door. She had no idea if the man could see them through those dusty front windows. She managed to stroll casually to the rear of the shop, then she pushed through the door, into the workshop.

Herr Schuster was at his jeweler's bench. "I am afraid the news is disappointing. The star sapphire—"

"Is there a back way out?" she asked.

"Excuse me?"

"Another exit?"

Jordan stepped in behind Clea. "There's a man following us."

Herr Schuster rose to his feet in alarm. "I have a back door." At a frantic shuffle, he led them through the workshop's clutter and opened the door to what looked like a closet. Dusty coats hung inside. He shoved the old garments aside. "There is a latch at the rear. The door leads to the alley. Around the corner is South Molton. You wish me to call the police?"

"No, don't. We'll be fine," said Jordan.

"The man—he is dangerous?"

"We don't know."

"The dagger—do you want it back?"

"It's not genuine?"

Regretfully Herr Schuster shook his head. "The sapphire is synthetic corundum."

"Then keep it as a souvenir. But don't show it to anyone."

A buzzer suddenly rang in the workshop. Herr Schuster glanced toward the front room. "Someone has come in the door. Hurry, go!"

Jordan grabbed Clea's hand and pulled her into the closet. Instantly the coats were slid back in place and the door shut on them. In the sudden darkness they blindly fumbled along the rear door for the latch and pushed.

They stumbled out into an alley. At once they tore

around the corner onto South Molton Street. They didn't stop running until they'd reached the Bond Street Underground.

Aboard the train to Tottenham Court Road, Clea sat in stunned silence as the blackness of the tunnel swept past her window. Only when Jordan had taken her hand in his did she realize how chilled her fingers were, like icicles in the warmth of his grasp.

"He won't give up," she said. "He'll never give up."

"Then we have to stay one step ahead."

Not we, she thought. *I'm the one Van Weldon wants. The one he'll kill.*

She stared down at the hand now holding hers. A hand with all the strength a woman could ever need, could ever want. In a few short days she'd come to trust Jordan in a way she'd never trusted anyone. And she understood him well enough by now to know the gentleman's code of honor by which he operated— an absurd concept under these brutal circumstances. He would never abandon a woman in need.

So she would have to abandon him.

She chose her words carefully. Painfully. "I think it would be better if…" The words caught in her throat. She forced herself to stare ahead. Anywhere but at Jordan. "I think I would be better off on my own. I can move faster that way."

"You mean without me."

"That's right." Her chin slanted up as she found the courage to keep talking. "I can't afford to spend my time worrying about you. You'll be fine holed up in Chetwynd."

"And where will you go?"

She smiled nonchalantly. "Some place warm. The south of France, maybe. Or Sicily. Anywhere I can be on a beach."

"If you live long enough to climb into a bathing suit."

The train pulled in to the next stop. Abruptly he pulled her to her feet and snapped, "We're getting off."

She followed him off the train and up the station steps to Oxford Street. He was silent, his shoulders squared in anger. So much for self-sacrifice, she thought. All she'd managed to do was turn him against her. And why the hell was he mad at her, anyway? It wasn't as if she'd rejected him. She'd simply offered him the chance to leave.

The chance to live.

"I was only thinking of *you,* you know," she said.

"I'm quite aware of that."

"Then why are you ticked off at me?"

"You don't give me much credit."

"There's nothing more you can do for me. You have to admit, it doesn't make sense for both of us to get our heads blown off. If we split up, they'll forget all about you."

"Will *you* forget all about me?"

She halted on the sidewalk. "Does it matter?"

"Doesn't it?" He turned to face her. They stood looking at each other, an obstruction to all the pedestrians moving along the sidewalk.

"I don't know what you're getting at," she said. "I'm sorry it has to end this way, Jordan. But I have to look out for number one. Which means I can't have you around. I don't *want* you around."

"You don't know what the hell you want."

"All right, maybe I don't. But I do know what's best for *you.*"

"So do I," he said, and reached for her. His arms went around her back and his mouth came down on hers in a branding kiss that held no gentleness, brooked no resistance.

Far from protesting, she welcomed the assault, thrilled to the surge of his tongue into her mouth, the hungry roving of his hands up and down her back. She could not hide her desire from him, nor could he from her. They were both helpless and hopeless, lost to the crazy yearnings that always burst forth whenever they touched. It had been this way from the start. It would always be this way. A look, a touch, and suddenly the tension would be sizzling between them.

His lips slid to her cheek, then her ear, and the

tickle of his hot breath sent a tremor of delight down her spine. "Have I made myself clear?" he whispered.

She moaned. "About what?"

"About staying together."

The need was still too strong between them. She pulled away and took a step back, fighting the urge to touch him again. *You and your crazy sense of honor,* she thought, staring up at his face. *It will get you killed. And I couldn't stand that.*

"I'm not exactly helpless, you know," she said.

He smiled. "Still, you have to admit I've come in handy on occasion."

"On occasion," she agreed.

"You need me, Clea. To beat Van Weldon."

She shook her head. "I've already tried. Now there's nothing else I can do."

"Yes, there is."

"The dagger's gone. I have no evidence. I can't see any way to get at him."

"There is a way." He moved closer. "Veronica Cairncross."

"What about her?"

"I've been trying to piece it all together. And I think you're right. She could be the key to all this. I've known Ronnie for years. She's a jolly girl, great fun to be around. But she's a gambler. And a big spender.

Over the last few years she's run up a fortune in debts. A scam like this could've saved her skin."

"But now we're back to the problem of how she commissioned that reproduction," said Clea. "How'd she get her hands on the original? It belonged to Van Weldon. Did she buy it from him? Borrow it from him?"

"Or steal it from him?"

Clea shuddered at the thought. "No one's stupid enough to cross Van Weldon."

"Somehow, though, that dagger found its way from Van Weldon into Delancey's hands. Veronica could be the link between them. That's what we have to find out." Jordan paused, thinking. "She and Oliver have a town house here in London. They spend their weekdays here. Which means they'd be in town now."

Clea frowned at him. She didn't like this new shift of conversation. "What, exactly, are you thinking?"

He eyed her hair. "I'm thinking," he said, "that it's time for you to try a wig."

ARCHIE MACLEOD HUNG UP the phone and looked at Richard Wolf and Hugh Tavistock. "They're in London. My man just spoke to an official from Lloyd's. Jordan and Clea Rice paid a visit there around four o'clock today. Unfortunately the man they met with—an Anthony Vauxhall—wasn't aware of the investigation. He just happened to mention their visit to his superior. By the time we found out, Jordan and Clea Rice had already left."

"So we know they're still alive," said Hugh.

"As of this afternoon, anyway."

They were sitting in Chetwynd's library, the room they'd turned into a crisis headquarters. Hugh had hurried back to Chetwynd that morning, and all day the three of them had sat waiting for word from their police contacts.

This last news was good. Jordan had made it safely to London.

Not that Richard was surprised. In the few months he'd known his future brother-in-law, he'd come to appreciate Jordan's resourcefulness. In a pinch there were few men Richard would rather have at his side.

Clea Rice, too, was a survivor. Together, they might just stay alive.

Richard looked at Hugh. The older man was looking drained and weary. The worry showed plainly in Hugh's round face. "That price on Clea Rice's head will be drawing every contract man in Europe," said Richard.

"Surely, Lord Lovat," said MacLeod, "you can marshal some help from your intelligence contacts. We have to find them."

Hugh shook his head. "My Jordan was reared in the lap of the intelligence business. All these years he's been listening. Learning. He's probably picked up a trick or two. Even with help, it won't be easy to track him down. Which means it won't be easy for Van Weldon to track him down, either."

"You don't know Victor Van Weldon the way I do," said MacLeod. "At this point, he'll be willing to pay a fortune to get rid of Clea Rice. I'm afraid money is the world's best motivator."

"Not money," said Richard. "Fear. That's what will keep Jordan alive."

"Blast it all," said Hugh. "Why do we know so little about this Victor Van Weldon, anyway? Is he so untouchable?"

"I'm afraid he is," admitted MacLeod. He sank into a chair by the fireplace. "Victor Van Weldon has always operated on the fringes of international law. Never quite crossing the boundaries into illegality. At least, never leaving any evidence of it. He hides behind a regiment of lawyers. Keeps homes in Gstaad, Brussels and probably a few places we haven't found out about. He's like some rare bird, almost never sighted, but very much alive."

"You can't dredge up any evidence against him?"

"We know he's involved in international arms shipments. Dabbles in the drug trade. But every time we think we have hard evidence, it disintegrates in our hands. Or a witness dies. Or documents vanish. For years it's been a source of frustration for me, how he manages to elude me. Only recently did I realize how many friends in high places he has, keeping him apprised of my every move. That's when I changed tactics. I picked out my own team of men. An independent team. We've spent the past six months gathering information on Van Weldon, ferreting out his Achilles' heel. We know he's sick—emphysema and heart failure. He hasn't much longer to live. Before he dies, I want him to face a little earthly justice."

"You sound like a man on crusade," said Richard.

"I've lost...people. Van Weldon's work." MacLeod looked at him. "It's something one doesn't forget. The face of a dying friend."

"How close are you now to building a case?"

"We have the foundations. We know Van Weldon took big losses last year. The European economy— it's affected even him. With his empire on the brink of ruin, he was bound to try something desperate. That's when the *Havelaar* went down. Eight men dead, a fortune lost at sea—all of it fully insured. I couldn't convince the Spanish authorities to foot the bill for a proper investigation. It would've required a salvage crew, ships and equipment. Van Weldon, we thought, had slipped away again. Then we heard about Clea Rice." MacLeod sighed. "Unfortunately, Miss Rice is not the sort of witness to base any prosecution on. Prison record. Family of thieves. Here we finally find a weapon against Van Weldon, and it's one that could backfire in court."

"So you can't use her as the basis of any legal case," said Hugh.

"No. We need something tangible. For instance, the artwork listed on the *Havelaar*'s manifest. We know bloody well it didn't go down with the ship. Van Weldon's stashed it somewhere. He's waiting for an opportunity to sell it off piece by piece. If we just knew where he's hidden it."

"It was supposedly shipped from Naples."

"We searched his Naples warehouse. We also searched—not always legally, mind you—every building we know he owns. We're talking about large items, not things you can just hide in a closet. Tapestries and oil paintings and even a few statues. Wherever he's keeping it, it's a large space."

"There must be a warehouse you don't know about yet."

"Undoubtedly."

"Interpol's not authorized to handle this alone," said Hugh. "You're going to need assistance." He reached for the telephone and began to dial. "It's not the customary way of doing things. But with Jordan's life at stake…"

Richard listened as Hugh made the contacts, called

in old favors from Scotland Yard's Special Branch, as well as MI5—domestic intelligence. After he hung up, Hugh looked at Richard.

"Now I suggest we get to work ourselves," said Hugh.

"London?"

"Jordan's there. He may try to reach us. I want to be ready to respond."

"What I don't understand," said MacLeod, "is why he hasn't called you already."

"He's cautious," said Richard. "He knows the one thing Van Weldon expects him to do is contact us for help. Under the circumstances, Jordan's best strategy is to keep doing the *unexpected*."

"Precisely the way Clea Rice has operated all these weeks," observed MacLeod. "By doing the unexpected."

VAN WELDON WAS WAITING for the call. He picked up the receiver. "Well?"

"They're here," said Simon Trott. "They were spotted leaving Lloyd's of London, as you predicted."

"Is the matter concluded?"

There was a pause. "Unfortunately, no. They vanished off Brook Street—a jewelry store. The proprietor claims ignorance."

The news made Van Weldon's chest ache. He

paused a moment to catch his breath, the whole time silently cursing Clea Rice. In all his years he'd never known such a tenacious opponent. She was like a thorn that couldn't be plucked out, and she seemed to keep burrowing ever deeper.

When he'd managed to catch his breath again, he said, "So she did go to Lloyd's. Did she take the dagger?"

"Yes. She must have been rather peeved to learn it was a fake."

"And the real Eye of Kashmir?"

"Safely back where it belongs. Or so I've been assured."

"The Cairncross woman brought us to the brink of disaster. She cannot go unpunished."

"I quite agree. What do you have in mind?"

"Something unpleasant," said Van Weldon. Veronica Cairncross was an opportunistic bitch. And a fool as well to think she could slip one over on them. Her greed had taken her too far this time, and she was going to regret it.

"Shall I see to Mrs. Cairncross myself?" asked Trott.

"Wait. First confirm the collection is safe. It must go on the market within the month."

"So soon after the *Havelaar?* Is that wise?"

Trott raised a good point. It was risky to release the artwork onto the market. To think of all those assets bundled away, untouchable, just when he needed them most! Last year he had overextended himself, had made a few too many commitments to a few too many cartels. Now he needed cash. Lots of it.

"I cannot wait," said Van Weldon. "It must be sold. In Hong Kong or Tokyo, we could fetch excellent prices, and without much notice. Buyers are discreet in Tokyo. See that the collection is moved."

"When?"

"The *Villafjord* is scheduled to dock in Portsmouth tomorrow. I will be on board."

"You…are coming here?" There was an undertone of dismay in Trott's voice. He *should* be dismayed. What had started as a minor difficulty had ballooned into a crisis, and Van Weldon was disgusted with his heir apparent. If Trott could not handle such simple matters as Veronica Cairncross and Clea Rice, how could he hope to assume the company's helm?

"I will see to the shipment myself," said Van Weldon. "In the meantime, I expect you to find Clea Rice."

"We have the Tavistocks under surveillance. Sooner or later, Jordan and the woman will surface."

Perhaps not, thought Van Weldon as he hung up. By now Clea Rice would be weary, demoralized. Her instinct would be to run as far and as fast as she could. That would take care of the problem—temporarily, at least.

Van Weldon felt better. He decided there was really no need to worry about Clea Rice. By now she'd be long gone from London.

It's what any sensible woman would do.

CHAPTER TWELVE

AT TWELVE-FIFTEEN Veronica Cairncross left her London flat, climbed into a taxi and was driven to Sloane Street where she had lunch at a trendy little café. Afterward she strolled on foot toward Brompton Road, in the general direction of Harrods. She took her sweet time in one shop to purchase lingerie, and in another shop to try on a half-dozen pairs of shoes.

A disguised Clea observed all of this from a distance and with a growing sense of exasperation. Not only did this exercise seem more and more pointless, but also her long black wig was itchy, her sunglasses kept slipping down the bridge of her nose and her new short-heeled pumps were killing her. Perhaps she should have slipped into that same shoe shop where Veronica had spent so much time and picked up a pair of sneakers for herself. Not that she could have afforded anything in there. Veronica clearly frequented only the priciest establishments. *What is it like to be so idle and so rich?* Clea wondered as she trailed the elegant figure up Brompton Road. *Doesn't the woman ever get tired of constant partying and shopping?*

Oh, sure. The poor thing must be bored to tears.

She followed Veronica into Harrods. Inside she lingered a discreet distance away and watched Veronica sample perfumes, browse among scarves and handbags. Two hours later, loaded down with purchases, Veronica strolled out and hailed a taxi.

Clea scurried out after her and after a few frantic glances, spotted another taxi, this one with tinted windows. She climbed in.

Jordan was waiting in the back seat.

"There she goes," said Clea. "Stay with her."

Their driver, a grinning Sikh whom Jordan had hired for the day, expertly threaded the taxi into traffic and maintained a comfortable two-car distance behind Veronica's vehicle.

"Anything interesting happen?" asked Jordan.

"Not a thing. Lord, that woman can shop. She's way out of my league. Any trouble staying with me?"

"We were right behind you."

"I don't think she noticed a thing. Not me or the taxi." Sighing, Clea sat back and pulled off the wig. "This is getting us nowhere. So far all we've found out is that she has time and money on her hands. And a lot of both."

"Be patient. I know Ronnie, and when she gets nervous, she spends money like water. It's her way of blowing off stress. Judging by all the packages she was carrying, she's under a lot of stress right now."

Veronica's taxi had turned onto Kensington. They followed, skirting Kensington Gardens, and headed southwest.

"Now where's she going?" Clea sighed.

"Odd. She's not headed back to the flat."

Veronica's taxi led them out of the shopping district, into a neighborhood of business and office buildings. Only when the taxi stopped and let Veronica off at the curb did Jordan give a murmur of comprehension.

"Of course," he said. "Biscuits."

"What?"

"It's Oliver's company. Cairncross Biscuits." Jordan nodded at the sign on the building. "She's here to see her husband."

"Hardly a suspicious thing to do."

"Yes, it seems quite innocent, doesn't it?"

"Are you implying otherwise?"

"I'm just thinking about Oliver Cairncross. The firm's been in his family for generations. Appointment to the queen and all that…."

She studied Jordan's finely chiseled face as he mulled it over. *Such eyelashes he has,* she thought. No man had a right to such long eyelashes. Or such a kissable mouth. She could watch him for hours and never tire of the way his face crooked up on one side when he was thinking hard. *Oh, Jordan. How I'm going to miss you when this is over....*

"Cairncross biscuits are internationally known," said Jordan. "They're shipped all over the world."

"So?"

"So I wonder which firm is used to transport all those cookie crates. And what's really inside them."

"Uzis, you mean?" Clea shook her head. "I thought Oliver was supposed to be the innocent party. The cuckolded husband. Now you're saying *he's* the one in league with Van Weldon? Not Veronica?"

"Why not both of them?"

"She comes out again," said their driver.

Sure enough, Veronica had reappeared. She climbed back into her taxi.

"You wish me to follow her?" asked the Sikh.

"Yes. Don't lose her."

They didn't. They stayed on Veronica's tail all the way to Regent's Park. There Veronica alighted from the taxi and began to walk across Chester Terrace, toward the Tea House.

"Back into action." Clea sighed. "I hope it's not another two-hour hike." She pulled on a new wig—this one shoulder length and brown—and climbed out of the cab. "How do I look?"

"Irresistible."

She leaned inside and kissed him on the mouth. "You, too."

"Be careful."

"I always am."

"No, I mean it." He pulled her around by the wrist. His grip was insistent, reluctant to let go. "If there was any other way I could do it instead of you, I would—"

"She knows you too well, Jordan. She'd spot you in a second. Me, she'd scarcely recognize."

"Just don't let your guard down. Promise me."

She gave him a breezy grin that masked all the fears she had rattling inside. "And you promise not to vanish."

"I'll keep you right in view."

Still grinning, Clea turned and crossed Chester Terrace.

Veronica was well ahead of her. She seemed to be merely wandering, strolling toward Queen Mary's Rose Garden, its season of bloom now past. There she lingered, every so often glancing at her watch. Oh, Lord, not waiting for another lover, Clea thought.

Without warning Veronica turned and began walking in Clea's direction.

Clea ducked under an arbor and pretended to inspect the label on the climbing rose. Veronica didn't even glance her way, but headed toward the Tea House.

After a moment Clea followed her.

Veronica had seated herself at a table, and she had a menu propped open in front of her. Clea took a seat two tables behind Veronica and sat facing the other way. At this hour the Tea House was relatively quiet, and she could hear Veronica's whiney voice ordering a pot of Darjeeling and iced cakes. *Now I'll waste another hour,* thought Clea, *waiting for that silly woman to have her tea.*

She glanced toward Cumberland Terrace. Sure enough, there was Jordan sitting on a bench, his face hidden behind a newspaper.

The waiter approached. Clea ordered a pot of Earl Grey and watercress sandwiches. Her tea had just arrived when a man crossed the dining terrace toward Veronica.

Clea caught only a glimpse of him as he moved past her table. He was fair haired, blonder than Jordan, with wide shoulders and a powerful frame— just the sort of hunk Veronica would probably go gaga over. Clea felt a spurt of irritation that yet another hour would be wasted while Veronica made cow eyes at her latest admirer.

"Mr. Trott," Veronica said crossly. "You're late. I've already ordered."

Clea heard the man's voice, speaking behind her, and in the midst of pouring tea, her hand froze.

"I have no time for tea," he said. "I came only to confirm the arrangements."

That was all he said, but his tone of command, the English coarsened by some unidentifiable accent, was enough to make Clea suck in a breath in panic. She didn't dare glance back over her shoulder; she didn't dare let him see her face.

She didn't need to see *his;* his voice was all she needed to recognize him.

She'd heard it before, floating above the sound of lapping Mediterranean waves and the growl of a boat's engine. She remembered how that same voice had cut through the darkness. Just before the bullets began to fly.

All her instincts were screaming at her to lurch from this table and flee. *But I can't,* she thought. *I can't do anything to draw his attention.*

So she sat unmoving, her hands gripping the table-cloth. So acutely did she sense the man's presence behind her, she was surprised that he didn't seem at all aware of *her.*

Her heartbeat thudding, she sat motionless at the table.

TROTT WATCHED VERONICA light a cigarette and take in an unhurried drag of smoke. She seemed not in the least bit worried, which only proved what a stupid bitch she was, he decided. She thinks she's untouchable. She thinks her husband's too important to our operations. What she doesn't know is that we've already found a replacement for Oliver Cairncross.

Casually she exhaled a cloud of smoke. "The cargo's all there. Nothing missing. I told you it would be, didn't I?"

"Mr. Van Weldon is not pleased."

"Why, because I borrowed one of his precious little trinkets? It was only for a few weeks." Calmly she exhaled another cloud of smoke. "We've been stuck with your bloody crates for months now—at no small risk to ourselves. Why shouldn't I borrow what's in them? I got the dagger back, didn't I?"

"This is not the time or place to speak of it," cut in Trott. He passed a newspaper across the table to Veronica. "The information is circled. We'll expect it to be ready and waiting."

"At your beck and call, your highness," said Veronica, her voice dripping with mockery.

Trott pushed his chair back, preparing to leave. "What about compensation?" asked Veronica. "For all our trouble?"

"You'll have it. After all items are accounted for."

"Of course they will be," said Veronica. She blew out another cloud of smoke. "We're not fools, you know."

CLEA HEARD the man's chair scrape back. He was rising to his feet. Instinctively she huddled closer to the table, afraid to be noticed. She forced herself to take a sip of tea, to pretend no interest whatsoever in the monster standing behind her.

When she heard him walk away, she went almost limp with relief. She glanced back.

Veronica was still sitting at the table, gazing down at a newspaper. After a moment she ripped off half a page, folded it and stuffed it in her purse. Then she, too, rose and left.

It took a while before Clea's nerves steadied enough for her to stand. Veronica was already walking out of the park. Clea started to follow, but her legs were shaking too hard. She took a few steps, faltered and stopped.

By then Jordan had realized something was wrong. She heard his footsteps, and then his arm was around her waist, supporting her, steadying her.

"We can't stay here," she whispered. "Have to hide—"

"What happened?"

"It was him—"

"Who?"

"The man from the *Cosima!*" Wildly she glanced around, her gaze sweeping the park for sight of the blond man.

"Clea, what man?"

She focused at last on Jordan. His gaze seemed to steady her. He held her face in his hand, the pressure of his fingers warming through her numbness.

"Tell me," he said.

She swallowed. "I've heard his voice before. The night the *Havelaar* went down. I was in the water, swimming alongside the lifeboat. He was the one who—the one who—" She blinked, and tears spilled down her face. Softly she finished, "The one who ordered his men to shoot."

Jordan stared at her. "The man with Veronica? You're absolutely certain?"

"He passed by my table. I recognized his voice. I'm sure it was him."

Jordan gave a quick glance around the park. Then he pulled Clea close, wrapping his arm protectively around her shoulder. "Let's get into the car."

"Wait." She went back to Veronica's table and snatched up the discarded newspaper.

"What's that for?" asked Jordan.

"Veronica left it. I want to see what she tore out."

Their taxi was waiting. As soon as they climbed in the back seat, Jordan ordered, "Move. See that we're not followed."

The Sikh driver grinned at them in the mirror. "A

most interesting day," he declared, and sent the cab screeching into traffic.

Jordan draped his jacket over Clea's shoulders and took her hands in his. "All right," he coaxed gently. "Tell me what happened."

Clea took a shaky breath and sank back against the seat. No one was following them. Jordan's hand, warm and steady, seemed to radiate enough courage for them both.

"Did you hear what they were saying?"

"No. They were speaking too softly. And I was afraid to get any closer. After I realized who he was..." She shuddered, thinking of the man's voice. In her nightmares she'd heard that same voice drifting across the black Mediterranean waters. She'd remember the explosion of gunfire. And she'd remember Giovanni, slumping across the lifeboat....

Her head came up. "I do remember something. Veronica called him by name. Mr. Trott."

"You're sure that was it? Trott?"

She nodded. "I'm sure."

Jordan's grip tightened around hers. "Veronica. If I ever get my hands around her elegant little neck..."

"At least now we know. She's the link to Van Weldon. Delancey paid for the Eye. She stole it back. Someone earned a nice profit. And the only loser was Guy Delancey."

"What about the newspaper?"

Clea looked down at the folded pages. "I saw Veronica tear something out."

Jordan glanced at the newspaper's date, then tapped their taxi driver on the shoulder. "Excuse me. You wouldn't happen to have a copy of today's *Times?*"

"But of course. And the *Daily Mail,* as well."

"Just the *Times* will do."

The driver reached over and pulled out a slightly mangled newspaper from the glove compartment. He handed it back to Jordan.

"The top of page thirty-five and six," said Clea. "That's what she's torn out."

"I'm looking for it." Jordan thumbed quickly through the driver's copy. "Here it is. Top of page thirty-five. Article about the Manchester slums. Building renovations. Another about horse breeding in Ireland."

"Try the other side."

Jordan flipped the page. "Let's see. Scandal in some ad agency. Drop-off in the fishing harvest. And..." He paused. "Today's shipping schedule for Portsmouth." He looked at Clea.

"That's it! That has to be it. One of their ships must be arriving in port."

"Or leaving." He sat back, deep in thought. "If Van Weldon has a vessel in Portsmouth, then it's here for either a delivery..."

"Or a pickup," she finished for him.

They looked at each other, both struck by the same startling thought.

"It's taking on cargo," she said. "It must be."

"It could be purely legitimate cargo."

"But there's the chance…" She glanced up as they pulled in front of their hotel. At once she was climbing out the door. "We have to call Portsmouth. Check which vessels are Van Weldon's."

"Clea, wait—"

But she was already hurrying into the building.

By the time he'd settled with their driver and followed her up to the room, Clea was already on the phone. A moment later she hung up and turned to Jordan in triumph.

"There's a *Villafjord* scheduled to dock at five this afternoon. She sails again at midnight. And she's registered to the Van Weldon company."

For a moment he stared at her without speaking. Then he said flatly, "I'm going to call the police." He reached for the phone.

She grabbed his hand. "Don't! Jordan."

"We have to alert the authorities. It could be the best chance they'll have to nail Van Weldon."

"That's why we can't blow it! What if we're wrong? What if his ship's here to take on a cargo of—of undies or something? We'll look like a pair of idiots. So will the police." She shook her head. "We can't tell them until we know *exactly* what's on board."

"But the only way to learn that is…" He froze in the midst of that thought. "Don't you even dare suggest it."

"Just one little tiny peek inside."

"*No.* This is the perfect time to call in Richard. Let him—or someone else—handle it."

"But I don't trust anyone else!"

Again he reached for the phone.

Again she grabbed his hand and held on tightly. "If we let too many people in on this," she said, "I guarantee there'll be a leak. Van Weldon will hear about it, and that'll be it for our big chance. Jordan, we have to wait till the last minute. And we have to be sure of what they'll find."

"You don't really think you can stroll aboard that ship and have a look around, do you?"

"When it comes to making unauthorized entries, I had the world's best teacher."

"Uncle Walter? He got caught, remember?"

"*I* won't get caught."

"Because you're not going anywhere *near* the *Villafjord*." He shook off her hand and began to dial the telephone.

Desperately she snatched away the receiver. "You're not doing this!" she cried.

"Clea." He heaved a sigh of frustration. "Clea, you have to trust me on this."

"No, you have to trust *me*. Trust *my* judgment. *I'm* the one with everything to lose!"

"I know that. But we're both tired. We're going to make mistakes. Now's the time to call the police and put an end to all this. To get back to our lives—our *real* lives. Don't you see?"

She looked into his eyes. *Yes, I see,* she thought. *You've had enough of running. Enough of me. You want your own life back, and I don't blame you.*

Defiantly she raised her chin. "I want to go home, too. I'm sick of hotels and strange beds and dyed hair. I want this all to be over with just as much as you do. That's why I say we do it *my* way."

"Your way's too bloody risky. The police—"

"I told you, I don't trust them!" Agitated, she paced over to the window, paced back. "I've survived this long only because I didn't trust anyone. *I'm* the only one I can count on."

"You can count on me," he said quietly.

She shook her head and laughed. "In the real world, darling, it's every man for himself. Remember that. You can't trust anyone." She turned and looked at him. "Not even me."

"But I do."

"Then you're crazy."

"Why? Because you're an ex-con? Because you've made a few mistakes in your life?" He moved toward her and took her by the shoulders. "Are you *afraid* to have me believe in you?"

She gave a nonchalant toss of her head. "I'd hate to disappoint anyone."

He cupped her face in his hands and lowered his mouth to hers. "I have complete faith," he whispered. "And so should you."

His kiss was sweet enough to break her heart. And that frightened her, because she knew now there could be no clean parting between them, no easy goodbyes. The break would be painful and haunting and bitter.

And inevitable.

He pulled back. "I'm going to have to trust you now, Clea. To do as I ask. To stay in this room and let me take care of this."

"But I—"

He silenced her by pressing a finger to her lips. "No arguments. I'm going to assert a little male authority here. Something I damn well should have done ages ago. You're going to wait for me. Here, in this room. Understood?"

She looked at his unyielding expression. Then she gave a sigh. "Understood," she said meekly.

He smiled and kissed her.

She smiled, too, as he walked out of the room. But

when she went to the window and watched him leave the building, her smile faded. *What makes you think I'm so damn trustworthy?* she thought.

Turning, she saw Jordan's jacket, which she'd left draped over a chair. Impulsively she thrust her hand in the pocket and pulled out the gold watch. She flipped open the dented cover and looked at the name engraved inside: Bernard Tavistock.

And she thought, This will end it. Here and now. It's going to end anyway, and I might as well do it sooner than later. If I take this watch, something he treasures, I'll cut the ties. Cleanly. Decisively. After all, that's what I am. A thief. An ex-con. He'll be relieved to see me go.

She thrust the watch into her own pocket. Maybe she'd mail it back to him someday. When she was good and ready. When she could think of him without feeling that painful twist of her heart.

Glancing out the window, she saw that Jordan was nowhere in sight. *Goodbye,* she thought. *Goodbye, my darling gentleman.*

A moment later she, too, left the room.

CHAPTER THIRTEEN

RICHARD WOLF was on the telephone to Brussels when the doorbell rang. He paid it no attention—the butler would see to any visitors. Only when he heard Davis's polite knock on the study door did Richard break off his conversation.

The butler, looking oddly uncertain, stood in the doorway. It was something Richard hadn't gotten the hang of, dealing with all these servants. His Yankee sense of privacy was always being violated by all the maids and butlers and underbutlers whom the Tavistocks insisted upon keeping underfoot.

"Pardon the interruption, Mr. Wolf," said Davis. "But there's a foreign gentleman at the door. He insists upon speaking to you at once."

"Foreign?"

"A, er, Sikh, I believe." Davis made a whirling gesture over his head. "Judging by the turban."

"Did he say what his business was?"

"He said he would speak only to you."

Richard cut the call short and followed Davis to the front door.

There was indeed a Sikh waiting on the front step, a short, pleasant-looking fellow with a trim beard and a gold tooth. "Mr. Wolf?" he inquired.

"I'm Richard Wolf."

"You called for a taxi."

"I'm afraid I didn't."

Without a word the Sikh handed an envelope to Richard.

Richard glanced in the envelope. Inside was a single gold cuff link. It was inscribed with the initials J.C.T.

Jordan's.

Calmly Richard nodded and said, "Oh, right. Of course. I'd forgotten all about that appointment. Let me get my briefcase."

While the Sikh waited on the doorstep, Richard ducked back into the study, slid a 9 mm automatic into his shoulder holster and reemerged carrying an empty briefcase.

The Sikh directed him to a taxi at the curb.

Neither of them said a thing as the car moved through traffic. The Sikh drove exactly the way one expected of a cab driver—calmly. Recklessly.

"Are we going some place in particular?" asked Richard.

"Harrods. You will stay there half an hour. Visit all the floors. Perhaps make a purchase. Then you'll return to my taxi. You will recognize it by the number—twenty-three. I will wait for you at the curb."

"What am I to expect?"

The Sikh grinned in the rearview mirror. "I do not know. I am only the driver." He paused. "We are being followed."

"I know," said Richard.

At Harrods Richard got out and entered the store. Inside he did as instructed, wandering about the various departments. He bought a silk scarf for Beryl and a tie for his father back in Connecticut. He was aware of two men lingering nearby, a short man and a blond man. They were good—it was a full five minutes before he noticed them, and only because he'd glimpsed them in a mirror as he tried on top hats. He lost them briefly in the gourmet foods section, but picked them up again in house-wares. If Jordan hoped to make contact, it was going to be difficult. Richard knew he could shake these guys if he wanted to. But then he'd probably shake Jordan, as well.

A half hour later he walked out of Harrods. He spotted taxi number twenty-three parked across the street, the Sikh driver still sitting patiently behind the wheel.

He crossed the street and climbed in the back seat of the taxi. "No luck," he said. "I was watched the whole time. Is there a backup plan?"

"This *is* the plan," said a familiar voice.

Richard glanced up in surprise at the rearview mirror, at the face of the bearded, turbaned driver. Jordan's brown eye winked back at him.

"Gotcha," said Jordan, and pulled the taxi into traffic.

"What the hell's going on?"

"Little game of wits. How am I doing so far?"

"Splendidly. You outsmarted me." Richard glanced back and spotted the same car following them.

"I see them," said Jordan.

"Where's Clea Rice?"

"A safe place. But things are coming to a head. We need help."

"Jordan, Interpol's already stepped in. They want Van Weldon's head. They'll arrange for the woman's safety."

"How do I know we can trust them?"

"They'd been watching over her for weeks. Until you two shook them off."

"Veronica's working for Van Weldon. Oliver may be, as well."

Richard, stunned, fell momentarily silent.

"You see, it reaches all levels," said Jordan. "It's like an octopus. Tentacles everywhere. The only people I can really count on are you, Beryl and Uncle Hugh. And you may regret hearing from me at all."

"We've been waiting for you to contact us. Hugh's calling in old favors. You'll be in good hands, I'll see to it myself. MacLeod's just waiting for the chance to move on Van Weldon."

"MacLeod?"

"Interpol. That was his man on the train platform. The one who saved your lives."

Jordan chewed on that piece of information for a moment. "If we come in, how will it be arranged?"

"Through your uncle. Scotland Yard will oversee. Whenever you're ready."

Jordan was silent as he dodged around a tight knot of traffic. "I'm ready," he said at last.

"And the woman?"

"Clea'll take some convincing. But she's tired. I think she's ready to come in, too."

"How shall we do it, then?"

"Sloane Square, the Underground. Make it an hour from now—eight-thirty."

"I'll let Hugh know."

They were coming up on the Tavistocks' London residence, one in a row of elegant Georgian town houses. The car was still following them.

Jordan pulled over to the curb. "One more thing, Richard."

"Yes?"

"There's a ship docking this afternoon in Portsmouth. The *Villafjord*."

"Van Weldon's?"

"Yes. My guess is, she'll be taking on cargo tonight. I suggest the police perform a little unannounced inspection before she leaves port."

"What's the cargo?"

"It'll be a surprise."

Richard stepped out and made a conspicuous point of paying for the ride. Then he walked up the steps and entered the house. As Jordan drove off, Richard saw that the car that had followed them remained parked outside the Tavistock residence. It was just as he'd expected. The men were assigned to watch him; they had no interest in any Sikh driver.

All the tension suddenly left his body. Only then did he realize how edgy he'd been.

And how close to the precipice they'd been dancing.

BACK AT THE HOTEL, Jordan parked the taxi a block away, and sat for a moment in the driver's seat, watching to see if any cars had followed him. When he saw nothing suspicious, he stripped off his beard and turban, got out and headed for the building.

Trust me, he thought as he climbed the stairs. *You*

have to learn to trust me. He knew it would be a long, slow process, one that might take a lifetime. Perhaps it was too late. Perhaps all the damage done in childhood had robbed Clea forever of her faith in other people. Could they live with that?

Could she?

Only then did he realize that, lately, all his thoughts of the future seemed to include *her.*

Sometime in the past week, the shift had occurred. Where once he would have thought *I,* now he thought *we.* That's what came of sharing so much, so intensely. It was both the reward and the consequence, this link between them.

Trust me, he thought, and opened the door.

The room was empty.

He stood staring at the bed, suddenly, painfully aware of the silence. He went into the bathroom; it was empty, as well. He paced back to the bedroom and saw that her purse was gone. And he saw his jacket, lying draped across a chair.

He picked up the jacket and noticed at once that it was lighter than usual. That something was missing. Reaching into the pocket, he discovered that his father's gold watch was missing.

In its place was a note.

"It was fun while it lasted. Clea."

With a groan of frustration, he crumpled the paper

in his fist. Blast the woman! She'd picked his pockets! And then she'd headed for…where?

The answer was only too frightening.

It was eight o'clock. She'd had a solid three hours' head start.

He ran back down the stairs to the taxi. First he'd swing past Sloane Square, to pick up some Scotland Yard assistance. And then it'd be on to Portsmouth, where a certain little burglar was, at this moment, probably sneaking up the gangplank of a ship.

If she wasn't already dead.

THE FENCE WAS HIGHER than she'd expected. Clea crouched in the thickening gloom outside the Cairncross Biscuits complex and stared up in dismay at the barbed wire lacing the top of the chain link. This was not the usual penny ante security one expected for a biscuit warehouse. What were they afraid of? An attack by the Cookie Monster? The fence ringed the entire complex, interrupted only by the main gate, which was padlocked for the night. Floodlights shone down on the perimeter, leaving only intermittent patches of shadow. Judging by the fortune invested in security, there was more than just biscuits being stored in that warehouse.

Right on the money, she thought. *Something else is going on in there besides the manufacture of teatime treats.*

It had required only a small leap of logic to lead her to the Cairncross warehouse on the outskirts of London. If Van Weldon's ship was taking on illicit cargo tonight, then here was the obvious holding place for that cargo. Legitimate trucks were probably in and out of here all the time, pulling up to that handy warehouse platform. If a truck showed up tonight to pick up a load of crates, no one in the neighborhood would bat an eyelash.

Very clever, Van Weldon, she thought. *But this time I'm one step ahead of you.*

She'd be ahead of the authorities, as well. By the time Jordan and his precious police converged on that Portsmouth dock, there'd be no telling how many people would know about the forthcoming raid. Or how much warning Van Weldon would have. Now was the time to view the evidence—before Van Weldon had a chance to change plans.

The sound of someone whistling sent Clea scrambling for the cover of bushes. From her hiding place she watched a security guard stroll past, inside the fence. He had a gun strapped to his hip. He moved at a leisurely pace, pausing to flick away a cigarette and crush the butt with his shoe. Then, lighting up another, he continued his circuit.

Clea timed the gap between his appearances. Seven minutes. She waited, let him go around again.

This time it was six minutes. Six minutes, max, to get through the fence and into the building. The fence was no problem; a few snips of the wire cutter she'd brought and she'd be in the complex. It was the warehouse that worried her. Those locks might take a while to bypass, and if the guard circled around too early, she'd be trapped.

She had to take the chance.

She snipped a few links in the fence, then hid as the guard came around. The instant he vanished around the corner she cut the last link, scrambled under with her knapsack and dashed across the expanse of pavement to the warehouse side door.

One glance at the lock told her she was in for some trouble. It was a brand-new pin tumbler, and six minutes might not be enough to bypass it. She set her watch alarm for five minutes. Holding a penlight in her teeth, she set to work.

First she inserted an L-shaped tension wrench and gently applied pressure to slide apart the plug and cylinder plates. Next she inserted a lifter pick, with which she gingerly lifted the first lock pin. It slid up with a soft click.

One down, six pins to go.

The next five pins were a piece of cake. It was the seventh one—the last—that kept tripping her up. She felt the minutes tick by, felt the sweat beading on her upper lip as she struggled to lift that seventh pin. Just one more click and she'd be in the door. Interrupt the effort now, and she'd be back to square one.

Her watch alarm gave a beep.

She kept working, gambling on the chance she'd conquer that last pin in the seconds that remained. She was so close, so close.

Too late, she heard the sound of whistling again. The guard was approaching her corner of the building!

She'd never make it back under the fence in time. Neither was there any cover along the building. She had only one route of escape.

Straight up.

Sheer panic sent her clambering like a monkey up a flimsy-looking drainpipe, seeking the cover of the shadows above.

As the guard rounded the corner, she pressed herself to the wall, afraid to move a muscle, afraid even to breathe. A few feet below, the guard stopped. Pulse hammering, Clea watched as he lighted a fresh cigarette and inhaled deeply. Then, with a satisfied sigh, he continued his circuit. He rounded the next corner without a backward glance.

Clea had to make a quick choice: should she try that bloody lock again or keep climbing? Glancing up, she traced the course of the drainpipe to the three-story-high roofline. There might be another way in from there. Though the drainpipe looked flimsy, so far it had supported her weight.

She began to climb.

Seconds later she scrambled up over the edge and dropped onto the rooftop.

A shadowy expanse of asphalt tile lay before her. She started across it, moving past the whirring fans of vents. At last she came to a rooftop door—locked, of course. Another pin tumbler. She set to work with her tension wrench and lifter pick.

In two minutes flat she had the door open.

At her feet a narrow stairway dropped away into the darkness. She descended the stairs, pushed through another door and entered the vast cavern of the warehouse. Here the area was lighted, and she could see rows of crates. All of them were stamped Cairncross Biscuits, London.

She grabbed a crowbar from a tool bin and pried open one of the crates, releasing the fragrant waft of cookies. Inside she found tins with the distinctive red-and-yellow Cairncross logo. The crate did, indeed, contain biscuits.

Frustrated, she glanced around at the other crates. She'd never be able to search them all! Only then did she spot the closed double doors in the far wall.

With mounting excitement she approached the doors. They were locked. There were no windows, so it was unlikely there was an office beyond.

She picked the lock.

A rush of cooled air spilled out the open door. Air-conditioned, she thought. Climate control? She found the light switch and flicked it on.

The room was filled with crates, each stamped with the Cairncross Biscuits logo. These crates, however, were a variety of sizes. Several were huge enough to house a standing man.

With the crowbar she pried off one of the lids and discovered a fluffy mound of wood shavings. Plunging both arms into the packing, she encountered something solid buried within. She dug into the shavings and the top of the object emerged, its marble surface smooth and gleaming under the lights.

It was the head of a statue, a noble youth with a crown of olive leaves.

Clea, her hands shaking with excitement, pulled a camera from her knapsack and began to snap photos. She took three shots of the statue, then reclosed the lid. She pried open a second crate.

Somewhere in the building, metal clanged.

She froze, listening, and heard the growl of a truck, the protesting squeal of a bay door being shoved open along its tracks. At once she killed the room lights. Opening the door a crack, she peered out into the warehouse.

The loading gate was wide open. A truck had

backed up to the platform, and the driver was swinging open the rear doors.

Veronica and the blond man were walking in Clea's direction.

Clea jerked back and shut the door. Frantically she waved her penlight around the room. No other exit. No place to hide except…

Voices were speaking right outside the door.

She grabbed her knapsack, scrambled into the open crate and pulled the lid over her head.

Through the cracks in the wood she saw the room's lights come on.

"It's all here, as you can see," said Veronica. "Would you care to check the crates yourself, Mr. Trott? Or do you trust me now?"

"I have no time for that. They must be moved immediately."

"I hope Mr. Van Weldon appreciates the trouble we've gone to, keeping these safe. He did promise there'd be compensation."

"You've already taken yours."

"What do you mean?"

"Your profit from selling the Eye. That should suffice."

"That was *my* idea! *My* profit. Just because I borrowed the bloody thing for a few weeks…"

There was a momentary pause. Then Clea heard

Veronica suck in a sharp breath. "Put the gun away, Mr. Trott."

"Move away from the crates."

"You can't—you wouldn't—" Suddenly Veronica laughed, a shrill, hysterical sound. "You *need* us!"

"Not any longer," said Trott.

Clea flinched at the sound of a gun firing. Three bullets in rapid succession. She pressed her hand to her mouth, clamped it there to stifle the cry that rose up in her throat. She felt as if all the air had been sucked out of the crate and she was suffocating in her fear, choking on silent tears.

Then she heard the sounds of terrified sobbing. Veronica's. She was still alive.

"Just a warning, Mrs. Cairncross," said Trott. "Next time, I'll hit my target."

Trott crossed to the doorway and called out, "In here! Get these crates in the truck!"

More footsteps approached—two men and a squeaky loading cart.

"The large one first," said Trott.

Clea heard the cart move closer, then the men grunted in unison. She braced herself as the crate tilted. She found herself wedged between the side of the crate and something cold and metallic: the bronze torso of a man.

"Christ, this one's heavy. What's in here, anyway?"

"That's not your concern. Just get it moved."

Every little bump seemed to squash Clea into a tighter and tighter space. Only when the crate at last thumped to a rest in the truck was she able to take in a deep breath. And take stock of her predicament.

She was trapped. With the men constantly shuttling back and forth, loading in the rest of the crates, she couldn't exactly stroll out unseen.

The scrape of a second crate being slid on top of hers settled the issue. For the moment she was boxed in.

By the glow of her watch she saw it was 8:10.

At 8:25, the truck pulled away from the warehouse. By now, Clea's calves were cramping, the wood shavings had worked their way into her clothes and she was battling an attack of claustrophobia. Reaching up, she strained to push off the lid, but the crate on top was too heavy.

She pressed her face to a small knothole and took in a few slow, deep breaths. The taste of fresh air took the edge off her panic. *Better,* she thought. *Yes, that's better.*

Something hard was biting into her thigh. She managed to worm her hand into her hip pocket and found what it was: Jordan's watch. The one she'd stolen.

By now he knew she'd taken it. By now he'd be hating her and glad she was out of his life. That's what she'd wanted him to think. What he should think. He was a gentleman and she was a thief. Nothing could close that gap between them.

Yet, as she huddled in that coffin of a space and clutched Jordan's pocket watch in her fist, her longing for him brought tears to her eyes.

I did it for you, she thought. *To make it easier for you. And me, as well. Because I know, as well as you do, that I'm not the woman for you.*

She pressed the watch to her lips and kissed it, the way she longed to kiss *him,* and never would again. She wanted to curse her larcenous past, her transgressions, her childhood. Even Uncle Walter. All the things that would forever keep Jordan out of her reach. But she was too weary and too frightened.

So she cried instead.

By the time the truck wheezed to a stop, Clea was numb in both spirit and body. Her legs felt dead and useless.

The other crates were unloaded first. Then her crate was tipped onto a cart and began a roller coaster ride, down a truck ramp, up another ramp. She knew there were men about—she heard their voices. An elevator ride brought her to the final destination. The crate hit the floor with a thump.

After a while she heard nothing. Only the faint rumbling of an engine.

Cautiously she pushed up on the lid. The weight

of the other crate had redriven the nails into the wood. Luckily she still had the crowbar. It took some tight maneuvering, but she managed to work the tip under the lid and yanked on the bar.

The lid popped open.

She raised her head and inhaled a whiff of diesel-scented air. She was in a storage bay. Beside her were stacked the other crates from the warehouse annex. No one was around.

It took her a few moments to crawl out. By the time she dropped onto the floor, her calves were beginning to prickle with renewed circulation. She hobbled over to the steel door and opened it a crack.

Outside was a narrow corridor. Beyond the corner, two men were laughing, joking in that foul language sailors employ when they're away from the polite company of women. Something about the whores in Naples.

The floor lurched beneath Clea's feet and she swayed sideways. The engine sounds were grinding louder now.

Only then did she focus on the emergency fire kit mounted on the corridor wall. It was stamped with the name *Villafjord.*

I'm on his ship, she thought. *I'm trapped on Van Weldon's ship.*

The floor swayed again, a rolling motion that made

her reach out to the walls for support. She heard the engine's accelerating whine, sensed the gentle rocking of the hull through the swells, and she understood.

The *Villafjord* was heading out to sea.

CHAPTER FOURTEEN

HUGH TAVISTOCK'S limousine was waiting at the side of the road just outside Guildford. The instant Jordan and his two Scotland Yard escorts pulled up in a Mercedes, the limousine door swung open. Jordan stepped out of the Mercedes and slid into the limousine's rear seat.

He found himself confronting his uncle Hugh's critical gaze. "It seems," said Hugh, "that I retired from intelligence simply to devote my life to rescuing *you*."

"And a fond hello to you, too," answered Jordan. "Where's Richard?"

"Present and accounted for," answered a voice from the driver's seat. Dressed in a chauffeur's uniform, Richard turned and grinned at him. "I picked up this trick from a certain relative-to-be. Where's Clea Rice?"

"I don't know," said Jordan. "But I have a very good idea. Did you confirm the shipping schedule for Portsmouth?"

"There is a vessel named *Villafjord* due to sail at midnight tonight. That gives us plenty of time to stop the departure."

"Why all this interest in the *Villafjord?*" asked Hugh. "What's she carrying?"

"Wild guess? A fortune in art." Jordan added, under his breath, "And a certain little cat burglar."

Richard pulled onto the highway for Portsmouth. "She'll jeopardize the whole operation. You should have stopped her."

"Ha! As if I could!" said Jordan. "As you may have surmised, she doesn't take to instruction well."

"Yes, I've heard about Miss Rice," said Hugh. "Uncooperative, is she?"

"She doesn't trust anyone. Not Richard, not the authorities."

"Surely she trusts *you* by now?"

Jordan gazed ahead at the dark road. Softly he said, "I thought she did…."

But she didn't. When it came down to the wire, she chose to work alone. Without me.

He didn't understand her. She was like some forest creature, always poised for flight, never trusting of a human hand. She wouldn't *let* herself believe in him.

That lifting of his pocket watch—oh, he understood the meaning of that gesture. It was part defiance and part desperation. She was trying to push him away, to test him. She was crazy enough to put him to this test. And vulnerable enough to be hurt if he failed her.

I should have known. I should have seen this coming.

Now he was angry at himself, at her, at all the circumstances that kept wrenching them apart. Her past. Her mistrust of him.

His mistrust of *her.*

Perhaps Clea had it right from the start. Perhaps there was nothing he could do, nothing she could do, that would get them beyond all this.

With renewed anxiety he glanced outside at a passing road sign. They were still thirty miles from Portsmouth.

MacLeod and the police were already waiting at the dock.

"We're too late," said MacLeod as Hugh and Jordan stepped out of the limousine.

"What do you mean, too late?" demanded Jordan.

"This, I take it, is young Tavistock?" asked MacLeod.

"My nephew Jordan," said Hugh. "What's happening here?"

"We arrived a few minutes ago. The *Villafjord* was scheduled to sail at midnight from this dock."

"Where is she, then?"

"That's the problem. It seems she sailed twenty minutes ago."

"But it's only nine-thirty."

MacLeod shook his head. "Obviously they changed plans."

Jordan stared out over the dark harbor. A chill wind blew in from the water, whipping his shirt and stinging his face with the tang of salt. *She's out there. I feel it. And she's alone.*

He turned to MacLeod. "You have to intercept them."

"At sea? You're talking a major operation! We have no firm evidence yet. Nothing solid to authorize that sort of thing."

"You'll find your evidence on the *Villafjord.*"

"I can't take that chance. If I move on Van Weldon without cause, his lawyers will shut down my investigation for good. We have to wait until she docks in Naples. Convince the Italian police to board her."

"By then it may be too late! MacLeod, this could be your best chance. Your only chance. If you want Van Weldon, move *now.*"

MacLeod looked at Hugh. "What do you think, Lord Lovat?"

"We'd need help from the Royal Navy. A chopper or two. Oh, we could do it, all right. But if the evidence isn't aboard, if it turns out we're chasing nothing but a cargo of biscuits, there's going to be enough red faces all around to fill a bloody circus ring."

"I'm telling you, the evidence *is* on board," said Jordan. "So is Clea."

"Is that what you're really chasing?" asked Hugh. "The woman?"

"What if it is?"

"We don't launch an operation this big just because some—some stray female has gotten herself into trouble," said MacLeod. "We move prematurely and we'll lose our chance at Van Weldon."

"He's right," said Hugh. "There are too many factors to weigh here. The woman can't be our first concern."

"Don't give me any bloody lecture about who's dispensable and who isn't!" retorted Jordan. "She's not one of your agents. She never took any oath to protect queen and country. She's a civilian, and you can't leave her out there. *I* won't leave her out there!"

Hugh stared at his nephew in surprise. "She means that much to you?"

Jordan met his uncle's gaze. The answer had never been clearer than at this very moment, with the wind whipping their faces and the night growing ever deeper, ever colder.

"Yes," said Jordan firmly. "She means that much to me."

His uncle glanced up at the sky. "Looks like some nasty weather coming up—it will complicate things."

"But…they'll be miles at sea by the time we reach them," said MacLeod. "Beyond English waters. There's no legal way to demand a search."

"No *legal* way," said Jordan.

"What, you think they'll just invite us aboard to comb the ship?"

"They're not going to know there *is* a search." Jordan turned to his uncle. "I'll need a navy helicopter. And a crew of volunteers for the boarding party."

Troubled, Hugh regarded his nephew for a moment. "You'll have no authority to back you up on this. You understand that?"

"Yes."

"If anything goes wrong—"

"The navy will deny my existence. I know that, too."

Hugh shook his head, agonizing over the decision. "Jordan, you're my only nephew…."

"And with a bloodline like ours, we can't possibly fail. Can we?" Smiling, Jordan gave his uncle's shoulder a squeeze of confidence.

Hugh sighed. "This woman must be quite extraordinary."

"I'll introduce you," said Jordan, and his gaze shifted back to the water. "As soon as I get her off that bloody ship."

THE MEN'S VOICES MOVED ON and faded down the corridor.

Clea remained frozen by the door, debating whether to risk leaving the storage area. Before they docked again, she'd have to find a new hiding place. Eventually someone would check the cargo, and when that happened, the last place Clea wanted to be was trapped in a crate.

The coast looked clear.

She slipped out of the storeroom and headed in the opposite direction the men had taken. The below-decks area was a confusing maze of corridors and hatches. Which way next?

The question was settled by the sound of footsteps. In panic, she ducked through the nearest door.

To her dismay she discovered she was in the crew's quarters—and the footsteps were moving closer. She scrambled across to the row of lockers, opened a door and squeezed inside.

It was even a tighter fit than the crate had been. She was crammed against a bundle of foul-smelling shirts and an even fouler pair of tennis shoes. Through the ventilation slits she saw two men step into the room. One of them crossed toward the lockers. Clea almost let out a squeak of relief when he swung open the door right beside hers.

"Hear there's rough weather comin' up," the man said, pulling on a slicker.

"Hell, she's blowin' twenty-five knots already."

The men, now garbed in foul-weather gear, left the quarters.

Clea emerged from the locker. She couldn't keep ducking in and out of rooms; she'd have to find a more permanent hiding place. Some spot she'd be left undisturbed...

The lifeboats. She'd seen it used as a hiding place in the movies. Unless there was a ship's emergency, she'd be safe waiting it out there until they docked.

She scavenged among the lockers and pulled out a sailor's pea coat and a black cap. Then, her head covered, her petite frame almost swallowed up in the coat, she crept out of the crew's quarters and started up a stairway to the deck.

It was blowing outside, the night swirling with wind and spray. Through the darkness she could make out several men moving about on deck. Two were securing a cargo hatch, a third was peering through binoculars over the port rail. None of them glanced in her direction.

She spotted two lifeboats secured near the starboard gunwale. Both were covered with tarps. Not only would she be concealed in there, she'd be dry. Once the *Villafjord* reached Naples, she could sneak ashore.

She pulled the pea coat tighter around her shoulders. Calmly, deliberately, she began to stroll toward the lifeboats.

SIMON TROTT STOOD on the bridge and eyed the increasingly foul weather from behind the viewing windows. Though the captain had assured him the passage would present no difficulties for the *Villafjord,* Trott still couldn't shake off his growing sense of uneasiness.

Obviously, Victor Van Weldon didn't share Trott's sense of foreboding. The old man sat calmly beside him on the bridge, oxygen hissing softly through his nasal tube. Van Weldon would not be anxious about something so trivial as a storm at sea. At his age, with his failing health, what was there left for him to fear?

Trott asked the captain, "Will it get much rougher?"

"Not by much, I expect," said the captain. "She'll handle it fine. But if you're that concerned, we can turn back to Portsmouth."

"No," spoke up Van Weldon. "We cannot return." Suddenly he began to cough. Everyone on the bridge looked away in distaste as the old man spat into a handkerchief.

Trott, too, averted his gaze and focused on the main deck below, where three men were working hunched against the wind. That's when Trott noticed the fourth figure moving along the starboard gunwale. It passed, briefly, under the glow of a decklight, then slipped into the shadows.

At the first lifeboat the figure paused, glanced around and began to untie the covering tarp.

"Who is that?" Trott asked sharply. "That man by the lifeboat?"

The captain frowned. "I don't recognize that one."

At once Trott turned for the exit.

"Mr. Trott?" called the captain.

"I'll take care of this."

By the time Trott reached the deck, he had his automatic drawn and ready. The figure had vanished. Draped free over the lifeboat was an unfastened corner of tarp. Trott prowled closer. With a jerk he yanked off the tarp and pointed his gun at the shadow cowering inside.

"Out!" snapped Trott. "Come on, *out*."

Slowly the figure unfolded itself and raised its head. By the glow of a decklight Trott saw the terror in that startlingly familiar face.

"If it isn't the elusive Miss Clea Rice," said Trott. And he smiled.

THE CABIN WAS LARGE, plushly furnished and equipped with all the luxuries one would expect in a well-appointed living room. Only the swaying of the crystal chandelier overhead betrayed the fact it was a shipboard residence.

The chair Clea was tied to was upholstered in green velvet and the armrests were carved mahogany. *Surely they won't kill me here,* she thought. *They wouldn't want me to bleed all over this pricey antique.*

Trott emptied the contents of her pockets and her knapsack onto a table and eyed the collection of lock picks. "I see you came well prepared," he commented dryly. "How did you get on board?"

"Trade secret."

"Are you alone?"

"You think I'd tell you?"

With two swift steps he crossed to her and slapped her across the face, so hard her head snapped back. For a moment she was too stunned by the force of the blow to speak.

"Surely, Miss Rice," wheezed Victor Van Weldon, "you don't wish to anger Mr. Trott more than you already have. He can be most unpleasant when annoyed."

"So I've noticed," groaned Clea. She squinted, focusing her blurred gaze on Van Weldon. He was frailer than she'd expected. And old, so old. Oxygen tubing snaked from his nostrils to a green tank hooked behind his wheelchair. His hands were bruised, the skin thin as paper. This was a man barely clinging to life. What could he possibly lose by killing her?

"I'll ask you again," said Trott. "Are you alone?"

"I brought a team of navy SEALs with me."

Trott hit her again. A thousand shards of light seemed to explode in her head.

"Where is Jordan Tavistock?" asked Trott.

"I don't know."

"Is he with you?"

"No."

Trott picked up Jordan's gold pocket watch and flipped open the lid. He read aloud the inscription. "Bernard Tavistock." He looked at her. "You have no idea where he is?"

"I told you I don't."

He held up the watch. "Then what are you doing with this?"

"I stole it."

Though she steeled herself for the coming blow, the impact of his fist still took her breath away. Blood trickled down her chin. In dazed wonder she watched the red droplets soak into the lush carpet at her feet. *How ironic,* she thought. *I finally tell the truth and he doesn't believe me.*

"He is still working with you, isn't he?" said Trott.

"He wants nothing more to do with me. I left him."

Trott turned to Van Weldon. "I think Tavistock is still a threat. Keep the contract on him alive."

Clea's head shot up. "No. No, he's got nothing to do with this!"

"He's been with you this past week."

"His misfortune."

"Why were you together?"

She gave a shrug. "Lust?"

"You think I'd believe that?"

"Why not?" Rebelliously she cocked up her head. "I've been known to tweak the hormones of more than a few men."

"This gets us nowhere!" said Van Weldon. "Throw her overboard."

"I want to know what she's learned. What Tavistock's learned. Otherwise we'll be operating blind. If Interpol—" He suddenly turned.

The intercom was buzzing.

Trott crossed the room and pressed the speaker button. "Yes, Captain?"

"We've a situation up here, Mr. Trott. There's a Royal Navy ship hard on our stern. They've requested permission to come aboard."

"Why?"

"They say they're checking all outbound vessels from Portsmouth for some IRA terrorist. They think he may have passed himself off as crew."

"Request denied," said Van Weldon calmly.

"They have helicopter backup," said the captain. "And another ship on the way."

"We are beyond the twelve-mile limit," said Van Weldon. "They have no right to board us."

"Sir, might I advise cooperation?" said the captain. "It sounds like a routine matter. You know how it is—the Brits are always hunting down IRA. They'll probably just want to eyeball our crew. If we refuse, it will only rouse their suspicions."

Trott and Van Weldon exchanged glances. At last Van Weldon nodded.

"Assemble all men on deck," said Trott into the intercom. "Let the Brits have a good look at them. But it stops there."

"Yes, sir."

Trott turned to Van Weldon. "We'd both better be on deck to meet them. As for Miss Rice…" He looked at Clea.

"She will have to wait," said Van Weldon, and wheeled his chair across the room to a private elevator. "See that she's well secured. I will meet you on the bridge." He maneuvered into the elevator and slid the gate shut. With a hydraulic whine, the lift carried him away.

Trott turned his attention to Clea's bonds. He yanked the ropes around her wrists so tightly she gave a cry of pain. Then quickly, efficiently he taped her mouth.

"That should keep you," he said with a grunt of satisfaction, and he left the room.

The instant the door shut behind him, Clea began straining at her bonds. It took only a few painful twists of her wrists to tell her that it was hopeless. She wasn't going to get loose.

Shedding tears of frustration, she slumped back against the chair. Up on deck, the Royal Navy would soon be landing. They would never know, would never guess, that just below their feet was a victim in need of rescue.

So close and yet so far.

She gritted her teeth and began to strain again at the ropes.

"YOU'RE CERTAIN YOU WANT to go in with us?"

Jordan peered through the chopper windows at the deck of the *Villafjord* below. It would be a bumpy landing into enemy territory, but with all this wind and darkness as cover, there was a reasonable chance no one down there would recognize him.

"I'm going in," Jordan said.

"You'll have twenty minutes at the most," said the naval officer seated across from him. "And then we're out of there. With or without you."

"I understand."

"We're on shaky legal ground already. If Van Weldon lodges a complaint to the high command, we'll be explaining ourselves till doomsday."

"Twenty minutes. Just give me that much." Jordan tugged the black watch cap lower on his brow. The borrowed Royal Navy uniform was a bit snug around his shoulders, and the automatic felt uncomfortably foreign holstered against his chest, but both were absolutely necessary if he was to participate in this masquerade. Unfortunately the other seven men in the boarding party—all naval officers—were plainly doubtful about having some amateur along for the ride. They kept watching him with expressions bordering on disdain.

Jordan ignored them and focused on the broad deck of the *Villafjord,* now directly beneath the skids. A little tricky maneuvering by the pilot brought them to a touchdown. At once the men began to pile out, Jordan among them.

The pilot, mindful of the hazards of a rolling deck, took off again, leaving the crew temporarily stranded aboard the *Villafjord.*

A man with blond hair was crossing to greet them.

Jordan slipped behind the other men in his party and averted his face. It would be bloody inconvenient to be recognized right off the bat.

The ranking officer of the naval team stepped forward and met the blond man. "Lieutenant Commander Tobias, Royal Navy."

"Simon Trott. VP operations, the Van Weldon company. How can we help you, Commander?"

"We'd like to inspect your crew."

"Certainly. They've already been assembled." Trott pointed to the knot of men huddled near the bridge stairway.

"Is everyone on deck?"

"All except the captain and Mr. Van Weldon. They're up on the bridge."

"There's no one below decks?"

"No, sir."

Commander Tobias nodded. "Then let's get started."

Trott turned to lead the way. As the rest of the boarding party followed Trott, Jordan hung behind, waiting for a chance to slip away.

No one noticed him duck down the midship stairway.

With all the crew up top, he'd have the below-decks area to himself. There wasn't much time to search. Slipping quickly down the first corridor, he poked his head into every doorway, calling Clea's name. He passed crew's quarters and officers' quarters, the mess hall, the galley.

No sign of Clea.

Heading farther astern, he came across what

appeared to be a storage bay. Inside the room were a dozen crates of various sizes. The lid was ajar on one of them. He lifted it off and glanced inside.

Swathed in fluffy packing was the bronze head of a statue. And a black glove—a woman's, size five.

Jordan glanced sharply around the room. "Clea?" he called out.

Ten minutes had already passed.

With a surging sense of panic he continued down the corridor, throwing open doors, scanning each compartment. So little time left, and he still had the engine room, the cargo bays and Lord knew what else might lie astern.

Overhead he heard the sound of rumbling, growing louder now. The helicopter was about to land again.

A mahogany door with a sign Private was just ahead. Captain's quarters? Jordan tried the knob and found it was locked. He pounded on it a few times and called out, "Clea?"

There was no answer.

She heard the pounding on the door, then Jordan's voice calling her name.

She tried to answer, tried to shout, but the tape over her mouth muffled all but the faintest whimper. Frantic to reach him, she thrashed like a madwoman against her bonds. The ropes held. Her hands and feet had gone numb, useless.

Don't leave me! she wanted to shriek. *Don't leave me!*

But she knew he had already turned from the door.

In despair, she jerked her body sideways. The chair tipped, carrying her down with it. Her head slammed against an end table. The pain was like a bolt of lightning through her skull; it left her stunned on the floor. Blackness swam before her eyes. She fought the slide toward unconsciousness, fought it savagely with every ounce of will she possessed. And still she could not clear the blackness from her vision.

Faintly she heard a thumping. Again and again, like a drumbeat in the darkness.

She struggled to see. The blackness was lifting. She could make out the outlines of furniture now. And she realized that the thumping was coming from the door.

In a shower of splinters the wood suddenly split open, breached by the bright red blade of a fire ax. Another blow tore a gaping hole in the door. An arm thrust in, to fumble at the lock.

Jordan shoved into the room.

He took one look at Clea and murmured, "My God…"

At once he was kneeling at her side. Her hands were so numb she scarcely felt it when he cut the cords binding her wrists.

But she did feel his kiss. He pulled the tape from

her mouth, lifted her from the floor and pressed his lips to hers. As she lay sobbing in his arms he kissed her hair, her face, murmuring her name again and again, as though he could not say it enough, could never say it enough.

A soft beeping made his head suddenly lift from hers. He silenced the pager hung on his belt. "That's our one-minute warning," he said. "We have to get out of here. Can you walk?"

"I—I don't think so. My legs…"

"Then I'll carry you." He swept her up into his arms. Stepping across the wood-littered carpet, he bore her out of the room and into the corridor.

"How do we get off the ship?" she asked.

"The same way I got on. Navy chopper." He rounded a corner.

And halted.

"I am afraid, Mr. Tavistock," said Simon Trott, standing in their path, "that you are going to miss your flight."

CHAPTER FIFTEEN

CLEA FELT Jordan's arms tighten around her. In the momentary silence she could almost hear the thudding of his heart against his chest.

Trott raised the barrel of his automatic. "Put her down."

"She can't walk," said Jordan. "She hit her head."

"Very well, then. You'll have to carry her."

"Where?"

Trott waved the gun toward the far end of the corridor. "The cargo bay."

That gun left Jordan no choice. With Clea in his arms he headed up the corridor and stepped through a doorway, into a cargo bay crammed full with packing crates.

"The landing party knows I'm on board," said Jordan. "They won't leave without me."

"Won't they?" Trott glanced upward toward the rumble of the chopper rotors. "They're about to do just that."

They heard the roar of the helicopter as it suddenly lifted away.

"Too late," said Trott with a regretful shake of his head. "You've now entered the gray world of deniability, Mr. Tavistock. We'll claim you never came aboard. And the Royal Navy will have a sticky time admitting otherwise." Again he waved the gun, indicating one of the crates. "It's large enough for you both. A cozy end, I'd say."

He's going to shut us inside, thought Clea. And then what?

A ditching at sea, of course. She and Jordan would drown together, their bodies locked forever in an undersea casket. Suddenly she found it hard to breathe. Sheer terror had drained her of the ability to think, to act.

When Jordan spoke, his voice was astonishingly calm.

"They'll be waiting for you in Naples," said Jordan. "Interpol and the Italian police. You don't really think it's as simple as tossing one crate overboard?"

"We've bought our way into Naples for years."

"Then your luck is about to change. Do you like dark, enclosed places? Because that's where *you're* going to find yourself. For the rest of your life."

"I've had enough," Trott snapped. "Put her down. Pry the lid off the crate." He picked up a crowbar and slid it across the floor to Jordan. "Do it. And no sudden moves."

Jordan set Clea down on her feet. At once she slid to her knees, her legs still numb and useless. Dropping down beside her, Jordan looked her in the eye. Something in his gaze caught her attention. He was trying to tell her something. He bent close to her and the flap of his jacket sagged open. That's when she caught a glimpse of his shoulder holster.

He had a gun!

Trott's view was blocked by Jordan's back. Quickly she slipped her hand beneath Jordan's jacket, grabbed the pistol from the holster and hugged it against her chest.

"Leave her on the floor!" ordered Trott. "Just get the bloody crate open!"

Jordan leaned close, his mouth grazing her ear. "Use me as a shield," he whispered. "Aim for his chest."

She stared at him in horror. "No—"

He gripped her shoulder with painful insistence. *"Do it."*

Their gazes locked. It was something she'd remember for as long as she lived, that message she saw in his eyes. *You have to live, Clea. For both of us.*

He gave her shoulder another squeeze, this one gentler. And he smiled.

"Come on, get the lid off!" barked Trott.

Clea hooked her finger around the pistol trigger. She had never shot anyone before. If she missed, if she was even slightly off target, Trott would have time to squeeze off his entire clip into Jordan's body. She had to be accurate. She had to be lethal.

For his sake.

His lips brushed her forehead and she savored their warmth, knowing full well that the next time she touched them they might carry the chill of death.

"It seems you need a jump start," said Trott. He raised his pistol and fired.

Clea felt Jordan shudder in pain, heard him groan as he clutched his thigh. In horror Clea saw bright red droplets spatter the floor. The sight of Jordan's blood seemed to cloud her vision with rage. All her hesitation was swept away by a roaring wave of fury.

With both hands she aimed the pistol at Trott and fired.

The bullet's impact punched Trott squarely in the chest. He stumbled backward, his face frozen in surprise. He weaved on his feet like a drunken man. The gun slipped from his grasp and clanged to the floor. He dropped to his knees beside it, made a clumsy attempt to pick it up again, but his hands wouldn't function. As he sank to the floor, his fingers were still clawing uselessly for the gun. Then they fell still.

"Get out of here," gasped Jordan.

"I won't leave you."

"I can't leave, period. My leg—"

"Hush!" she cried. On unsteady legs she stumbled over to Trott's body and snatched up his gun. "There's no getting off this ship, anyway! They've heard the shots. They'll be down here any minute, the whole lot of them. We might as well stick together." She tottered back to his side.

He sat huddled in a pool of his own blood. Tenderly she took his face in her hands and pressed a kiss to his mouth.

His lips were already chilled.

Sobbing, despairing, she cradled his head in her lap. *It's over,* she thought as she heard footsteps pounding toward them along the corridor. *All we can do now is fight till the bitter end. And hope death comes quickly.* She bent down to him and whispered, "I love you."

The footsteps were almost at the cargo door.

With a strange sense of calmness she raised the gun and took aim at the doorway....

And held her fire. A man in a Royal Navy uniform stood blinking at her in surprise. Behind him stood three other men, also in uniform. One of them was Richard Wolf.

Richard shoved through into the room and saw Jordan and the growing pool of blood. Turning, he yelled, "Call back the chopper again! Have the Medevac team standing by!"

"Yes, sir!" One of the naval officers headed for the intercom.

Clea was still clutching the pistol. Slowly she let the barrel drop, but she did not release the grip. She was almost afraid to let go of the one solid thing she could count on. Afraid that if she did let go, she would drop away into some dimensionless space.

"Here. I'll take it."

Dazed, she looked up at Richard. He regarded her with an almost kindly smile and held out his hand. Wordlessly she gave him the pistol. He nodded and said softly, "That's a good girl."

Within fifteen minutes a team of medics had appeared, helicoptered in from the nearby Royal Navy ship. By then, Clea's legs had regained their circulation and she was able to stand, albeit unsteadily. Her head was aching worse than ever, and a medic tried to pull her aside to examine the bruises on her temple, but she shrugged him away.

All her attention was focused on Jordan. She watched as IV lines were threaded into Jordan's veins, as he was lifted and strapped onto a stretcher. In numb silence she squeezed onto the elevator that carried his stretcher up to the deck.

Only when one of the officers held her back as they

lifted Jordan into the chopper did she understand they were taking him from her. Suddenly she panicked, terrified that if she lost sight of him now, she would never see him again.

She shoved forward, elbowing aside the naval officer, and would have run all the way to the chopper were it not for a grip that firmly closed around her arm.

Richard Wolf's.

"Let me go!" she sobbed, trying to fight him off.

"He's being transported to a hospital. They'll take care of him."

"I want to be with him! He needs me!"

Richard took her firmly by the shoulders. "You'll see him soon, I promise! But now *we* need you, Clea. You have to tell us things. About Van Weldon. About this ship."

The roar of the rotor engine drowned out any other words. With despairing eyes, Clea saw the chopper lift away into the wind-buffeted darkness. *Please take care of him,* she prayed. *That's all I ask. Please keep him safe.*

She watched the taillights wink into the night. A moment later the rumble had faded, leaving only the sounds of the wind and the sea.

"Miss Rice?" Richard prodded gently.

Through tears Clea looked at him. "I'll tell you everything, Mr. Wolf," she said. And an anguished laugh suddenly escaped her throat. "Even the truth."

IT WAS TWO DAYS before she saw Jordan again.

She was told that Jordan had lost a great deal of blood, but that the surgery had gone well, without complications. She could learn no more.

Richard Wolf installed her in an MI6 safe house outside London. It was a sweet little stone cottage with a white fence and a garden. She considered it a prison. The three men guarding the entrances did nothing to dispel that impression.

Richard had told her the men were a necessity. The contract on her life might still be active, he'd explained. It was dangerous to move her. Until Van Weldon's topple from power became general knowledge, Clea would have to be kept out of sight.

And away from Jordan.

She understood the real purpose of the separation. It did not surprise her that his aristocratic family would, in the end, prevail. Clea was not the sort of woman one allowed into one's family. Not if one had a reputation to uphold. No matter how much Jordan cared about her—and he *did* care, she knew that now—her past would come between them.

The Tavistocks had only Jordan's well-being in mind. For that she could not fault them.

But she did resent them for the way they had taken control of her freedom. For two days she tolerated her pleasant little prison. She paced in the garden, stared at the TV, leafed without interest through magazines.

By the second day in captivity, she'd bloody well had enough.

She picked up her knapsack, marched outside and announced to the guard posted in the front yard, "I want out."

"Afraid that's quite impossible," he said.

"What're you going to do about it, Buster, shoot me in the back?"

"My orders are to ensure your safety. You can't leave."

"Watch me." She slung the knapsack over her shoulder and was pushing through the gate when a black limousine rolled into the driveway. It came to a stop right in front of her. In amazement she watched as the chauffeur emerged, circled around and opened the rear door.

An elderly man stepped out. He was portly and balding, but he wore his finely tailored suit with comfortable elegance. For a moment he regarded Clea in silence.

"So you are the woman in question," he said at last.

Coolly she looked him up and down. "And the man in question?"

He held out his hand in greeting. "I'm Hugh Tavistock. Jordan's uncle."

Clea momentarily lost her voice. Wordlessly she accepted his handshake and found the man's grip firm, his gaze steady. *Like Jordan's.*

"We have much to talk about, Miss Rice," said Hugh. "Will you step into the car?"

"Actually, I was just leaving."

"You don't wish to see him?"

"You mean...Jordan?"

Hugh nodded. "It's a long drive to the hospital. I thought it would give us a chance to get acquainted."

She studied him, searching for some hint of what was to come. His expression was unreadable, his face a cipher.

She climbed into the limousine.

They sat side by side, not speaking for a while. Outside the window, the countryside glided past. The brilliant hues of fall were tingeing the trees. *What do we possibly have to say to each other?* she wondered. *I'm a stranger to his world, as he is to mine.*

"It seems my nephew has formed an attachment to you," said Hugh.

"Your nephew is a good man," she said. She stared out the window and added softly, "A very fine man."

"I've always thought so."

"He deserves..." She paused and swallowed back tears. "He deserves the very best there is."

"True."

"So…" She raised her chin and looked at him. "I'll not be difficult. You must understand, Lord Lovat, I have no demands. No expectations. I only want…" She looked away. "I only want him to be happy. I'll do whatever it takes. Even if it means vanishing."

"You love him." It was not a question but a statement.

This time she couldn't keep the tears at bay. They began to fall slowly, silently.

Sighing, he sat back in the seat. "Well, it's certainly not without precedent."

"What do you mean?"

"A number of women have fallen for my nephew."

"I can see why."

"But none of them were quite like you. You do realize, don't you, that you are almost single-handedly responsible for bringing down Victor Van Weldon? For smashing an arms shipment empire?"

She shrugged, as if none of it mattered. And at the moment, it didn't. It all seemed irrelevant. She scarcely listened as Hugh outlined the ripple of developments since the *Villafjord* was boarded. The arrests of Oliver and Veronica Cairncross. The new investigation into the *Max Havelaar*'s sinking. The cache of surface-to-air missiles found in the Cairncross Biscuits warehouse. Unfortunately, Victor Van Weldon would probably not live long enough to go to trial. But he had, in some measure, met justice. The final rendering would have to come from his Maker.

When Hugh had finished speaking, he looked at Clea and said, "You have performed a service for us all, Miss Rice. You're to be congratulated."

She said nothing.

To her surprise he chuckled. "I've met many heroes in my time. But none so uninterested in praise."

She shook her head. "I'm tired, Lord Lovat. I just want to go home."

"To America?"

Again she shrugged. "I suppose that *is* my home. I…I don't know anymore…."

"What about Jordan? I thought you loved him."

"You yourself said it's not without precedent. Women have always been falling in love with your nephew."

"But Jordan's never fallen in love with them. Until now."

There was a silence. She frowned at him.

"For the past two days," said Hugh, "my normally good-natured nephew has been insufferable. Belligerent. He has badgered the doctors and nurses, twice pulled out his intravenous lines and commandeered another patient's wheelchair. We explained to him it wasn't the right time to bring you for a visit. That

contract on your life, you know—it made every
transfer risky. But now the contract's off—"

"It is?"

"And it's finally time to fetch you. And see if you
can't restore his good humor."

"You think I'm the one who can do that?"

"Richard Wolf thought so."

"And what does Jordan say?"

"Bloody little. But then, he's always been close-
mouthed." Hugh regarded her with his mild blue eyes.
"He's waiting to speak to you first."

Clea gave a bitter laugh. "How distressing it must
be for you! A woman like me. And your nephew.
You'd have to hide me in the family closet."

"If I did," he said dryly, "you'd find half my ancestors lurking in there with you."

She shook her head. "I don't understand."

"We Tavistocks have a grand tradition of choosing
mates who are most…unsuitable. Over the centuries
we've wed Gypsies, courtesans and even a stray
Yank or two." He smiled. For the first time she recognized the warmth in his eyes. "You would scarcely
raise an eyebrow."

"You'd…allow someone like me in your family?"

"It's not my decision, Miss Rice. The choice is
Jordan's. Whatever will make him happy."

How can we predict what will make him happy?

she thought. *For a month, or a year, he might find contentment in my arms. But then it will dawn on him who I was. Who I am...*

She clutched her knapsack in her lap and suddenly longed for escape, longed to be on the road to somewhere else, anywhere else. That was how she'd survived these past few weeks—the quick escape, the shadowy exit. That, too, was how she'd always resolved her romantic relationships. But now there was no avoiding the encounter that lay ahead.

She'd simply have to be straight about this. Lay her cards on the table and be brutally honest. She owed it to Jordan; it was the kindest thing she could do.

By the time they reached the hospital, she had talked herself into a benumbed sense of inevitability. She stood stiff and silent as they rode up the service elevator. When they got off on the seventh floor and walked toward Jordan's hospital room, she was composed and prepared for what she knew would be a goodbye. Calmly she stepped into the room.

And lost all sense of resolve.

Jordan was standing by the window, a pair of crutches propped under his arms. He was fully dressed in gray trousers and a white shirt, no tie— casual for a Tavistock. At the sound of the door's opening, he turned clumsily around to face her. The crutches were new to him, and he wobbled a bit, struggling to find his balance. But his gaze was steady on her face.

Her escorts left the room.

She stood just inside the door, longing to go to Jordan, yet afraid to approach. "I see you came through it" was all she said.

He searched her face, seeking, but not finding, what he wanted. "I've been trying to see you."

"Your uncle told me. They were afraid to move either one of us." She smiled. "But now Van Weldon's gone. And we can go back to our lives."

"And will you?"

"What else would I do?"

"Stay with me."

He stood very still, watching her. Waiting for a response.

She was the first to look away. "Stay? You mean… in England?"

"I mean with *me*. Wherever that may happen to be."

She laughed. "That sounds like a rather vague proposition."

"I'm not being vague at all. You're just refusing to recognize the obvious."

"The obvious?"

"That we've been through bloody hell together. That we care about each other. At least, I care about *you*. And I'm not about to let you run."

She shook her head and laughed—not a real laugh. No, it felt as though her heart had gotten caught in her throat. "How can you possibly care about me? You're not even sure who I am."

"I know who you are."

"I've lied to you. Again and again."

"I know."

"Big lies. Whoppers!"

"You also told me the truth."

"Only when I had to! I'm an ex-con, Jordan! I come from a family of cons. I'll probably have kids who'll be cons."

"So…it will be a parenting challenge."

"And what about *this?*" She reached into her knapsack and took out the pocket watch. She dangled it in front of his face. "I *stole* this. I took something I knew you cared about. I did it to prove a point, Jordan. To show you what an idiot you are to trust me!"

"No, Clea," he said quietly. "That's not why you stole it."

"No? Then why did I take it?"

"Because you're afraid of me."

"I'm afraid? *I'm* afraid?"

"You're afraid I'll love you. Afraid you'll love *me.* Afraid it'll all fall apart when I decide you're hopelessly flawed."

"Okay," she retorted. "Maybe you've got it figured

out. But it does make a certain amount of sense, doesn't it? To get the disillusionment over with right at the start? You can put a nice romantic spin on all of this, but sooner or later you'll realize what I am."

"I know what you are. And I know just how lucky I am to have found you."

"Lucky?" She shook her head and laughed bitterly. "Lucky?" Holding up the pocket watch, she let it swing in front of his face. "I'm a thief, remember? I steal things. I stole this!"

He grabbed her wrist, trapping it in his grip. "The only thing you stole," he said softly, "was my heart."

Wordlessly she stared at him. Though she wanted to pull away, to turn from his face, she found that her gaze was every bit as trapped as her hand.

"No, Clea," he said. "This time you don't run away. You don't retreat. Maybe it's the way you've always done things. When life gets rough, you want to run away. But don't you see? This time I'm offering you something different. I'm giving you a home to run *to*."

She stopped struggling to free herself and went very still. Only then did he release her wrist. Slowly. They stood looking at each other, not touching, not speaking. His gaze was all that held her now.

That and her heart.

So many times I've tried to run away from you, she

thought. *And it was really myself I was running from. Not you. Never you.*

Tenderly he stroked her face and caught the first tear as it slid down her cheek. "I'm not going to force you to stay, Clea. I couldn't, even if I wanted to. But I've already made a decision. Now it's time you made one, too."

Through the veil of tears blurring her vision, she saw his look of uncertainty. Of hope.

"I...want to believe," she whispered.

"You will. Maybe not now, or next year, or even ten years from now. But one of these days, Clea, you will believe." He edged his crutches forward and pressed his lips to hers. "And that, Miss Rice," he whispered, "is when your running-away days will finally be over."

She looked at him in wonder through her tears. *Oh, Jordan, I think they already are.*

She threw her arms around his neck and pulled him close for another kiss. A sealing kiss. When she pulled away, she found he was smiling.

It was the smile of the thief who had stolen *her* heart. And would forever keep it.

'It's scary just how good Tess Gerritsen is.'
—Harlan Coben

Twenty years after her father's plane crashed in the jungles of Southeast Asia, Willy Jane Maitland was finally tracking his last moves. She recognised the dangers, but her search for the truth about that fateful flight was the only thing that mattered.

Closing in on the events of that night, Willy realises that she is investigating secrets that people would kill to protect. And without knowing who to trust, the truth can be far from clear cut...

MIRA

They'd said her husband was dead...

So why was she sure he was still alive?

A ringing phone in the middle of the night shakes newlywed Sarah Fontaine awake. Nick O'Hara from the US State Department is calling with devastating news: Geoffrey Fontaine, Sarah's husband of two months, has died in a hotel fire…in Berlin.

Sarah forces a confrontation with Nick that finds them criss-crossing Europe on a desperate search for Geoffrey. Trying to stay one heartbeat ahead of a dangerous killer, they become quarry in the clandestine world of international espionage, risking everything for answers that may prove fatal.

MIRA

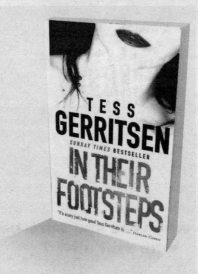

Had she condemned
her patient to die? Or was
it murder?

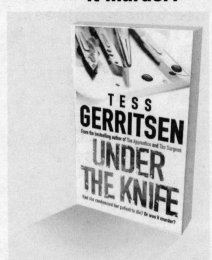

For David Ransom, it begins as an open-and-
shut case. Malpractice. As attorney for a grieving
family, he's determined to hang a negligent doctor.
Then Dr Kate Chesne storms into his office, daring
him to seek out the truth – that she's being framed.

First it was Kate's career that was in jeopardy.
Then, when another body is discovered, David
begins to believe her. Suddenly it's much more.
Somewhere in the Honolulu hospital, a killer
walks freely among patients and staff. And now
David finds himself asking the same questions
Kate is desperate to have answered.
Who is next? And why?